Psi Another Day

a Psi Fighter Academy novel

Psi Another Day

a Psi Fighter Academy novel

D. R. Rosensteel

Entangled Publishing, LLC
2614 South Timberline Road
Suite 109
Fort Collins, CO 80525
Visit our website at www.entangledpublishing.com.

Edited by Guillian Helm and Stacy Abrams
Cover design by Kelley York

Print ISBN   978-1-62266-042-1
Ebook ISBN   978-1-62266-043-8

Manufactured in the United States of America

First Edition May 2014

This book is dedicated to the real Rinnie and Susie, and to all of you who are true Psi Fighters at heart.

Vanquish Evil, Do Right, Protect the Innocent.

Chapter One

Murder Me Elmo

My life changed forever the night the stalker came to town, although I didn't realize it at the time. I say *came to town*, but I know now it was someone who had been there all along. I actually had no intention of getting involved. I thought the cops had it covered. They spotted some guy all over the city dressed up in funny costumes. Clowns, rock stars, flamboyant dinosaurs. People thought it was an advertising stunt until he tried to pull a little girl into his creeper van. Luckily, she screamed and the neighbors came running. Squad cars showed up, but he disappeared without a trace. It was all over the news, and the whole town was put on alert. Police patrols were everywhere. Even that didn't stop him. He showed up a few days later at my little sister's elementary school.

That's where I drew the line. Little sisters, especially mine, were off limits for creeps. The police were in over their heads, so I decided they needed a specialist to step in. The guy was obviously no ordinary stalker.

Fortunately, I'm no ordinary teenager. My name is Rinnie Noelle. I'm a Psi Fighter. We protect the innocent, kind of like Batman. But we don't do capes. Capes are for weirdos.

Andy and the Kilodan said I wasn't ready. Andy is my mentor and favorite sparring partner. He's like a big brother to me—overprotective and annoying, but in a sweet way. The Kilodan is the Psi Fighters' leader, you know, like Captain America is the Avengers' leader? Except that the Kilodan doesn't actually have a name. He's just "the Kilodan." And he's always masked. I've known him since I was six, but I've never seen his face. He's *really* big on secret identities.

They wanted me to fix the problems at my high school instead of taking down the stalker. Major, fly-catching yawn. Don't get me wrong. The drugs and violence at school are beyond annoying. But what crime fighter wants to put bullies in detention when she can save the world from nefarious villains? I wanted to test my skills on bigger trouble.

Long story short, I got permission to be Andy's backup on this mission. Something told me there was more to this stalker than there appeared to be. I had no evidence, just a feeling. Turns out, I was right. Feelings are my specialty.

• • •

I slipped through Sinclair Park, masked and armored, and feeling a little freaky. Not from the outfit. That was awesome. The high-tech mask, midnight blue hood with matching tabard, and formfitting body armor made me all but indestructible. But

Sinclair Park was an eerie place. It started out as a cemetery during the Revolutionary War. All sorts of famous dead people were buried there. Then, some rich family bought it in the 1950s and built a playground in the middle of it. They apparently didn't see a problem mixing toys with tombs. Monkey bars, sandbox, freshly dug grave…maybe I'm weird, but that creeped me out. A little too much Mr. Rogers meets Stephen King for my taste. The Kilodan insisted we'd find the stalker there. How he knew, I didn't have a clue, but he had this annoying way of always being right.

As the twilight sky darkened, I reached my observation point, a high-tech mausoleum at the edge of the woods. Yes, I said mausoleum. Andy took some poor soul's gateway to the Great Beyond and turned it into a surveillance center. I love Andy, but seriously, normal was not his style.

Floodlights clicked on with a low hum down by the playground, startling me. I quickly touched the bronze nameplate, calmed my mind, and concentrated. The door slid open and I slipped through. It closed silently behind me the moment I cleared the opening. The inside was about ten by twelve, and well lit for a final resting place. Reminded me of something out of *Dark Shadows*. The granite bench where the coffin was supposed to go sat in the center. It had been converted to a sofa. No way was I sitting there. A pinball machine with a picture of Elvis Presley in a black leather jacket with black leather wristbands, playing a brown and gold guitar, sat in the far corner. Four bronze doors were bolted to the long marble wall behind the couch. They were labeled, from left to right, "1956—Got Famous," "1959—Made Fried Squirrel Famous," "1973—Made Hawaii Famous," "1977—Left the Building." They had Andy written all over them.

I hit a button on my armor. All four bronze doors slid upward and disappeared into the ceiling, revealing high-resolution monitors. They flashed to life, displaying the woods and playground across the long back wall like a mural.

If you've never hunted a ferocious stalker from inside a high-tech tomb, I don't recommend it. There were no rotting corpses or rattling skeletons, but there were spiders. I hate spiders. I was covered from head to toe in a space age fabric so strong it made Kevlar look like cheap aluminum foil, but I'd have gladly traded it for a good old-fashioned can of Raid.

I stared through the mausoleum's monitors out onto a scene that made my spider-infested sepulcher seem even spookier. Sinclair Park is built on a wooded hillside, with a little valley slashed right down the middle. The cemetery lies at the top of the valley, and the playground is at the bottom. When the sun goes down, it looks like something out of a horror movie. Not the new kind, where the vampires are hot. The old kind, where they have bloodstained fangs and smell like road kill on an August afternoon. Mist flowed down from the trees like a shadowy stream, washing eeriness from the tombstones and depositing it on the playground in the hollow below. If a werewolf (again, the scary kind, not the kind that looks awesome with no shirt) had stalked across the lawn, it totally wouldn't have surprised me.

In the midst of that Tim Burton-ish setting, a small group of children played. Sans parents. What was up with that? You'd think after a series of creeper sightings, there would be parents. And even if the whole town hadn't been freaked out by a rampant stalker, what kind of mother lets her child play alone in a cemetery after dark? Even birds guard their young. And they have smooth brains.

"Sound," I said. Instantly, the clamor of children laughing and playing came across the mausoleum's hypersensitive audio receivers. The floodlights cast an eerie yellow glow around the children. I scanned the tree line for what seemed an eternity. Nothing. No vampires, no werewolves, no stalkers. As first missions went, this one was rating a low five. If there had been a full moon, I might have given it a six. Andy's voice echoed over my mask's radio. "This could get very dangerous, very quickly."

"Hey, 'Danger' is my middle name. *Grave* danger. Get it?"

"This isn't practice, sweetheart."

I scanned the monitors, but couldn't find Andy. Trees, swings, monkey bars, kids. No masked vigilante. "What good is all this high-tech bad guy hunting gadgetry if I can't see you on it?"

"Hold on," Andy's voice came back. "Look now."

An orange-ish glow appeared on the monitor. It took the shape of a stick figure waving. I said, "Enhance," into my mask's microphone. The stick figure blurred and refocused. Andy popped onto the screen with amazing clarity, dressed in his bone-white mask and black armor. "Where were you?"

"I came out of Shimmer."

Shimmer is like stealth mode. A nice feature Andy built into our armor.

"Forgot your cloak of invisibility?"

"Get serious. This guy is deadly."

Normally, Andy is a total goof, so his uncharacteristically somber mood caught me off guard. This was my first real mission, but it's not like I'm a total newb. I pressed a button on the side of my mask. Low voltage current tickled my throat, and I felt my vocal cords thicken. "So am I," I said, pleased with the venomous sound of my electronically altered voice.

"This is not a game!" Andy's voice was stern. "Children's lives are at stake. Stick to the plan."

The plan was for Andy to capture the stalker without any witnesses. My job was to watch him while Andy took him down. Okay, sticking to the plan. Slight problem, though. "I don't see him."

"Repeat?"

I tapped my mask. "Do you see him?"

"You're breaking up. Switch to infrared. Look along the tree line. By the big oak."

"Red," I said. The monitors instantly glowed with night vision. I scanned the trees above the playground. There he was, just like Andy said. He lurked about fifty yards from the children, outside the range of the floodlights, hiding himself in the shadows of a massive oak. "Enhance. Zoom." Wow. The ghoulish night vision didn't do the stalker justice. Once the high res color enhancers zoomed in on him, I got a close-up I wasn't quite ready for. I only saw the back of his head, but that guy had some serious fashion issues. His hair was huge, bright red, and looked like he had used a ten million volt Taser for a straightener. Had to be a mask. "What's he dressed like this time?"

"Not close enough to tell." Andy's figure moved swiftly across the monitor. "I'm switching back to Shimmer. Keep your eyes open. He'll be out of my line of sight for two minutes. I'm coming in from the north. Warn me if anyone heads his way. And don't move. No matter what. Got it?" Andy vanished from the screen.

"Got it." Suddenly, I couldn't see the stalker. I quickly scanned the monitors, but found nothing with weird hair.

"Wide," I said, switching out of night vision into wide mode. Only trees. "Red," I said, as panic started to set in. The screen went back to night vision, and I saw movement. "Enhance. Zoom." The sicko was back in view, slinking nearer to the children, careful to stay in the shadows. He settled into a small recess in the landscape surrounded by heavy brush and trees. The perfect hiding spot—impossible to see from the playground. This guy was good.

"He moved," I said.

Andy didn't respond.

"Andy. Fetch."

No response.

The red-haired creeper stooped behind another huge tree and set something on the ground at the edge of the recess. Suddenly, an eerie children's song I only half-recognized piped across the mausoleum's speakers. A little girl looked up from the sandbox. Not good.

"Andy, you gotta move *now!*" Static crackled and died, and fresh panic hit me like an avalanche. I scanned the tree line, but Andy was nowhere to be seen. Normally, that wouldn't bother me. Andy practically invented the art of stealth. Nobody could see him if he didn't want them to, even without his uniform's Shimmer mode. But he was relying on me, and I was not going to let a single one of those children disappear.

"Andy, if you can hear me, I'm going in."

I touched the hidden latch on the mausoleum's marble wall. It rolled open, and the smell of wet leaves gushed in. The evening had a slight chill, moist with the drifting fog.

As I bolted from my hideout toward the red-haired freak, darting silently between the trees, panic gave way to excitement. This was almost too easy. The Kilodan was wrong—I *was* ready. I had trained ten years for this. I grinned beneath my mask. That freak's stalking days were officially over. I moved in behind him like the mist. Slowing my pace, I eased myself so close I could smell him. Gross. Just to be safe, I drew my Amplifier.

The weirdo stood icily still, watching the little girl on the playground, unaware that if he backed up, he'd trip over me. His breathing was slow and calculating. Head and shoulders taller than me, he wore a classy designer jacket and matching jeans. Nice outfit, but it clashed with his scent. Rancid Gym Sock, by Estee Stalker. Soap was apparently not part of his repertoire.

Neither were scruples. The creep wore an Elmo mask. That was just wrong. The scratchy music came from some sort of old tape recorder, and I realized it was the theme song to Sesame Street. Using a beloved childhood character to lure innocent rug rats gave a whole new meaning to the word "scum." Brought to you by the letters P-U.

I thought about dropping him by pinching a nerve on his neck. Nice and clean. He'd never know what hit him. In hindsight, that would have been a better approach. Yeah. Instead, I grabbed his mask by the red fur and plucked it off. A grimy mop of dark, unwashed hair lay plastered against his head, and its stench hit me like a nuclear blast, obliterating the sweet green smell of the woods. I almost threw the mask back on him to save what remained of my sinuses. He grabbed at his head, then spun around in confusion, his face scrunched up with anger.

"Shhhh." I held a gauntleted finger to my masked lips.

The creeper's expression changed like he had flipped a light switch, and his breathing accelerated. He smiled down at me, and his face became so adorable I almost overlooked his stench.

"Do you want to play with me?" he whispered. His eyes were deep brown, sparkling. I put him at about forty, but he seemed very childlike. My first impression was that he'd probably clean up pretty well with the right combination of soap, love, and an industrial pressure washer. His sweet voice made me wonder whether we had the right guy.

Then he balled up his fist and tried to take my head off. Definitely the right guy.

I slapped his punch aside with a quick wave of my armored hand and slammed my fist into his stomach. It was soft. The creep had zero abs. Lucky for him I pulled the punch. He doubled over, gagged once, and tried unsuccessfully to breathe. I dropped to the ground and swept his feet out from under him. He landed hard and lay unmoving.

I hit the button on my mask.

"This is not a game." My transformed voice thundered like an avenging angel, more horrifying than I had intended, and chills ran down my spine. Thankfully, it had the same effect on him. The Elmo-wannabe crawled to his knees, cringing. He wiped his mouth with his hand, then raised it as though he thought I would hit him again. I planned to, but not the way he expected. I had to hold him until Andy found us.

Fear me, I thought, and clamped my hand around his wrist. My body tingled as my mask filled with mental static. Psychic force rushed down my arm and ripped into him. His eyes bulged with terror.

"You're not real!" he gasped, wildly shaking his head, struggling to pull away. His filthy hair stuck out like a scarecrow's. I focused hard, pounding the cruelest delusions I could imagine into his mind. I felt his fear growing. That was good. That was how it worked during practice. In moments, he would be in a fetal position, too terrified to move.

"Get away!" he panted. The man recoiled, tearing out of my grip. He leapt to his feet, backpedaled and tripped, but caught himself. I moved in to end it. Fumbling at the zipper on his jacket, he ripped out a pistol and pointed it at my chest.

That was not good. That never happened during practice.

Without thinking, I flicked my wrist, and the word "sorrow" echoed through my mind. Masters of the Mental Arts form psionic weapons from thoughts and emotions. Unfortunately, I am not a Master. I didn't mean to draw the emotion that triggered the Psi Fighter's most powerful Psi Weapon, but Andy and I had just practiced the technique in training, and I couldn't think of anything else. A ghostlike whip of psychogenic mist exploded from my Amplifier and solidified around the stalker's arm. I yanked and held tight. His gun spiraled through the air, and he fell to the grass, shaking violently. My Memory Lash slithered up his arm, coiling around him like a misty python.

Please! The stalker's terrified thoughts filled my brain before his voice reached my ears. He sobbed like a little girl, thrashing as the Memory Lash tightened. His memories flooded my mind like a blast of putrid wind, siphoned by the Lash…tiny faces in a wire cage, little girls crying for their mothers. A hideous skull surfaced and disappeared. A little blond face flashed into my head, dirty and crying, screaming that she would tell his mommy. Horror gripped him, fear that his mother would find out—

His terror filled me in a way I had never experienced in practice. I *became* him, horrified of my mother, paralyzed by what she'd done to me in the past. Her enormous face came at me from all directions. The little girl wouldn't stop screaming. I ripped open the cage door, picked up a claw hammer, and hurled it with all my strength. The claw lodged in the wooden frame beside her head. Terror filled the girl's eyes, and she clamped her hands over her screaming mouth. An overwhelming sense of glee flooded into my mind, and I slammed the cage door shut.

That twisted feeling jolted me like high voltage electricity, and I fought to become me again. I threw my Amplifier to the ground, trying to escape the horrible images, but I couldn't push the stalker's memories out of my head. My legs shook, the world spun, and I dropped to my knees, trying not to vomit in my mask.

"Get up!" Andy's irritated voice snapped me from the trance. His mask, a bright angelic face with laughing eyes, peered down at me, cocked at a furious angle.

I knew without looking that the smelly creeper was gone.

"Andy, I'm sorry."

He jerked me to my feet. "You ignored my orders. Why?"

"But my radio—"

"I told you to check the charge," he spat, towering over me. "Why would you use a Memory Lash? You know you can't handle it!"

"It was all I could think of." My whole body quivered. "He had a gun. I'm sorry, Andy, I…"

Andy sighed. His big body relaxed, and he rested his gauntleted fist on my shoulder. "It's okay. Did the Lash change him?"

"No sorrow, no remorse," I said. "He enjoys terrorizing. I think he likes being afraid. Andy, I saw his face."

"I know." Andy picked up the dropped Elmo mask. "That thing smells awful. Who is this Jim Henson reject?"

"Didn't recognize him. But Elmo isn't his only disguise."

"Yeah, I know. Clowns, purple dinosaurs."

"I saw a skull mask in one of his memories. Like a pirate's Jolly Roger. Probably wears it to frighten the children."

Andy's body went rigid. "A death's head? Are you sure?"

"Yeah," I mumbled. Now that I was released from the effects of my backfired attack, I tried to remember what I had seen. I knew I shouldn't, but I couldn't help it. Children were caged, and I had just let their kidnapper escape. "Idiot!" I said under my breath. "Andy, he's holding little girls captive. If they die, it's my fault." I picked my broken Amplifier out of the grass and pulled at it with my mind, hoping that some memory fragments remained.

How could I have let him get away? How could I have been so stupid? That poor child, the way her eyes bulged when the hammer nearly killed her, the sickening joy the stalker felt, the horror of his mother...suddenly, a gateway opened and the terrible things I had seen in the stalker's mind flooded out. My legs buckled, my hands shook... Instantly, the memories became too vivid—the hammer felt deadly in my hand—I was there again, enjoying it, and it terrified me—and I struggled to separate myself from him. "Andy, the little girls—please stop it! I can't keep him out—Andy, help me! Andy—"

Andy was on me in an instant, arms around me, masked forehead pressed against my own, whispering into my mind, "Every mission has its own horror. Don't dwell there. You know how to push it away. Now push. Like we practiced."

Calmness flowed through me, but I knew it wasn't of my own doing. I concentrated, filling myself with thoughts of home, the Academy, my family, until I regained control. My storm of emotions calmed. I forced the memories out, and I was me again.

"Thank you," I muttered. "The Kilodan was right. I wasn't ready. Why is he always right?"

"Benefits of being our glorious leader," Andy said. "You were lucky this time. Rinnie, you don't realize how powerful you are. You have *got* to stay in control. You could hurt somebody."

I smiled, knowing Andy couldn't see it under my mask. "I'm okay now. I guess I never took that part of the training seriously."

"I know. You never had a reason. Now you do." He lifted my chin with his finger. "You know, the Kilodan is also right about your school. You could stop it all. Make the high school safe."

"Smooth change of subject."

Andy folded his hands. "It's what I do."

I shook my head. "Sorry, not interested. I've got a stalker to pummel. It's personal now."

"And being bullied every day isn't?"

I thought about a typical day at school. Name-calling, humiliation, the joy of being a total outcast. Algebra. "Life can't always be a box of chocolates. Anyway, that's different. Out here, I'm masked."

Andy laughed. "Our masks are just tools."

"This *tool*"—I jabbed a finger at my mask—"is the only thing that hides my identity. In case you're forgetting, I don't dress like this at school."

"There are ways to stay hidden without wearing a mask. Underdog didn't wear a mask. Nobody knew his identity."

"Underdog had it easy. He had a telephone booth to duck

into. I have a cell phone. It's a little tight."

"Duck into your locker," Andy said.

I did a finger wag at him. "Somebody would notice a blond girl going in and a masked vigilante coming out. I'd be captured and interrogated by the Knights until I told them your name. They would hunt you down, torture you for days, and finally kill you and hang your rotting corpse in the streets as a reminder to us all. Worse yet, I'd get detention. You know we aren't allowed to fight in school."

Walpurgis Knights, our fiercest enemy. Their leader is very likely the deadliest human alive. They call him Nicolaitan. Like us, the Knights also create weapons from thoughts and emotions, but they prefer jealousy, hatred, and guile, the darkest of emotions. They are especially sensitive to the use of Psi Weapons, which is why the Psi Fighters never use them while unmasked.

"Your concern for my safety overwhelms me," Andy said. "As does your cluelessness about your school."

"I know enough to keep my mask on. The Kilodan is *never* unmasked. I've known him for ten years, and I've never seen his face. Or heard his real voice. *He* knows how to keep his identity hidden. I'm just following his example."

"The rest of your classmates would love to fight back," Andy said. "They just need a leader."

"The rest of my classmates aren't in danger of being murdered in their sleep."

"I thought 'Danger' was your middle name."

"Not according to the jerks at school."

"So you'll take the assignment?"

"Do I have a choice?"

"Not really."

Chapter Two

A Day in the Life

I'm sixteen, but sometimes I feel a lot older. I like Elvis Presley and the Three Stooges. I like old superhero comic books. But I do not like spiders of any age. Unfortunately, my life is infested with them. Some of the spiders attend my school. One of them goes by the name of Mason Draudimon. He's my year, and has picked on me for as long as I can remember. I used to come home and cry on my bed, but I never let anybody see. Especially Dad. Well, I'm adopted, so he's not my birth father, but I still call him "Dad." If he knew Mason picked on me, he would pay the boy a little visit, and *that* would not be pretty. He is so overprotective. But in a really sweet way.

If Andy and the Kilodan had their way, Dad would never need to visit Mason. They pulled me from the stalker case. They were cool about it. Unfortunately, they wanted me to permanently stop Mason instead. Yuck. Oh, yeah, and they wanted me to master the Memory Lash. Double yuck.

I knew I'd never win the Memory Lash argument, so I didn't even try. I'd have to learn to deal with the anguish of that thing regardless. Came with being a Psi Fighter. Mason, however, was another matter. I *really* didn't want that assignment, so I told the Kilodan that being targeted by Mason didn't bother me. He reminded me that I'm not the only one Mason picks on. Touché. He hit a soft spot, and he knew it. To tell the truth, I would have saved the rest of the kids from him and his goons long ago, but here's the thing—I was *completely* comfortable kicking bad guy butt while wearing the mask and armor of a Psi Fighter. I could have polished the floors with Mason's forehead and never broken a sweat if I was in uniform. But I wore jeans and frilly tops to school. If I fought crime dressed like that, everyone would know my secret, right? Happened once. Won't happen again.

When I was six, the Walpurgis Knights kidnapped me. One of them saw me practicing…figured out that I was a Psi Fighter in training. Stupid move on my part, even for a six-year-old. I've grown considerably more careful since then. The Knights are like the bad guys *plus*, like the comic book super villains on a steady diet of prune juice and fiber. They are just miserable people. The Psi Fighters rescued me, but two died trying. My real parents. I miss them. I thought the Kilodan would back off the Mason assignment when I reminded him. No such luck.

The Psi Fighters are nothing like comic book superheroes. We're more like awesome vigilantes. We practice the Mental Arts, which are like martial arts with extra caffeine and awesome sauce. We punch and kick and do that ninja art-of-invisibility stuff, but we also make weapons just by thinking. Andy invented this gizmo he calls "the Amplifier." It channels our thoughts and emotions into weapons. Some weapons are harder to control than others—I especially have trouble with the Memory Lash. The problem is, when I use it, it shows me my opponent's most horrifying memories. The stalker's memories were just too real. Who knows what I'd see if I used it on Mason? That boy had issues. And Kathryn, my best friend in the entire universe, loved to point them out every time we saw him.

"Okay, Rin." Kathryn stood next to me in the hallowed halls of Greensburg High School during our break before morning assembly. "Let's say you're the first person on earth. God gave you the job of naming all creatures that slink or slither. What do you call *that* slathering beast?" She pointed to the large figure lumbering our way, elbowing through the crowd like a coupon-toting shopaholic at a fifty-percent-off sale.

"Let's see," I said. "Long hairy arms, stubby hind legs, unibrow...Mason is a wombat."

We burst out laughing. Kathryn Hollisburg has been my best friend since forever. We know everything about each other. I know her secret shopping hot spots. She knows my secret identity. She is beyond beautiful, built like a supermodel, and über popular, although she totally misses that fact. Kathryn is as genuinely unsnobbish as a person can be.

Then there's me. Born Lynn Morgan, my last name became Noelle when I was adopted after my parents' murder, and my first name became Rinnie when my adorable new little sister Susie couldn't say Lynn. I am, in my professional opinion, a tad *under*developed for sixteen, and on the line between popular and unpopular, I fall somewhere in the vicinity of despised. But only by the Excessively Cool, who are jealous of my friendship with Kathryn.

Mason Draudimon is another story. We have a deep, ongoing love-hate relationship—he loves to abuse me, and I hate his guts. Totally. Of course, I'm in the minority. The cool girls think he's a hottie. They babble about his gorgeous sapphire eyes, the way his hair swoops away from his face like an eagle's wings, how he's built so strong and sleek and pantherish…all of which is true, but when you've been picked on by someone since the fifth grade, your view becomes slightly skewed. To me, he'll always be a smelly, grub-eating marsupial of the genus Vomitus Wombaticus.

The thing is, he's not just mean, he's privileged. As the untouchable son of the mayor, Mason could find a cub scout helping a little old lady cross the street, mug the old lady, take the scout's lunch money, and three quarters of the city officials would swear he was at the soup kitchen feeding the poor when the crime occurred. Everyone is afraid of his father. Even the teachers are helpless against him, which Mason totally takes advantage of. He has no respect for anyone in authority. With two exceptions—Mason worships Captious the math teacher and Miliron the science teacher. They have doctorates. Mason loves people with brilliant minds. He has made it clear to the world that he'll earn a PhD and cure mental illness. Academic achievement is Mason's top priority. He's a man on a mission.

Unfortunately, part of that mission includes inventing new and exciting ways to abuse people. Rumor has it Mason was emotionally scarred by his cruel mother, who, rumor also has it, resides in Old Torrents, the mental hospital outside of town. So he takes his anger out on the kids at school. It's his mean streak that makes him ugly. I should probably feel sorry for him, but I don't. I wish a meteor would hit him.

Greensburg had this marvelous (according to the School Board) campus that squished the elementary school, middle school and the high school next to each other. Consequently, the younger kids enjoyed the agony of sharing the halls with the older kids. That beautiful arrangement allowed Mason and his thugs to mistreat all ages, as they saw fit. And they saw fit a lot.

As he stalked toward us, Mason broke into a nasty smile that grew bigger and bigger, like the Grinch when he had his wonderful, awful idea. The Grinch had his dog Max, and Mason had *his* dog, Bobby. Bobby Blys was a small, mouse-haired boy with a lightbulb-shaped head and abundant ears. He was a brain, and I think Mason admired him for it. But he was also a little geeky—actually, a lot geeky—and a favorite target of Mason and his goons. His buzz cut and Mr. Magoo glasses didn't help. They just made his ears more noticeable. Not that they needed help…he could hang glide in a weak breeze.

Bobby knelt facing an open locker down the hall from us. Mason stopped beside him and whispered something I couldn't hear. Bobby looked up at him and shook his head. Mason smiled, reached out and slammed the door on Bobby's face just after a teacher disappeared into his classroom. Besides being helpless, the teachers are completely buffaloed when it comes to Mason. His public displays of nastiness are legendary, and so is his timing. He never gets caught.

"The jerk," Kathryn fumed. "Why can't he leave Bobby alone? He thinks he's so tough."

"Mason's a coward," I said, glaring at him. "He never picks on anybody who can fight back."

"Time to put a stop to it." Kathryn whipped an umbrella

from her book bag.

"What are you gonna do with that, open it and give him bad luck?"

"Hey, these things are deadly in the right hands. *You* stomp him, then. I mean, you *are* a major butt-kicking machine, aren't you? I'll cover your back."

"You know I can't." Not that I wouldn't have liked to. Stuffing Mason's head up his nether regions would bring me unbridled joy. It was times like these that made me wish I didn't have a secret identity to guard.

"If I practiced every night to kick major butt, I'd definitely kick butts that needed major kicking," Kathryn said. "Whatever happened to 'With great power comes great responsibility'?"

"That's for people who have issues with radioactive spiders."

"You have issues with *any* kind of spider."

"Okay." I took Kathryn by the umbrella and pulled her toward Bobby and Mason. "Maybe if we give Mason dirty looks, he'll go away."

Bobby closed his locker door and got up to leave, rubbing the egg-sized knot on his head. Without a word, Mason pushed him up against the lockers. Bobby's lip quivered. He stared up at Mason with wide, watery eyes.

"You should reconsider," Mason said, his face suddenly grim. "This project means a lot to the community. You know how civic-minded I am."

"You don't know what you're making." Bobby's knees shook. "It's illegal, Mason. I heard Tammy Angel bragging. She said—"

"Angel is a perfectly law-abiding citizen, just like me." Mason pinched Bobby's trembling cheeks in his huge hands and stretched his mouth into a grin. "We're one big happy family."

"Let him alone, Draudimon!" Kathryn screamed.

Mason turned and beamed. He released Bobby's cheeks and whacked him on the side of his head. "Gotta talk to your girlfriend, Roberto. I think she likes me."

"Your dog doesn't even like you," I snapped, as Mason stepped toward us. Kathryn stared at me in disbelief and proceeded to walk backward until she disappeared around the corner. So much for covering my back.

"Smile when you say that, Peroxide," Mason said, reaching for me. "My dog's dead. Hey, I wonder if you'd look like Mrs. Bagley if I put your hair up in a bun. Let's find out. Did you know that one day I aspire to be a hairdresser?"

I backed against the wall. Peroxide. That was hardly fair. It wasn't my fault I had super white blond hair. It just grew that way. Beautiful visions of kicking Mason right in his nomenclature danced in my head. Retribution for giving me that nasty name. Of course, *properly* kicking said anatomy might expose my secret. Clark Kent had it so much easier. As long as he kept his glasses on, there was no way he'd be mistaken for Superman.

Still, even Clark fought back if a life were in danger. And getting a new hairdo from an unlicensed wombat clearly put my life in danger of eternal humiliation. Mason was hand-delivering me a reason to do what the Kilodan wanted me to do. If I only used my less potent skills...one little judo chop would drop Mason like a bad cell phone connection. Then the school would see that Mason wasn't so tough, and they wouldn't be afraid of him anymore. At least, that's how it worked in the movies.

I sunk nervously into my fighting stance, wondering how

accurate movie wisdom was.

"Oh, horror, Peroxide's actually defending herself this time," Mason said, covering his mouth with both hands.

"You wouldn't beat up a girl half your size, would you?" Appealing to his manliness might save me the hassle of dusting the lockers with his face.

"Not a pretty one. Maybe I should ask you out instead."

"Better stick to something you have a chance of success with."

"You won't tell me no." Mason raised an eyebrow. "Ever been in a fight in school?"

"Uh, not really." I'd been in a gazillion battles during practice sessions at the Academy. I had even fought against a real bad guy, which didn't turn out so well. But never in school. *Never* unmasked. Maybe I needed to rethink my strategy. If the Knights figured out that I was a Psi Fighter because I kicked Mason's wombat butt, they'd raid the Academy and murder everyone, and I'd never hear the end of it.

Maybe it wouldn't hurt to let Mason rearrange my hair just a teensy bit. Humiliation is supposed to be good for the soul. I closed my eyes as Mason's grimy fingers cupped my face, and found myself wondering—does he really think I'm pretty? Ew!

Mason's hands slid gently up my cheeks, lifting my hair on both sides. I shivered. Spiders crawling up my face could not have grossed me out more.

"Nice ears," he said softly.

"Back off, Mason," a quiet voice warned. I jumped. A muscular boy stood next to me. Kathryn squeezed beside him. He was smaller than Mason, but Mason dropped my hair and backed away. His cocky expression melted like chocolate in a blast furnace.

"Hey, Egon," Mason said. "What up?"

Egon said nothing. He simply stared at Mason, expressionless.

Mason began bobbing his head like an over-caffeinated pigeon. "Just havin' fun. You know I like to have fun."

"Have it somewhere else," Egon whispered.

Mason swallowed. His Grinchy grin disappeared.

Egon said nothing.

Mason turned slowly and loped down the hall, not looking back. Relief swept me. My secret was safe. My hair was happily unbunned. The day was plodding along nicely.

"Toodles, Peroxide," Mason hollered as he disappeared around the corner. "Call me!"

"It's not bleached," I muttered, glaring at the floor. What a jerk. One day, Mason would get what he had coming to him. I would pound him into paste. I would hit him so hard he'd become a vegetarian. I'd batter him so bad I'd be cited for cruelty to wombats. I turned to tell Kathryn what would happen if I ever met Mason when I was masked, and found myself staring up into Egon's mesmerizing green eyes.

Suddenly, my feet were very large and my knees very knobby. My heart stopped working, and I could feel the beginnings of rigor mortis setting in. "I, umm...thank you," I mumbled, slouching badly.

Egon's eyes smiled at me and he nodded. "See ya." He gave me a little two-fingered wave that made me tingle, then simply floated away, riding off into the desert sun that was setting in my frazzled brain. I suddenly had to pee really badly.

Kathryn squealed, "Omigosh, did you see the way he checked you out?"

"Who *is* he?" I felt my mouth for slobber. "He is absolutely gorgeous…"

"And famous," Kathryn said. "Egon Demiurge is an intergalactic Mixed Martial Arts champion or something. Apparently he just moved here to train. They say he's so good, they're making it an Olympic sport just for him. Nobody, and I do mean nobody, will mess with him in this school. I'll bet he'd give *you* a workout."

"Oh, I could never fight him," I whispered, staring absently down the hall.

"I wasn't talking about fighting," Kathryn said, grinning. "He's a senior, you know."

A smile tugged at the corners of my mouth. Of all my friends, Kathryn was the first to take it to the gutter.

"Thanks," a small voice said from behind me. I turned and found myself eye to eye with a thoroughly red-faced Bobby Blys.

"Hey, Bobby."

"Thanks," he repeated.

"No problem. Mason's such a jerk. What was that all about?"

"Hi-eeeeee, Bobby," Kathryn squealed, hipping me out of the way. I grunted.

"Oh, hi, Kitty," Bobby said quietly, blushing like a bruised strawberry.

"That was so brave, Bobby!" Kathryn smiled as though her happy sauce had kicked into high gear.

"Don't see what's so brave about getting smacked around by a yeti." Bobby rubbed the rapidly swelling lump on his head.

"Actually, Mason's a wombat," I told him. "Although, now that you mention it, he *is* abominable."

Kathryn elbowed me in the ribs and giggled. "Oh, don't

you just adore Bobby's sense of humor?"

"So, what's up with Mason?" I asked Bobby, rubbing my ribs.

He looked away. "Nothing, I...quit the Class Project. He's mad."

The Class Project. Besides being obsessed with beating up people who were smaller than him, Mason had a thing for this goofy school project that was sponsored by some hospital or something. Students learned about it in Chemistry, then were allowed to continue the work outside of class for extra credit if they wanted to. And Mason had launched a personal crusade to make sure they wanted to. "I heard you tell him he doesn't know what he's making. So...what's he making?"

"I'm not positive." Bobby folded his arms. "Mason thinks the Class Project is supposed to help the mentally ill. But if my research is right, the compound made in our lab can be altered in a more advanced lab—" He slowly shook his head. "If Tammy Angel is telling the truth..."

"Such a brilliant mind! Well, let's not be late for assembly, Rin." Kathryn took me by the hand and led me away like a puppy. "See you in Math Club, Bobby."

We walked toward the auditorium, Kathryn grinning blankly at the tile floor like she had left her brain in her locker.

"Kitty?" I said, raising an eyebrow. "And when did this happen?"

Kathryn giggled. "When Bobby joined Math Club."

"Kathryn, you've been in Math Club together since it was invented."

"But I never really talked to him until recently. He sort of avoided me."

"Probably didn't think he was your type. You know your

dating history."

Kathryn got the oddest look on her face. "What are you talking about, my *history*?"

Like I said, Kathryn was completely oblivious to her own popularity. "Student body president. Track captain. Football captain. Debate Team captain." I ticked each guy she's ever dated off my fingers. "Every awesome boy in the school wants to be with you. No wonder Bobby avoided you."

"But Bobby is so not like them."

"Exactly. You are gunning for a complete dweeb this time, Kathryn. Shows character. I'm proud of you."

"I do *not* gun. Those boys asked me out. I don't even know why."

"I do. You have cleavage."

Kathryn backhanded my shoulder. "Bobby is real, Rin. He's deep. He gets me for who I am. Problem is, I think the attraction is purely intellectual. We have such amazing discussions, but they're all about logic and math and philosophy."

"He calls you Kitty. Nobody who has an intellectual attraction would call you Kitty."

"Bobby says I'm a woman of great poise, elegance, and wit, like Kitty Carlisle."

"Who's that?"

"A woman of great poise, elegance, and wit, obviously. I don't know, some actress from the Thirties. Maybe you can help me, Rin. How can I get him to notice me?"

"You could always try stalking him."

Kathryn bit her lower lip and nodded. "Has potential."

Chapter Three

A Warning

The school's auditorium was actually very cool. Designed to seat seven hundred kids, it resembled a Greek amphitheater. Hand-carved faces of people too beautiful to have ever been real decorated the ceiling like an ancient work of Michelangelo. Murals with exotic species of trees and flowering vines covered the walls. The balcony, with its gorgeous red velvet seats, had a perfect view of the stage and the audience below. Unfortunately, it was permanently reserved for the Excessively Cool. Plebeians like me got to sit in the peasant section at ground level, which would also have been gorgeous if it weren't plastered with spit wads and other glop whose origin I preferred not to know.

Principal Ophia Bagley paced the stage like a hungry tiger in its cage. The teachers were positioned strategically across the auditorium, two in the front row, the rest scattered along the outside aisles, attempting to give the illusion they were in control. I noticed they also had easy access to the exits in case trouble broke out.

Trouble, as usual, sat up in the balcony—Mason and his posse, three girls who called themselves the Red Team. They loved the balcony, because it made those of us who sat below them easy marks for their chewing gum missiles that, once embedded, had to be surgically removed from our hair.

My seat was as comfortable as a dentist's chair, but it was near the front, where I would be a more difficult target. The downside to that strategy was my proximity to the stage. It would be hard to ignore the boring speech Mrs. Bagley delivered weekly. I was closer yet to Dr. Captious, my arrogant Algebra teacher. He sat smugly in the first row next to Dr. Miliron, the head of the Class Project.

"Awesomeness at three o'clock," Kathryn whispered.

I looked to my right as Egon took the seat next to me. Instantly, all neural functions ceased. I gripped Kathryn's wrist, trying not to squeal.

"Easy, girl," she said.

"So," Egon whispered in my ear, sending chills down my spine, "looks like this is the only class we have together."

Under ordinary circumstances, I would have gotten it. Egon was being cute. The proper response would have been to make a joke about this being my favorite course, or the homework being tolerable. Instead, all my flummoxed mind could conjure was, "I know, right?"

Kathryn patted my arm. "Deep breaths, Rin. Deep breaths."

As the principal tapped the microphone, Egon chuckled

and said, "Here comes yet another enthralling show."

I smiled and relaxed my death grip enough for Kathryn to get the circulation back in her wrist.

Mrs. Bagley continued to stare out over the crowd. To say the woman had a harsh look about her was unfair, but not totally inaccurate. She reminded me of the lady in the painting with the pitchfork-toting husband—except the lady in the painting looked happier.

Tall and thin, Mrs. Bagley wore a gray flowered dress and black granny shoes with hard, square heels. Bobby pins held her hair in a bun so tight that closing her eyes must have been painful. According to rumor, she had been an adult from birth, but I knew she was not as harsh as she seemed. I had personally witnessed moments where a kind of softness, caring and genuine affection for the students accidentally leaked through her schoolmarmish exterior.

This was not one of those moments.

"Stu-*dents*," she said finally in a staccato voice. She waited until the auditorium quieted. "I have good news for you, and I have news that is less than satisfactory."

"What's the good news, Old Bag?" a voice from the back shouted. The auditorium echoed with laughter at the nasty nickname.

"For me, Mr. Rubric," she said calmly, "good news would be a relaxing breakfast of sausage, eggs, and a honey-covered biscuit, eaten after the joyful discovery that my milk carton had your picture on it."

Direct hit. I gave it a ten.

"But we're not here to celebrate," she continued. "We have received a letter from the state. People in my position do not look favorably on letters from the state, especially when said letter tells me that we have failed to meet the minimum pass rate on our standardized tests. This is distressing to me. Do any of you know what this means?"

"We have idiots for teachers," a voice yelled from the balcony, and roars of laughter filled the auditorium. Dr. Captious laughed quietly, and whispered to Dr. Miliron, who smiled and nodded.

This sort of banter between the teachers and students would never happen in a normal school. But I didn't go to a normal school. The teachers had lost control long ago. The few who still tried, like Mrs. Bagley, were outnumbered by the ones who had just given up. They complained that they weren't allowed to teach anymore, that discipline was a thing of the past. Mason's dad was part of the problem. He always said, "Patience, tolerance, and redirection. Not punishment." Being the mayor, he had as much influence on the teachers and school board as Kathryn had on the students, which was considerable.

Mrs. Bagley banged on the microphone so violently a bobby pin popped. A curl launched from the side of her head like a broken spring from a cuckoo clock. "It *means* there are bigger problems here than you are aware of!"

"It *means* we can all sleep in. What's the bad news?"

Mrs. Bagley tightened her lips, glaring. "I have asked for your cooperation before, but have run into certain…" She waved her hand toward the balcony. "Obstacles. Your teachers and I are equipped to deal with poor grades, however, our problem goes beyond grades. I find that I have lost my patience with asking the school board for help, and being referred to committee after agonizing committee. I have grown intolerant of our hallowed policy against punishing troublemakers who are immune to redirection. So I've found outside assistance to take back our school. If policy cannot help us, law surely can. Without further ado, I give you Police Chief Amos Munificent, a man who has full authority to do what needs to be done. If you show him the same respect you have shown me, I can assure you that you shall all receive detention for the rest of your natural lives." She backed away from the microphone smiling, clapping her hands, looking expectantly out at the audience to do the same. Captious and Miliron clapped, and several people in the front row joined in.

I clapped, too. This was good. My problem was solved. The police would come in and take over, and I could tell Andy and the Kilodan that my services were no longer needed.

I was officially off the hook.

Police Chief Munificent emerged from the backstage shadows and walked to the microphone. Maybe "waddled" is a better word. He was beyond overweight, his shirttail was half in, half out, and his crooked hat made him look like a mall guard wannabe. Stylin' he was not. I try not to judge people by their appearance, because I think you have to be a complete bonehead to do that, but to tell the truth, my excitement at being off the hook started to droop a little. Maybe he was having a bad hair day, but the man was seriously not what I expected. No *way* could he handle this crowd.

Then I noticed his eyes. Andy taught me to look at my opponents' eyes if I wanted to see what they were really capable of. The Police Chief had the eyes of a man who meant business. He scrutinized the students in the auditorium, grimacing like we were all suspects in some horrible crime. When his gaze reached me, his face softened. He nodded and smiled as though he knew me.

"Who's your new bud?" Kathryn asked.

"Not a clue," I said, shaking my head.

"His name's Egon," Egon whispered, elbowing my ribs gently.

My head turned so quickly I was certain my neck had snapped. Egon just called himself my new bud. Was he flirting with me? I *hoped* he was flirting with me. But I couldn't know for sure without taking extreme measures—I could scan him. No, the Kilodan would murder me. I could ask Kathryn. But how totally lame would that be with him sitting right there? Egon smiled slyly at me, green eyes melting me right into the auditorium seat.

Mr. Munificent pulled the microphone close to him and said, "I'll get right to the point. Mrs. Bagley is correct. The problem goes beyond bad grades. Kids are being assaulted and forced to take drugs. I don't like it."

"Neither do the kids we beat up," the voice in the balcony said. The auditorium echoed with laughter.

Munificent stood silently, gazing out into the sea of students. He shook his head finally and said, "You kids don't have a clue, do you? The bullying and the drugs are just a decoy. This is about something much bigger."

"Bigger than your gut?" the voice said.

The chief smiled like a mongoose facing off against a snake, knowing it had found an easy meal. "Look, genius, I'm not a man who's afraid to do his job. Give me a reason, and I'll slap cuffs on you. And believe me, I'll enjoy it. Here's the deal. The drug floating around this school is called Psychedone 10. It's a twisted mutation of LSD. Ordinary LSD just makes people stupid. But this poison that you kids are into, this atrocity, this cancer…it makes people wicked. Ten years ago, I hunted a masked kidnapper who terrorized the city. He fed this drug to his victims, all children. They committed obscenities you can't even imagine. We stopped them, but he disappeared without a trace. Now he's back, and you kids are his target." A hush fell over the auditorium. The Chief raised an eyebrow and said in a low voice, "What, no snappy comeback, tough guy?"

I scooted forward in my seat, suddenly interested.

"He's using you kids to do his dirty work," the Chief said. "You know why? Because you have enough idiots among you to make it easy."

So the stalker had been around before. I wondered if the memories I saw were old—visions of the girls he kidnapped ten years ago. No matter, he was still out there. Kids were still in danger.

"A piece of advice," Munificent said. "You punks who think it's cool to push drugs or beat people up, you're the ones who'll take the rap for what this guy is doing. You're his cover. He wants us to focus on you instead of him. And it's working. The fact that I'm here now proves it. I should be out finding him. I'm the only one left on the force who understands that the man is pure evil. He'll recruit you against your will, and when he's done with you, he'll kill you, and your friends will be blamed. I need your help to find out who he is. I need to stop him this time."

"It was Professor Plum with a pipe!" the voice from the balcony shouted.

Amos Munificent glared up at the balcony, suddenly irritated. "Mason, for once in your life, shut up! This is serious. Not even your father can protect you from this man. You don't know who we're dealing with. I would think that someone with your history would take this more seriously."

"Ooh," Kathryn said. "Draudimon got told!"

"Shhh!" I elbowed her.

Munificent gazed out at the crowd and said quietly, "I'm looking for a man who covers his face with a skull mask. He's wanted in connection with the attempted kidnapping of a ten-year-old girl. We believe he is behind the drugs in this school, as well. One of you knows him. You have no idea how much danger you're in. I need to stop him before anyone dies. Before you die. I need your help."

So he knew about Elmo and his nasty skull mask. Not surprising. Andy and the Kilodan always let the cops know what's up. We're their best source. The stalker's image spun through my head like a pinwheel...Elmo mask, skull mask, no mask. Andy and I had gone through every mug shot in the database, but I couldn't identify the stalker. He told me that he was working on something that would help, but I felt so useless. Tears welled up. It was my fault the stalker escaped. I had to find him.

Then it hit me.

The Kilodan was right. Crud, the man was always right. The clue I needed to find the stalker was right here at school. Munificent said one of us knew him. I just had to figure out who.

A crypt-like silence had descended on the auditorium. Most of the students had stunned expressions. Only Dr. Captious had an arrogant smirk, but he always had an arrogant smirk. I turned to the balcony. The Red Team girls were grinning smugly, but Mason Draudimon's ghastly pale, wide-eyed expression shocked me—he was absolutely terrified. What was up with that?

Even if the police had somehow connected Mason to

the stalker, that wouldn't explain his reaction. His dad would pull strings and he'd be off the hook. So what was it about Mr. Munificent's announcement that terrorized Mason? The drug connection made no sense. Everyone knew the drug dealers were Art Rubric and Chuckie Cuff. Mason hated drugs. There had to be something else. I needed to know what that something was.

Being off the hook had totally lost its appeal. I officially put myself back on.

Suddenly, I felt a warm shoulder leaning against me, and breath against my cheek. "If you need a bodyguard," Egon said into my ear, "I know a few moves."

. . .

With the exception of Social Studies, Business, and one study hall, Kathryn and I have every class together. It's a nice arrangement, because I often need her to lean on. Sometimes metaphorically, other times, like today, literally. We went straight from the assembly to gym class, which I suffered through against my will. On my best day, I stunk at any sport that didn't involve ancient weapons or hand-to-hand combat. But after the assembly, my concentration had dropped below zero, and concentration was a prerequisite for this particular gym class. Miss Jackson, our teacher, was a former dodgeball diva.

I want to be clear about this—dodgeball is not a game. It's an evil cult activity that decent people shouldn't associate themselves with. In ancient times, they called it "stoning." Fortunately, I was confident that the damage I suffered to internal organs was minimal, and the throbbing red welts in the center of my back would heal in a decade or so. I limped into the empty girls' locker room, leaning on Kathryn, moaning in exaggerated agony.

"We are awesome dodgeball players, aren't we, Rin?"

"You played. I was a casualty. I thought they outlawed dodgeball in civilized schools."

Kathryn shrugged. She helped me to the bench. "Since when is this place civilized? We all know that gym class was modeled after the medieval torture chamber. Damp, musty walls, scurrying insects, odors of death and critter poop—now, before the rest of the class moseys in here, let's get back to the assembly."

"We weren't talking about the assembly."

Kathryn threw her arms wide. "You were thinking about it. The welts prove it. I've seen you practice kung fu. Nobody can touch you if you don't want them to. I know you're all flustered over Egon offering to guard your body, and I'm thrilled for you, but that wouldn't transform you into an instant easy target. Now, indulge me. The way I heard it, there is some connection between the stalker, the drugs, and Mason. Is that the way you heard it?"

"Flustered is an understatement. But you're right, the assembly left me wondering. It doesn't feel right. I got the connection between the stalker and the drugs. But not Mason. Something else is going on with him. Did you see the look on his face?"

"Okay, great minds think alike. I saw it, too. Mason's not afraid of anything. Suddenly the police mention a kidnapper and drugs, and Mason's afraid. I smell guilt in the air. Aren't you supposed to have some sixth sense about this stuff? Did you check the batteries on your bad guy meter?"

"But the drug connection is pretty far-fetched. Everybody knows that Mason doesn't do drugs."

"Right. The three things he is most proud of are his grades and his drug-free lifestyle."

"That's two things."

"And the fact that he can get away with murder. I assumed you assumed that one."

"Yeah, he's a role model."

"So, this proves that Mason, the drugs, and the skull-headed guy are connected."

I shook my head. "It doesn't prove anything."

"It proves that Bobby was right. The Class Project is a sinister plot to get everyone addicted to this Psycho-whatsis 10 and take over the world."

"That's not what Bobby said."

Kathryn took me by the shoulders and looked straight into my eyes. "Read between the lines, Rin. How can you do what you do with such a total lack of women's intuition?"

Sometimes Kathryn and I are on completely different wavelengths. "Kathryn, do you think that, even as out of control as this school is, the teachers would knowingly let us make illegal drugs?"

"Knowingly? No. Cluelessly? Absolutely."

"The connection to drugs doesn't make sense. There has to be something else."

"It makes perfect sense if what Bobby and Munificent said is true. The stalker's into drugs. The Class Project is all about drugs. Mason is all about the Class Project. Henceforth, hitherto, and ipso facto, Mason knows the stalker. Duh. He may not do drugs, but he's certainly working for someone who appreciates them. And I think he's doing it against his will. We all know Mason is an evil wombat. But this time, Mason's afraid. He knows his dad can't save him."

"The Class Project isn't about drugs, though. Even Bobby said the chemicals made in the Class Project are harmless."

"He also implied that a lab with more advanced equipment could make something nasty from them."

"So you're saying the psycho stalker is Mason's boss."

"I'm saying, if you want to know who the smelly man in the Elmo mask is, ask Mason."

I thought about it for a minute, then patted Kathryn's head. "I hate to say it, lady, but you should be a Psi Fighter."

Footsteps and laughter echoed off the tiled walls. The rest of the survivors were returning from the pelting. As girls streamed into the locker room, we changed from our ghastly gold and brown gym uniforms, Kathryn into her Hollisters with holes machined in various strategic locations, me into my boring, hole-free jeans from Walmart. My mom's voice echoed in my mind. *I don't care what Kathryn wears. You are not going to school with holes in your clothes.*

Parents simply do not understand fashion.

Lockers clanged all around us as students rushed to get to the next class. A well-endowed cheerleader changed a few lockers down from me. She didn't have a single dodgeball wound on her, although she had contributed to the majority of mine. She was a pro with those inflatable red implements of destruction, and I was her favorite target. I smiled. "Hi, Tammy. Good game."

Tammy eyed me like I was a festering sore. She turned away and, noticing that Kathryn wasn't looking, said, "Hey, Kathryn. *Love* your outfit!"

"'Sup, Tam," Kathryn muttered, pulling on her shoes. "To the potty, Rin. Back in a sec."

I'm used to being ignored by the Excessively Cool people, especially Tammy Angel.

Being ignored can be quite useful, the Kilodan once told me. *You can hide in plain view and see things you might not otherwise see.*

Maybe so, but it can also be quite annoying. Tammy is captain of the cheerleaders even though she's a junior, and next to Kathryn, the hottest girl in school. She's also undisputed leader of the Red Team. How they got that stupid name, I can only guess. She has zero time for the Uncool, and I am at the very top of that list. You'd think that being best friends with the most popular girl in school would rub a little of the magic off on me, but it's just the opposite. Tammy hates my relationship with Kathryn and makes certain that all her friends feel the same way. She thinks *she* should be Kathryn's BFF. Apparently they used to be tight in preschool or something, which makes it even sadder.

As I pulled my backpack from my locker, a pale girl with greasy hair and sunken eyes joined Angel.

"Tammy, can we talk?"

"Hey, hey, Erica," Tammy said.

Erica Jasmine, previously a sweet girl, currently a witch with a capital B. I had watched her go downhill for a few weeks. She wasn't the only one. Other formerly nice kids had turned mean, suddenly snapping at people for no reason. Until today's assembly, I was convinced that it was either the Bubonic Plague or terrible constipation. Now I knew it was that Psychedone 10 stuff.

Angel put her arm around Erica, and said in a singsongy

voice, "I know why you're here."

Erica backed out of Angel's hug. "Tammy, I...can't anymore. My parents know—"

"Erica," Tammy said. "I thought we talked about this. Uncool is no longer acceptable in this school. The Cool Rule. And *I* rule the Cool. If you ever want to be a member of the Red Team, you'll have to get on the Star Ship Angel." She pulled a small baggie from her pocket. "And this is your ticket."

Shocked, I pinned myself against the locker, hiding behind the open door and happy for once to be unnoticed.

Erica glanced at her feet. "I don't like what this stuff does to me."

"Small price to pay for Coolness. Hang with us. Eighty-six the Loser Squad. They're no good for you anymore. Here you go." Tammy slid the baggy into Erica's hand. "Get healthy."

Erica's tired, sunken eyes suddenly changed. They grew bright and she glared into Tammy's. "No, Tammy. I'm done. You can't make me anymore. I'll go to the police." She shoved the baggy back into Tammy's hand.

"No problem." Tammy smiled. "Maybe I'll talk to your little sister instead."

What was Angel up to? She and the Red Team were the school's most notorious bullies, but they weren't into drugs. Angel headed the school's Students Against Drugs committee. She personally put up all the "Hugs not Drugs" and "Users are Losers" posters. She was even more anti-drugs than Mason was.

The anger fell from Erica's face. "Not my sister," she whispered, and pulled a wad of cash from her pocket.

"Where are your manners, Erica?" Tammy snatched the money and waved it in Erica's face. "The Red Team demands respect."

Erica's lip quivered as she reached out with cupped hands. "Please, Tammy?"

"Hey, your momma taught you the magic word." Tammy flipped the baggy at Erica. It bounced off her chest and landed on the floor.

"Erica, no!" a voice shouted from across the room. A skinny girl I knew only as Tish stood beside the bench in the next row of lockers. She had pasty white skin, unnaturally black hair, and a dozen silver hoops, balls, and figurines sticking out of various parts of her face. It looked positively painful. "*You're* dealing?" she shrieked at Angel. "What's your problem? I thought you guys didn't do drugs."

Tammy Angel smiled and pulled another baggie from her pocket. "I don't. These are supplements. All natural. Maybe you could use a hit."

"I heard what they said at the assembly. That stuff's dangerous."

"Not as dangerous as, oh, say, not knowing your place." Tammy strolled toward the black-haired girl, smiling sweetly. "Do we need a lesson in the social graces?"

Code for *don't make me call my dogs*. Angel was a master manipulator who never did her own dirty work. She preferred subtle (and sometimes not so subtle) intimidation. Her father was an insanely powerful lawyer who protected her the way Mason's dad protected him. But her high-society act was just a front.

It dawned on me that Tammy might know what was going on with Mason. I had a sudden urge to see what was on her so-called mind. Somewhere in that gully of emptiness and decay, I might find something useful. I reached into my backpack and drew my Amplifier.

Fear me, I thought, and the image of a short spear flashed into my mind. Psychic energy ripped through my body. My hair crackled with static and poofed like I had entered a massive electrical field. Which was why I never left home without my trusty brush.

Mental force rampaged down my arm, into my hand, through my fingertips. Sparks jumped to the Amplifier's electrodes and red mist exploded silently from the tip, forming a short pointed dart. I took a step toward Tammy, holding the dart behind my back, but immediately relaxed and extinguished my weapon. What was I thinking? Using Psi Weapons while unmasked was a sure way to bring the Knights to my doorstep. Knights are as sensitive to the use of Psi Weapons as Obi Wan is to disturbances in the Force.

"No, please," Tish gasped. "I misunderstood. I didn't see anything."

"How convincing," Tammy said, rolling her eyes. "So happy it was a simple mistake. Still, we must learn our position in this wide, wide world, mustn't we?" Tammy turned and called daintily through cupped hands, "Girls! Cleanup in aisle five."

They rounded the lockers like they were walking down a runway—Boot Millner, a stocky blond beauty queen wannabe, top-notch runner and too-cool-for-school jerk, whom I'd had the displeasure of knowing since seventh grade; and Agatha Chew, captain of the girls track team, a formerly decent human recently converted to the dark side. The Red Team. Tammy's venomous minions.

"Hey, Tam," Boot said. "What'cha got goin' here?"

"Outpatient surgery." Tammy smiled sadistically, snapped her fingers, and pointed at Tish.

Boot circled Tish like a vulture, then stopped behind her,

grabbing Tish by both wrists and pinning them behind her back. "The things we must do to keep order. Honestly, Tammy, I don't know how you stay so dedicated. You're a saint."

Angel closed her eyes and clasped her hands like she was praying. "For the greater good."

"Please, don't." Tish struggled helplessly against Boot's grip.

Agatha laughed. "You may proceed, Dr. Angel."

"So many procedures, so little time." Tammy popped open her locker and gazed inside. "Hmmm, I believe this is suitable, medically speaking. Mummy's Magic Mix—concentrated garlic sauce, a touch of curry, and a very large yellow onion, shaken not stirred."

The other girls laughed when Tammy pulled out the hermetically sealed, explosion-proof squeeze bottle that everyone knew housed her favorite torture device. According to Kathryn, the Angel household had some unique discipline tactics. Growing up, Tammy was never grounded when she was bad (which I have to believe was daily). Instead, she was taken shopping and forced to watch while her mother bought herself expensive gifts with Tammy's allowance. And while Tammy thrived on foul deeds, she never used foul language. Whereas normal kids got their mouths washed out with soap, the Angel kids got the Magic Mix.

Tammy held the container at arm's length, squeezed ever so slightly, and shot a stream of brownish goo onto the floor. "Locked and loaded," she said. A stench I can't even begin to describe saturated the air. Greensburg's sewage treatment plant smelled like buttercups compared to that. Tish's eyes grew wide and teary as Tammy said, "Open wide!"

"I told you I didn't see anything!" Tish choked back tears.

"Please."

"I know, I know," Tammy mocked. "It will all be over soon. Please try to understand, this is really for the greater good."

"No," Tish whispered. She shook her head and black tears streaked her face.

"Be a dear, Aggy," Tammy said. Agatha grimaced, reached out and gingerly plucked the squeeze bottle from Tammy's outstretched hand.

"I'm going in!" Agatha moved toward Tish, holding the bottle high in the air. Tish squeezed her eyes and mouth shut.

I stepped closer to the girls, deciding that it was time to be noticed. "Practicing mental proctology without a license?"

"Mental *what*?" Tammy snapped, momentarily losing her Extreme Coolness. "Don't use words you don't understand, Peroxide."

"The art of walking around with your head up your butt," I said, swishing my hand. "It's in the dictionary. Oh, I forgot. You can't read. Love to stay and chat, but Tish and I have to go. Toodles." I stiffened my fingers and poked a pressure point on Boot's wrist.

"Hey!" Boot barked, and her grip on Tish popped open.

Agatha raised the Magic Mix, glaring defiantly like she was about to squirt me. So I jabbed my thumb into her shoulder. Solid impact. Nice crunch. But I should have hit her harder, so I only gave it a seven. Agatha squealed as her arm dropped and hung like an unfettered fruit rollup, scrambling to grab the Magic Mix with the hand that still had feeling.

Tish glanced at me in disbelief and ran from the locker room. I turned to follow her.

"Peroxide has come without an appointment," Tammy said. "Boot, dear, please make her feel welcome. After all, we wouldn't want her to leave with a bad taste in her mouth. Or would we?"

Suddenly, Boot seized me from behind, wrapping her beefy arm around my throat and squeezing hard.

Boot was Tammy's Number One Enforcer because she was so freakishly strong. I couldn't breathe, and things quickly started to go black. I grabbed Boot's elbow to take the pressure off my throat, and gulped in a lungful of air. Bad move. Passing out would have been so much more pleasant. Being mauled by rabid Chihuahuas would have been more pleasant.

The instant I opened my mouth to breathe, Agatha squirted that stinking concoction into it. The stench was awful, but it was nothing compared to the taste. Garlic is good in small quantities on, say, white pizza where it belongs. But when it's enhanced with yellow onion juice and concentrated into Mummy's Magic Mix, I can tell you an unwashed gym sock would have tasted better. My throat burned. My eyes burned. A beautiful vision of my elbow slamming into Boot's ribs flashed through my mind, but fear gripped me. Suspension. Fines. What if I hurt Boot? Happy thought, but my dad would kill me.

"C'mon, Rin," a voice said as the bell rang. Kathryn rounded the lockers in her usual bouncing gait. "We'll be late for our Language Arts test. Very uncool, ladies. Release the prisoner, please. You don't need detention."

"Oh, hi, Kathryn," Boot said, letting me go.

Tammy's Extreme Coolness returned in a heartbeat. "Hey, hey, Kathryn! We were just getting to know Rinnie, you know, seeing if she might fit in."

"Oh, she's definitely not Red Team material," Kathryn said.

"I don't know," Tammy said. "Everyone has potential. We

try not to judge."

"Need a mint," I mumbled as I followed Kathryn from the locker room, wiping my tongue on my sleeve. "A vat of disinfectant. A wire brush. Yuck!"

Humiliation, I decided, was not good for the soul. Humiliation stunk.

Chapter Four

The Psi Fighter Academy

After a day of embarrassment and disgrace, I *really* looked forward to a relaxing evening of major butt-kicking. As I climbed the white marble steps to the Greensburg Public Library, I felt as though I was entering a lost world. The library was old, over two hundred years, and built entirely of beautiful hand-carved white marble. The walls came alive with wildly detailed engravings of a great battle between humans and mythical creatures. The massive pillars reminded me of the Parthenon. A great stone lion stood between them, guarding the library entrance. It looked so real, I swore its eyes followed me as I approached.

Heavy oak doors swung inward on silent hinges at my touch. The smell of dust and very old books escaped into the sunlight with not even a hint of garlic. I always felt a sort of nostalgia, because I had dim memories of going there with my parents before they died. I breathed deeply and stood tall as I passed between the doors. Waving to the librarian, I hurried past rows and rows of books, straight for the bathroom. I went into the second stall, closed the door, and sat down on the toilet.

Second stall to the right and straight on till morning.

I giggled quietly as I reached toward the roll of toilet paper, resting my hand against the silvery plate above it. Tiny electrodes dotted its cold surface. My mind grew silent and I concentrated, releasing a light stream of psychic energy through my fingertips. Suddenly the wall behind me opened and the toilet spun around. I found myself facing a black-walled mine shaft, and smiled. Only Andor Manchild would build a secret entrance like this. Andy had a flair for the abnormal.

The toilet rolled forward into the shaft and jerked to a stop. The wall closed silently behind me, and I remembered too late that I had forgotten the most important part of the ride. Again. Tinny theme park music suddenly blasted me from all sides. I gripped the seat just in time. The toilet dropped abruptly through the floor, shooting water everywhere. I plummeted down, my hair in my face, and my stomach in my throat. Warm wind and black rock and the smell of creosote rushed past me. I squealed with a mixture of terror and joy, clenching the toilet seat, wondering why Andy's twisted sense of technology didn't include seat belts. Air brakes hissed and the toilet came to a jarring halt, splashing the remaining water into the air like a geyser, drenching my entire southern hemisphere.

A metallic voice echoed from hidden speakers, "I hope you enjoyed the ride. Please exit to the left."

"Eeeewwww," I said in disgust, standing up. My saturated

jeans were cold and clinging. I forced my legs apart as I duckwalked away from the toilet. Now deep beneath the library floor, the air was surprisingly warm. The shaft I had just come down disappeared above me into blackness. The water that didn't manage to marinate my clothes lay in a clear puddle around the toilet behind me.

"Better than last time," I said to the wall. My voice echoed in the distance.

The shadowy tunnel ahead of me was framed in huge wooden beams bolted together with black iron plates. I rubbed my hand across the coal wall, and it came away clean. Illuminated by a single yellow bulb, a sign hung against the wall. It read:

Old Salem Academy of Psi Fighters
Vanquish Evil
Do Right
Protect the Innocent

Tacked to the bottom of the sign, a small paper with scribbled handwriting said:

...and Always Flush First

Something in the shadows caught my eye, and a chill went down my spine. I decided it was because I was drenched. Then the shadow moved and a low, rumbling laugh echoed down the length of the tunnel. In the darkness, a large, diabolical figure dressed in black armor leaned against the wall, staring at me, breathing like Darth Vader. His eyes reflected the yellow light.

I smiled. "Hi, Andy. Trying to sneak up on me again?"

"I am master of stealth," Andy said in a deep voice as he

stepped slowly, menacingly into the light. "I am one with the darkness, silent as dust."

"You *are* dusty."

"I can do that stealth stuff, too." Andy looked at my pants and smiled. "Forget to flush again?"

"I was, like, in a hurry, okay?"

"Hey, you know, like, no Valley Girl talk down here, you dig?"

I cringed. "Valley Girl and Burned-Out Hippie are a *really* bad combination. Although it suits you. Ready for class?"

"It's what I live for." He cocked his head to the side as though something had occurred to him. "Only water this time?"

"Yeah."

"That's an improvement, then, isn't it?"

"Uh huh," I said, remembering the only other time I had forgotten to flush. It was a long time ago, and I was in a massive hurry, and, well, it was embarrassing.

I glanced up at the inscription carved into the polished wood of a massive overhead beam.

NO ONE MAY ENTER EXCEPT BY INVITATION.

Andy reached up and touched the engraving. "We need a human skull hanging there, don't you think?"

"Or a bottle of Mummy's Magic Mix."

"Bad day at school again?"

"Normal day at school again."

"Let's go take it out on some unsuspecting Academy students. Then you can tell me how your new mission is going."

"Better than the last one."

"Life is just full of surprises." Andy pinched his nose shut.

"Tell me, did you brush your teeth today?"

"Ha ha."

Andy clapped his hands. Bright halogen lights instantly illuminated a long tunnel with hand-waxed wooden beams and a polished anthracite floor.

I buried my face in my hands. "Please don't tell me you installed a clapper."

"Light switches are so yesterday."

I walked beside Andy through the tunnel, which seemed to go on forever. The place was incredibly clean and well lit for an abandoned mine that, according to official city records, didn't exist. Occasional passages shot off to the left or right. A steel door sealed one passage, a red neon sign above it reading K-MART. Behind the door lay Andy's home away from home, the tech lab where he invented our gadgets. James Bond had Q. We had Andor Manchild. Q was *way* more normal.

"Police Chief came to school today," I said.

"Uh huh."

"You knew?"

"I know many things, youngling," Andy told me. "What do you think I do all day, sit around and watch old movies?"

"You don't?"

"I do. Society underestimates the educational value of the Three Stooges."

"Then you knew that the stalker is behind the drugs and violence in my school. Did you also know Mason is involved?"

"Mayhap," Andy said quietly, peering at me from the corner of his eye. "And maybe I know more."

The tunnel ended abruptly at a huge coal wall with a shiny metal plate embedded in its center. Andy placed his hand against the plate and closed his eyes. His hair poofed like he had bad static cling. A surge of excess mental energy reflected off the coal and hit me like a blast of wind. I was always amazed at how someone so goofy could be so incredibly powerful. The wall opened without a sound, and we entered the training room of the Old Salem Academy of Psi Fighters.

An enormous bookshelf covered the front wall. In the center of the room, a lone stack of cement slabs rested on the floor. Around it, a small group of students warmed up. Some practiced unarmed combat. Others simply sat on the padded floor, stretched into a Russian split. Several engaged in battle with Amplifiers. They looked amazing in their Psi Fighter uniforms.

I entered my assigned dressing closet and began to peel off my wet clothes. My reflection stared back at me from the closet's full-length mirror, apparently as upset with her day as I was with mine. Tall and thin, she looked like any other sixteen-year-old with anemic hair. There was no hope in that area… she could color it, but then Mason would just make up another nasty name, like Clairol. She didn't need another name. Her feet were maybe a little too big, and her knees a bit knobby. And she slouched a little. Okay, maybe a lot. But only because today stunk.

To tell the truth, I didn't look at all like a Psi Fighter. I was just a basic person. Ordinary. Not somebody you'd notice, like Kathryn, who was drop-dead beautiful…luxurious hair, perfect knees, upright spine.

I really needed the uniform.

I took it down from its hanger and pulled it on. The midnight blue outfit was formfitting, loose enough in the right places for unhindered movement, tight enough in other places to look awesome. The built-in shin and thigh armor was lightweight and flexible, but nearly indestructible. The long tabard was fashioned from heavier fabric than the pants, armored front and back. I liked the feel of its snug fit. Plus it made my boobs look like they actually existed.

I pulled on my gauntlets, complete with forearm guards, wondering if the Kilodan would let me add little pointy things like Batman had. Suddenly, I felt whole.

My mask smiled down at me from the top shelf, waiting patiently for my next mission. The Psi Fighter mask isn't meant to be scary. We don't look like NHL rejects, or giant bats with bad dispositions and excessively long ears. Our masks are beautiful. They're all different, modeled after little children, like the cherubim. Mine has wide, innocent eyes and a pouty smile. Made from the same tough stuff as my armor plates, it could easily stop a bullet or a Psi Weapon assault (too bad it didn't also stop a backfired Mental Lash). But my favorite feature is its voice-altering electronics. I can inspire terror in my opponent with the voice of Death Incarnate. I can also sing the Campfire Song like SpongeBob.

"Much better," I said as I emerged dressed in my not-so-ordinary uniform.

"A little swordplay before class starts?" Andy asked, tying a red bandana around his head.

"It's what I live for."

Andy hit a switch on his chest armor, and "Burnin' Love" blasted from a hidden sound system in the classroom walls. I started to dance, then drew my Amplifier and concentrated as Elvis belted out my favorite fighting song.

To Vanquish Evil, to Do Right, to Kick Andy's Butt, I thought. An electric guitar appeared in my mind, but I decided against bludgeoning Andy with a stringed instrument. Instead,

I pictured Zorro's rapier. Suddenly, I felt its weight, its sharp edge. My hair poofed from emotional static as the smoky blue blade pulled from my mind and exploded through the tip of the Amplifier. I swished the yard of pure psychic energy through the air in salute to Andy, who had formed his own weapon in the shape of a pirate's cutlass.

He returned the salute, and attacked with a fierce slash at my head. "Arrrr, prepare to be boarded."

"I'm always bored dead when I'm with you," I said, blocking the attack with an easy flick of my wrist. When our blades met, wild laughter and hideous screams filled the air.

"You can pun, but you can't hide!" Andy slashed, then stabbed, then slashed again. He attacked fiercely, forcing me back toward the wall. I parried every blow, riposting relentlessly, my own blade laughing as Andy's emitted grunts and angry squeals.

"Elvis brings out the aggression in you, doesn't he?" Andy grinned.

I fired a lightning-fast side kick into his chest, knocking him backward. "What makes you say that?"

"Ooo, nice one," Andy said. "Hurt your foot?"

"My foot's fine. How's your pride?" I kicked again, this time at Andy's head.

"Gadzooks, you're a feisty lass," he said as he ducked and nearly shish-kabobed me with his wailing cutlass. "Lucky for me your sword is only as sharp as your mind."

The misery of my day faded into oblivion as my battle with Andy kicked into high gear. Pure joy energized me as I cut loose in a way I could never do in school. Punches and kicks flashed through the air. Smoky blades licked in and out like the tongues of holographic serpents, parrying and riposting, thrusting and slashing. The psychic weapons seemed to take on lives of their own, emitting wild screams or hysterical laughter each time they collided. The other students stopped practicing and gathered around to watch us battle, cheering each time an attack was made, laughing at the sounds emitted by the weapons, imitating the verbal sparring that danced between Andy and me, entirely caught up in the exhilarating world of the Psi Fighter.

Then a gong rang out. "Line up!" a voice shouted.

"Oh crud, just when I had you where I wanted you," Andy said, taking his place at the front of the class.

"Standing victoriously over your uncoordinated body?" I whispered as I took my place beside him. Every student has his or her specialty. Some are recon. Others are intelligence. Andy and I are fight demonstrators. Took me ten years in the most accelerated program any Psi Fighter had ever been through to get there.

The students assembled into formation quickly, and the room went silent. Psi Fighter training is intense, sometimes brutal, always exciting. We are a small, very elite team that hovers around a dozen. Admission is by invitation only. There is only one requirement: you must be faithful and trustworthy. Surprisingly hard to find in today's world.

The Four entered, dressed in the armor and mask of the Psi Fighter. Our leaders. The Four rarely show up in class at the same time. When they do, we never know what to expect. Sometimes they teach, sometimes they simply observe.

They stopped at the head of the class next to the stack of concrete slabs. The Four were the most secretive of all the Psi Fighters, their identities hidden even from the students. With their expressionless angelic masks, they all looked alike. But I knew from the way the last one moved, from the way he oozed raw power and incredible confidence, that he was the Kilodan. The Four bowed to the class. We returned the greeting.

"We will begin with a light warm-up," the Kilodan said in a voice like Mufasa from *Lion King*. "Down for two hundred pushups."

I groaned. This had to be observation night. The Four believed in a strong body and mind. I dropped to the floor, wishing they believed in chocolate chip cookies and hot cocoa.

Chapter Five

The Mental Arts

"Tonight," the Kilodan said, after we had finished an unusually brutal warm-up, "we return to basics. Before you can strike effectively with your body, you must learn to unleash the power of your mind. Without your mental strength, a kick is just a kick, a punch merely a punch…ordinary martial arts. But we practice the discipline that is forerunner to all martial arts. Anyone with a black belt can do this." He stood over the concrete slabs, raised his open hand to his masked cheek, and dropped it lazily, almost soundlessly, through the entire stack.

Anyone. Right. Most black belts have to put a bit more effort into it.

The Kilodan dusted off his glove and faced the class. "The ability to break inanimate objects is irrelevant. It requires nothing more than a bit of brawn. But, breaking an opponent who is physically superior to you requires quite another talent.

Lynn and Andor, if you please…Andor, simple, brute strength."

The Kilodan was the only person who called me "Lynn." It made me feel sort of…I don't know, professional. I faced Andy.

Normally, Andy was just a big goof. But during demonstrations and actual missions, he could be very intimidating. He moved like a lion when he walked, and when he stood, he looked like he wanted to kill something. He smiled cruelly at me and flexed his massive chest. His armor stretched and groaned.

"I'm going to crush you, little girl," he whispered.

"Of course, you are," I said.

Suddenly, he dove at me. Andy was fast, but I was faster. I slammed my strongest side kick into his armored gut. That kick would have knocked anyone else through a wall, but kicking Andy was like kicking a mountain. He crashed into me and slammed me to the floor, laughing. I pushed both hands against his chest armor with all my strength, but I couldn't budge him. So I concentrated.

I knew I was being mean, but I couldn't think of any other way to escape. My hair poofed as I pounded images of my own lifeless body into Andy's mind. Andy's eyes grew wide. Horror filled his suddenly pale face, and he gaped down at me. He raised himself to his knees, shaking in horror, covering his mouth with his forearm.

"Noooo!" he screamed, his face a mask of anguish. I pulled my hands away, and Andy's expression changed immediately. Color came back to his cheeks, and he started to laugh.

"You love me," I said, grinning, feeling a bit ashamed of myself.

"Yes, I do, you little brat!" He picked me off the ground, crushing me with a hug. "But if you *ever* do that to me again, I *will* kill you!"

"Put her down, please, Andor," the Kilodan mumbled. "Students, listen carefully…this ought to be good. Lynn."

"Well," I said, smiling at Andy, "sometimes I get a little too overconfident about my speed. I'm faster than Andy, and my plan was to knock him on his butt. But he's just too strong. When he had me down, I was completely helpless. So I did a Heart Piercer. I made him think he had killed me."

"That was just nasty," Andy said. "Next time I try to annihilate you, be civil."

"You can see," the Kilodan talked over us, "how useless a punch or kick is against so powerful an opponent. But the mind has no such limitations. If you channel your thoughts and emotions into weapons, your abilities will be most impressive. But if you can turn your *opponent's* thoughts and emotions into weapons, you will be invincible. Andor, please explain."

Andy folded his hands, closed his eyes, and began to speak as if reciting a passage he'd memorized for a school play. "Each Psi Weapon is unique. Some disrupt your opponent's perception. Others affect their memory or distort their reasoning. All tug at emotion in one form or another. The Heart Piercing Dagger, as demonstrated by my heartless partner, causes the victim, in this case me, to believe he has done something terrible to a person he cares deeply about, in this case the selfish brat. If I didn't love the thankless creature as though she were my own annoying little sister, the technique would have had no effect on me at all. As it stands, my heart has been shattered and my soul left bitter and empty by her thoughtless attempt at—"

"A bit less embellishment, perhaps?" the Kilodan muttered.

Andy nodded, clearing his throat. "Yes, let's move on to

the Thought Saber. Cool technique. Usually takes the form of a sword, although it can be anything that comes to mind. Use this weapon and you *hear* the emotions—screams of anguish, shouts of joy. It can slice through steel, but won't cause physical harm to a person. However, the Thought Saber does have the interesting side effect of temporarily severing the connection between mind and body. Variations of the technique include War Hammers, which, of course, only Knights and other low IQ brutes use. Dark Emotions feed that sort of barbaric weapon. As you know, Dark Emotions…jealousy, guile, greed…are the realm of the Knights. Psi Fighters use the Pure Emotions.

"Which brings us to the Mental Blast, technique of choice for unleashing Pure Emotion. If you use joy or anger, the Mental Blast will knock an opponent off his feet. If you use something as powerful as fear, you must be careful not to kill him. That's a no-no, considered bad form by those in power at the Academy. Unchain sheer fury, and you will completely blow away your opponent's mind."

Then Andy got very serious and looked straight at me. "And our most powerful weapon, the only one that can actually change a person's heart. The Memory Lash. An emotional whip. Crack the whip, and you'll raise memories like welts. Your opponent becomes his own victim. He remembers the most heartless things he ever did. He feels everything his victims felt: the agony, the terror, the sorrow. If he is capable of remorse, he will change in ways you can't imagine. This is not a technique to take lightly. You will *see* everything he sees, *feel* everything he feels. It can be ugly. Be sure you're up to it before you use it.

"And now, a happier topic." Andy pulled his Amplifier

from his belt. "The beautiful little piece of modern technology that makes all this possible."

Like everything that was Andy's, his Amplifier reflected his personality. Mine resembled a slim midnight blue fountain pen with silver bands and a really cool cap, crystal with a white rose embedded inside. However, Andy's was a miniature light saber, burnished gold with intricate symbols and precious stones along the barrel. He held his Amplifier in the air, and a monstrous cutlass burst from it. Andy twirled the cutlass, and it became a whip, then a spear, then a shield. He spun the shield, and it transformed into a guitar. The whole class started to applaud.

"Thank ya," he said, dropping to one knee. "Thank ya very much." He leapt into the air, strummed the guitar, and it imploded back into the Amplifier's tip.

"You were saying," the Kilodan murmured, the slightest hint of emotion coming through.

Andy's face turned red. "Most Amplifiers," he explained, "look like a fountain pen or some other ordinary, everyday object. Easy to carry, easy to hide, completely undetectable. For a long time, only those who had mastered the Mental Arts could turn their thoughts into physical weapons. The rest of us had to touch our opponent to transfer mental attacks, the way my cold and uncaring partner just demonstrated. However, thanks to a technological genius, a master of psitronics—in fact, dare I say it? A babe magnet, the standard to which all women compare their men—"

The Kilodan sighed. "The point, Andor..."

Andy raised an eyebrow. "I personally find the history of the Amplifier fascinating. But for those of you who are less concerned with our glorious past, let me just say that the Amplifier gives the fledgling black belt the ability to channel thoughts and emotions into physical weapons. The technology behind it is very intricate, from the silver and gold encephalographic electrodes to the resonating core, which amplifies your thoughts the way a toilet bowl amplifies the sound you make when you—"

"Thank you, Andor." The Kilodan shook his head and turned to the class. "To understand a technique, you must experience it. Pair up. We will begin with the Memory Lash."

Yuck. I drew my Amplifier and faced Andy. "So," I said sweetly and innocently, trying not to make it too obvious that I desperately did not want to do a Memory Lash. "Might I inquire as to your knowledge of the connection between Mason, the stalker, and the drugs in my school?"

Andy pursed his lips. "You might."

"I just did."

"Don't want to do a Memory Lash, huh?"

"Nope. And your answer would be?"

"The Knights are back."

"As in Walpurgis?"

"*Si.*"

"And you know this how?"

"I am all-knowing. I am all-seeing."

"Enlighten me."

Andy frowned. "Ten years ago it was drugs and kidnapping. This time, it's drugs and kidnapping. Consider yourself enlightened."

I just stared at him. "'Splain."

"The Walpurgis Knights kidnap children and train them to be Knights."

"'Kay." I knew that.

"They use mutated hallucinogens to change their personalities. Nice people can't be Knights."

"'Kay." I didn't know that.

"What do you know about Draudimon?" Andy asked.

"Mr. Munificent insinuated that someone at school is involved with a man in a skull mask. I think it's Mason. Mr. Smelly had a skull mask. If Mason knows who he is, I'll get it out of him. Preferably, by force."

"Mr. Smelly doesn't wear the skull mask," Andy said.

"Well, he did in the memory I saw."

"That wasn't his mask. I believe that was a memory of someone he met. The man in the Elmo mask and the man in the skull mask are two different people."

I was confused. "Why do you think that?"

"This isn't the first time a man in a skull mask caused us a lot of trouble."

"Well, I only care about the stalker. If Mr. Smelly doesn't wear the skull…crud. Mason can't help me there."

"Oh, contrariwise. If Munificent is right, and he always is, our best clue is in your school. And if you're right, which has happened on occasion—"

"Hey!"

"Elmo and Skullface are definitely linked, but for some reason, they're targeting different victims. The Knights always kidnapped young children, like when they took you. But the drug ring seems to be targeting teens. May be part of the same scheme, may not be. I don't know, but if it is, the Knights have changed their M.O."

"M-what?"

"Modus operandi." Andy slapped my forehead. "Do you not watch crime dramas? As I was saying, if you're right, you'd better become good buddies with Mason. He may be our best connection to the man with the death's head for a face. And I can settle an old score."

Hot anxiety suddenly burned in my chest. "What do you mean?"

"I fought a man in a skull mask the night your parents died. I suspect that you saw your parents' killer in the stalker's mind."

This was news I hadn't seen coming.

Chapter Six

Odd Connections

Learning that the stalker was connected to my parents' killer left me unusually energized the next day. I was ready to take on the world. Whether or not I was ready to take on an algebra test was another question.

Even with my nose buried deep in my algebra book, I heard the light tap of shoes crossing the floor as I sat in the library waiting for Kathryn to do some last-minute studying. As usual, the silly girl was trying to sneak up on me just to prove she could do it. Unfortunately for her, I had trained for ten years to be aware of everything in my surroundings. Unless I was badly distracted, I was very hard to sneak up on. Suddenly the footsteps stopped and I had an overwhelming feeling that I was being watched. I peeked up from my algebra book and stared directly at—*not* Kathryn.

"Hey," Egon said.

"Oh! Hello." I pretended I hadn't heard him coming. I also pretended I wasn't in total shock that he was speaking to me.

"Sorry. Didn't mean to startle you." He pulled out the chair across from me and quietly sat down. Then he simply stared at me, not the expressionless way he had stared at Mason when he rescued me, but with a very subtle sparkle in his green eyes and the hint of a smile on his lips. Not an actual smile or sparkle…I had the impression that the real thing was being reined in, waiting for just the right moment to explode all over me. I played with the pages of my book, wondering what to say. Egon never blinked. If I'd been holding a dictionary instead of a math book, it would have been opened to a dissertation on the word *awkward*.

"Come here often?" he finally said.

"Umm, yeah. Every day." It's a library. We're in school.

Oh, *moron*, he was making a joke. Little Miss Ingénue, yep, that's me.

Egon leaned forward in his chair and unleashed a very charming smile at me. "I didn't really get a chance to talk to you at the assembly, and I was wondering, you know…"

"Wondering?"

"I kind of offered to be your bodyguard, and I was hoping you didn't take it the wrong way. I mean, you don't even know me, and that could have come off as being very rude. It's just that I tend to say stupid things in a crowd because I'm not really comfortable around people. You know what I mean?"

"No." I honestly didn't. "I mean, you're famous." According to Kathryn—I had never heard of him before. "You have to be used to crowds."

Egon giggled. It was a hysterically girlish giggle, but I didn't say anything.

"I guess when I'm the center of attention, my tough guy side comes out. I've been trained to act that way for the media. That's not the real me, Rinnie. I was hoping to get to know you a little better. After all, every bodyguard has to know who he's protecting."

"I know, right?" I had no idea where this was going, but I must say, I was enjoying it.

Egon rested his chin on both hands. "So, tell me all about yourself."

Oh, crud. *That's* where it was going.

"Not much to tell," I said. Technically, not much I *could* tell. "I go to school, I have practice after school. I hang out with Kathryn. We study together. I don't know, my life isn't all that exciting."

"What do you practice?" Egon's smile was so sweet.

"Kung fu. There's a little school in town."

Egon folded his hands. "Kung fu, huh? I know some kung fu people on the MMA circuit."

"MMA?" I said, pretending I didn't know what he was talking about.

"Mixed martial arts. Cage fighters. Hey, maybe you'd like to get into the competition. I'll bet you're pretty good!"

"I'm not *that* good!" I laughed.

"Just pretty, then?"

Heat rose in my face, and hard as I tried, I couldn't stop my lips from pulling into a stupid grin.

"Well, you are," Egon whispered.

I covered my face with my hands, embarrassingly flazzled. I totally had to change the subject. "Let's talk about *you*. Where did you live before you moved here?"

Egon sat back and took a deep breath. "Oh, here and there.

I actually grew up in Greensburg, but we moved away. My dad wanted me to follow the MMA circuit. He got me into it when I was younger, and I guess I was pretty good. But I went through trainers like water."

"Why? Were they too hard on you?" I giggled, knowing firsthand what hard training looks like.

"No, I was a quick learner. I kept getting better than them. Within six months they couldn't last thirty seconds in the ring with me, and I had to find a new trainer."

"Impressive," I said.

"Not really. I found out that most of my trainers were ex-fighters who couldn't make it in the ring. They weren't that great to begin with. But they taught me one thing that a great fighter probably couldn't have—how to act like you deserve the reputation."

"And how is that helpful?" I asked.

"Comes in handy when you're facing a tougher fighter," he said softly. "Like when I stopped Mason from picking on you. He's a pretty intimidating dude. He's a lot stronger than me, so I knew I had to play mind games."

"What do you mean?"

"Mason knows I have a reputation for being tough."

"You have a reputation for being unstoppable. That's what Kathryn told me."

"See, that's the thing. Nobody at this school has ever seen me in the ring. They don't know whether I'm a champion or just mediocre. So I use that to my advantage. I act like a tough guy, and people actually believe I am. If you want to know, I was shaking in my boots when I saved you from Mason. I had seen him knock people around before. I knew what he was capable of. He probably could have kicked my butt all over the school, but he didn't know that."

Wow. To Egon's credit, he was showing real humility for a pro fighter. "I don't know whether I believe you're afraid of Mason. You had a pretty convincing tough guy act. You stayed very cool."

"That's what I'm telling you, Rinnie. That's the media act. I'm totally not at all cool. This"—he flourished his hands at himself—"is the real me. Give me a pair of thick glasses and an ascot and I can be a dweeb with the best of them."

"Egon, nobody wears ascots anymore. Not even dweebs."

"See, I'm not even qualified to be a dweeb."

I smiled, staring at the tabletop. I quickly glanced up and Egon caught me. He smiled and looked away.

"Rinnie, I've been wanting to ask you something."

The smile began tugging at my face again. "You have?"

He reached across the table and touched my arm. "I was just wondering if you'd like to hang out some time. I mean, it's okay if you don't—if you're busy. I understand."

I hoped that he didn't feel my arm shaking. "That would be nice."

Egon's eyes lit up like stars. "Cool. Hey, I gotta get to class."

Yeah. Cool. In a very hot way. I melted into blissful oblivion as Egon walked away from my table and disappeared through the library doors.

"You can come out now," I said quietly.

Kathryn stepped out from behind the shelves. "How did you know I was there?"

I gave her a double palms up. "It's my job."

• • •

The algebra classroom sat on the sunny side of the school. Soft yellow light filtered in, reflecting warmly off the walls, casting a primrose hue across the linoleum floor. Old books stacked by the window, heated by the sun, gave off a pleasant musty scent that reminded me of the Greensburg Library. Under any other circumstance, the classroom would have been very calming. Unfortunately, it belonged to Dr. Captious, an annoying little man with the ego of a dragon and the temperament of a toy poodle.

"Books on the floor, eyes straight ahead," he yipped, bouncing on his toes, hands behind his back, gazing at the ceiling. "This is your first algebra test this term, students. The required material is extremely difficult, beyond the ability of the average student. But fear not."

"Here it comes," Kathryn whispered.

I choked back a laugh.

"You are in my class," Dr. Captious continued, "because you are qualified to receive exceptional instruction. Which you have. If you do well on my test, it is because *I* am an excellent teacher. If you do poorly, it is because *you*…are a poor student."

I tried to imagine the type of animal Kathryn would use to describe Dr. Captious. He stood just over five and a half feet tall, and nearly as wide, with a pasty complexion, flat black eyes, and embarrassing hair. Hard as I tried, all I could picture was a cue ball with a bad comb-over.

As Dr. Captious reverently lifted a stack of tests from his desk, the classroom door burst open, and an animal I recognized strolled in. He glanced in my direction and a slight smile tugged at his lips. My first instinct was to stick my finger down my throat to show him how much I welcomed his charming face, but I controlled myself. If Andy was right, I might have to get close to Mason, which meant, nauseating as the thought was, I needed to play nice.

"Do you have a late pass, Mr. Draudimon?"

"Sorry, Dr. Captious," Mason said. "Won't happen again."

"I'm counting on it," Dr. Captious said. "Take your seat."

Mason calmly gave me a noogie (the swine) on his way to his desk in the last row. As soon as he was seated, Dr. Captious began his ordeal of passing out tests. Normal teachers just hand them out. Captious makes a ceremony of it. He walked up and down each row, stopping in front of every student, handing over the test like he was awarding a trophy. Then he came to an empty desk and his expression turned smug. Erica Jasmine's desk. Probably afraid of another run-in with the Red Team, so she took the day off. Happened all the time. Dr. Captious apparently thought she'd ditched because of the test.

"Family crisis," Mason said without looking up. He was doodling on his desk. Mason always doodled in class.

Captious's face showed a hint of color as he turned toward Mason. "And you know this how, Mr. Draudimon?"

"I like to keep up on social events in our community. You know what a community-minded fellow I am."

"May I assume that was the cause of your tardiness? Let's you and I have a social event after class." Captious turned and pattered to the front of the room. "Now students, when I count to three, you may begin. Three!"

And he wondered why people failed his class. I picked up my pencil, read the first test question, and got to work.

Forty-two minutes later, the bell rang.

"Pencils down," Dr. Captious yapped from the back of the room. "Hand me your papers on the way out the door."

As the other students filed out, I sat at my desk, watching

Kathryn touch up her makeup. Mason gave me another noogie on his way past and pressed a folded piece of paper into my hand. I gave him a nasty look as he walked away, and opened the paper.

Oh. Wow. I turned to Kathryn. "A smiley face. What is he up to?"

Kathryn rolled her blue eyes. "It's probably poisoned. Rin, every time we're in this class, I rub all my makeup off. Cappy gives me anxiety. I think I need to transfer."

"I know, it's like he emits caffeine rays or something. Okay, we're out of here!"

We turned to leave the empty classroom when the sound of hushed voices in the hall stopped us.

"This is not common knowledge, Mason. How did you know about Erica?"

"Angel knows the family. She stopped me on the way to class."

"Who else knows?"

"Probably the whole school. She's been out of control lately. Don't know what she's into."

"Wonderful. I would like you to find out. Fill me in tonight."

Footsteps clopped down the hall. Then the late bell rang and Kathryn said, "Oh, crap!" Late is one thing we never were. We rushed toward the classroom door.

"Dr. Captious," I said, handing him my test. "May we please have a late pass?"

Captious's gaze went to me, then to Kathryn. He smiled a poodley little smile.

"Of course, ladies. I trust you did well on the test? I believe you'll both be extremely successful in my class." He pulled a pad from his pocket, scribbled on it, and handed it to me. "In fact, I'm certain of it."

"Thank you," we both chimed as we headed down the hall. I crammed the late slip and Mason's smiley face into my pocket, wondering what was up with Captious. Suddenly, my head went wacky. Pictures flashed through my mind like a choppy old movie.

A fat man in a dark office.

His hair matted with sweat.

Reminded me of the stalker. Then I realized…it was Munificent.

His bloodshot eyes moved in quick jerks.

He crammed something into a drawer.

"How could I let it happen again?" he said. He turned when the door opened.

An unseen man's voice echoed through the room. "You couldn't stop it the first time."

"Didn't know who you were back then," Munificent whispered. He drew his gun. "I do now."

"Timing is perfect." A hand stretched out unnaturally far and disappeared into Munificent's chest.

Munificent dropped the gun, clutched his heart and struggled for breath. His eyes rolled into his head. He dropped to his knees.

The room spun slowly and stopped on a man's reflection in a mirror. He was dressed in black, and in place of his face was a skull.

"Earth to Rin. Earth to Rin."

Kathryn's voice snapped me back. My heart was racing. I didn't know where it came from or why, but I was pretty sure I had just had a vision of the same person I saw in the stalker's mind. If Andy was right, that was my parents' killer. Memories

of the night they died began to surface, but I forced them
down. I realized I was shaking.

"You okay?" Kathryn touched my shoulder.

"Yeah, just daydreaming."

"About earthquakes?"

I changed the subject. "Hey, what's up with Mason and
Captious?"

"They've been buds for a while. They both hang out at the
Shadow Passage."

"Not possible," I said. The Shadow Passage was a video-
arcade-slash-gym. "Captious wouldn't know a video game from
a dump truck, and his idea of a workout is reaching for his next
Twinkie."

"True."

"So, why does he hang out there?"

"Works with troubled youth. Molding young minds, and
that sort of thing. It's also the Official Hangout of the Cool of
the School. They even have their own section."

I patted Kathryn on the head. "Remind me not to go
there."

"Rinnie!" a voice called from behind.

Tish walked toward us, followed by a boy I knew only as
Whatsisface. He had the most oddly shaped body I had ever
seen. His neck was excessively long, his shoulders narrow and
sloping, hips and belly very wide. He tottered on unnaturally
short legs. A Friar Tuck hairdo rested like a beanie on his
undersized head. No wonder he was a major target of Mason's
goons.

"Hi, Rinnie," Tish said. "I never thanked you for the other
day. You shouldn't have bothered. It's not worth the hassle."

"I, umm…you're welcome?" I looked at Tish for a sign that

I had responded correctly, but her woe-is-me eyes remained unchanged. I did a double take and noticed that the dark circles under them were painted on. What kind of fashion statement was that?

"Stay away from the front of the cafeteria," Whatsisface said. The dark circle under his left eye was definitely *not* painted on. "Art Rubric and Chuckie Cuff are charging a toll."

"Thanks," I said. "I'll do that."

"Did you hear about Erica Jasmine?" Tish's eyes filled with tears. "Her little sister Christie was kidnapped this morning. Right inside the elementary school."

Kathryn and I caught each other's gazes. She looked as terrified as I felt.

"Mr. Munificent was right," Whatsisface murmured, rubbing his black eye. "As if things aren't bad enough here without a kidnapper to worry about."

• • •

The rest of the day was agonizingly long. I wanted so badly to text my little sister Susie, but she didn't have a cell. That evening while the other students were doing their warm-up stretches, I made it a point to train with her before class started. Susie was ten years old and, like me, had been a student at the Academy since she was six. She was my little buddy, and there was no way the stalker was going to touch her. I couldn't personally guard her all the time, so I decided to make sure she could guard herself.

The Kilodan wasn't big on breaking inanimate objects with our bare hands, but he *was* big on breaking them with our minds. We practiced on boards like the regular martial arts people did. I chose a nice, heavy oak slab about two inches thick, and dangled it on a wire from the Academy ceiling. If Susie could shatter that, she could shatter Elmo.

"Will the Kilodan find Christie?" Susie asked.

"He's the best hunter we have," I said. Christie and Susie were friends from school. "He can find anybody."

"I should go after her myself," Susie growled. "If the kidnapper is lucky, the Kilodan will find him before I do. I won't be as nice."

"Susie, you know you aren't allowed. Be patient. I know it's scary, but the Kilodan will handle it." She sounded so much like me, I couldn't imagine that we weren't blood relatives. Whereas I am blond and pale, Susie has gorgeous black hair and tans better than anyone else in my family. She blinked at me with her deep chocolate eyes.

"Don't be scared," Susie said, reaching up to touch my cheek. "I won't let him get you."

"My bodyguard." I hugged her. "Now let's practice, in case you have to save me."

"Okay." Susie turned to the board. "Board, prepare to be boarded."

I covered my face with my hands. "I gotta keep Andy away from you. Okay, elbow down, fist vertical, and imagine that your arm is a cannon."

Susie was still six years away from her black belt, too young to have an Amplifier. Her Mental Arts skills were powerful, but completely unpredictable. She dropped into her fighting stance, hands clenched, fists tight, knees stiff.

"Relax," I said. "He took your friend. Find your anger."

"Okay." Susie squinted and pursed her lips, concentrating

with everything she had. She extended her closed fist slowly toward the dangling board, then bared her teeth like a lion cub about to attack. Her face became so furious I almost giggled.

"Focus..."

Her arm stiffened and her feet shifted. Her breathing quickened. Her whole body shook like a jackhammer.

"Blast it!" I shouted, trying not to laugh at my vibrating little sister. Susie's shoulders lurched violently, her fist flashed open, and a tiny *pop* echoed against the Academy walls.

Hmm.

A cricket chirped in the distance.

On the plus side, the board wobbled a little, which was actually pretty impressive for a first try, but I knew Susie wouldn't be satisfied.

"Aw, crud," she groaned. "How come I can't do it? My hair didn't even poof."

"Are you kidding? That was awesome!" I said. "I couldn't get it to move until I was twelve."

"I didn't break it. C'mon, show me!"

I smiled, and kissed her cheek. "It's all in your head."

I eased into my fighting stance and slowly raised my half-opened fist to the suspended board. I didn't have to try hard to find my anger. I thought about the children I saw in Elmo's mind. Instantly, my body tingled as mental force ignited the rage inside me, ripping down my arm, gathering speed like a jet engine winding up for takeoff. Sparks snapped as though I was traveling down a plastic sliding board. My hair frizzed, my body twitched, my hand opened, and the board exploded with a sonic boom, sending fragments across the Academy floor.

"Cool!" Susie screamed. "Lemme try again! I wanna—"

"Line up!" a voice bellowed. The other students took their

places on the practice floor.

"Oh, crud, time for class," Susie said. "Can we practice again later?"

"Definitely."

Andy and the Kilodan entered and bowed to the class. Andy hit a button on his chest armor and the theme song from the *Addams Family* played softly in the background. I did a mental eye roll. I could always predict the weirdness of the lesson by the music Andy selected. Tonight promised to be unusual.

"Fear," the Kilodan began, "is a terrifying weapon."

"Scares me half to death," Andy quipped.

The Kilodan elbowed him and continued as though nothing stupid had been said. "Most fear is an illusion, yet we convince ourselves otherwise. Fear makes us see things that do not exist. It creates monsters in our minds. Turn your opponent's irrational anxieties against him, and you will gain an easy victory. Today we practice the Dart of Paranoia, a technique that makes imaginary terror *feel* very real. Lynn and Andor."

I smiled as I drew my Amplifier. I loved battling Andy with the Dart of Paranoia. It never mattered who won, the outcome was always hilarious. Last time I skewered Andy with the Dart, he started dancing around, screaming that somebody had copied daytime soap operas over his Three Stooges DVDs.

I faced Andy.

Fear me, I thought. My hair fluffed, and psychic flames rippled down my arms. Red mist shot from my Amplifier, and took the shape of a short, fiercely pointed spear. I eased into my fighting stance, holding the Dart of Paranoia in both hands. Andy's weapon had taken the form of a banderilla, the brightly colored barbed dart used in bullfights. Andy loved theatrics. Without warning, he attacked, stabbing fiercely at my heart. I parried with a lazy flick of my own Dart, and blew him a kiss.

Andy smiled. "A thought just crossed my mind."

"Short journey," I said, and lunged forward, slashing at Andy's leg. "Tell me all about it."

Andy twirled his banderilla, knocking my attack aside. "I think it's my turn to win."

"Even a blind pig finds a truffle occasionally," I said, resuming my guard. Andy thrust low with his banderilla, and I flicked my Dart to block. He stopped short and slashed high.

"Oink!" he yelled triumphantly. His Dart brushed my forearm and I started to laugh, knowing I should not have fallen for such an obvious trick. I tried to think of an appropriate insult, but then the whole world changed.

The laugh caught in my throat and my vision blurred and refocused.

Mason stood grinning at me. "Smile, Peroxide."

"It's not bleached!" I covered my face as Mason reached out for my hair.

Rinnie, it's okay, it's not real.

I thought I heard Susie's little voice in the distance. I looked up, trying to find her, but a huge face blocked my view, laughing and pointing. "I'll take your sister," a man in an Elmo mask whispered. Wires of cold fear tightened around my chest, restricting my breathing.

"You will not!" I screamed, and closed my eyes tightly. Uncontrolled terror filled me, and I thrust my palm forward. A sharp crack echoed through the room.

"Rinnie!"

Suddenly, there was silence. I opened my eyes, and found

everyone staring. But they weren't looking at me.

I followed their gaze to find Andy's limp body lying against the wall, his chest armor shattered.

"Oh, no," I whispered. "Andy—"

The Kilodan knelt beside Andy's body. I couldn't tell if he was breathing. The class began to murmur. My heart thumped so hard I thought it might burst through my uniform. Then slowly, Andy opened his eyes and looked down at his demolished chest armor.

"Good one," he said weakly. "Do I know how to work the Dart, or what? I'll bet you never watch Sesame Street again."

"Oh, Andy, I'm so sorry," I sobbed, tears running down my cheeks. "It was so real."

"You just proved my point," the Kilodan murmured impassively. He helped Andy to his feet, then clapped his hands. "Class dismissed."

Susie and the other students looked shocked, but bowed obediently, then filed through the main door. I wanted to know what point I had just proved, but it was obvious that there would be no discussion, so I bowed and turned to leave.

"Wait, Rinnie." The Kilodan's electronically altered voice leaked the slightest hint of emotion. Fear gripped me and I stopped in my tracks. Other than mild exasperation with Andy's teaching style, the Kilodan didn't show feelings. He *never* called me Rinnie. That couldn't be good. I didn't think he even knew I had another name. I slowly turned to face him.

"I asked you to stop the trouble at your school," the Kilodan said. "I was wrong to ask."

"It's okay. I know the man in the skull mask is connected to the kidnapper. Mason is my link to him. I won't make the same mistake I made ten years ago. Nobody will die because of me this time. I'll be careful."

"What mistake?" the Kilodan asked.

"I did something stupid that linked me to the Psi Fighters. I don't remember what, but I was always practicing when I was little. If I had just been more careful, they'd be alive today."

"Is that what you think? Honey, your parents didn't die because of anything you did." His voice shook, even through the mask's electronic modifiers. At first, I thought he was angry. But then I noticed the way he held his head. He seemed to be fighting tears. For the first time in my life, I wondered if the Kilodan might actually be human.

"Yeah. They did."

"Your parents saved a little boy. It was completely accidental. By that time, the town was in terror, and the Knights had become very bold. A Knight pulled the boy off the street right in front of them, in broad daylight."

Hmm. This was news. "My mom and dad weren't masked, were they?"

"There was no time."

"Why would they do that?" I asked. "Isn't our first priority to protect our identity?"

"Our first priority is to protect the innocent."

"Okay. So they saved the boy, captured the Knight...and?"

The Kilodan glanced away. "The Knight escaped. He recognized their Mental Arts skills, and knew they were Psi Fighters. You were kidnapped the next day. They received a ransom note saying he wanted to trade you for the boy they rescued, that you could be found in Dead End Alley. Your parents knew it was a trap, but went anyway."

By now, tears were streaming down my face. "Why? Why would they risk their lives like that?"

"You were more important to them than their secret identities. Or ours. We don't consider risk when someone we love is in danger."

"What happened to the Knight?"

The Kilodan inhaled sharply, and I instantly felt his rage bounce off me, like the searing summer heat rebounding off asphalt. Just as quickly, it was gone.

"He was extremely powerful," Andy said. "We know now it was Nicolaitan. Nobody else could have escaped both of them. And it seems that he has resurfaced."

"Nicolaitan?" I looked back and forth between Andy and the Kilodan. "The leader of the Walpurgis Knights? He's the one with the skull mask? He killed my parents? And he's back?"

"Yes," Andy whispered.

"You knew?" I was suddenly livid. "And you didn't tell me?"

Andy's eyes narrowed. "We weren't certain that he was back until you saw the skull mask in Elmo's memory. And I didn't tell you Nicolaitan murdered your parents because—"

"You want me to find him," I said. "I'm on it."

"Because I knew you'd say that," Andy said.

"No, we do *not*!" The Kilodan pointed a gloved finger at Andy. "See, I *told* you this would happen."

"Look, Big K," Andy began. "I—"

"Big K? What am I, a bowl of cereal?"

Andy bowed deeply, and spoke in Darth Vader's voice. "Forgive me, my master."

The Kilodan turned to me as if to say, *Forget you saw that.* Then he let out a long, electronically altered sigh that sounded like a deflating whoopee cushion, and became his emotionless old self again. "Andor is the reason I asked you to get involved at your school. He believes you are ready. I, however, do not."

I glanced at Andy and was suddenly filled with affection. Andy believed in me. Andy stood up for me. Andy supported—

"What do you mean, you 'do not'?" I said, spinning toward the Kilodan.

"You are headstrong and impulsive."

"And?"

The Kilodan slowly placed both fists on his hips. "I do not believe you are ready to do battle with a Walpurgis Knight."

"Who said anything about fighting a Knight? I thought I'd just have to find Nicolaitan, and you'd take it from there."

"It is not possible to simply *find* a Walpurgis Knight. Once he or she has been found, you will be drawn into battle whether you want to or not. Especially when the Knight is Nicolaitan."

I was suddenly very uneasy. "Okay, I'll stick to Mason. He's our key to finding the skull guy and Mr. Smelly, right?"

"The man who wears the skull mask is closer than we originally thought," the Kilodan said. "We believe that Nicolaitan has placed an apprentice in your school."

My jaw nearly bounced off the floor. No words came to me. No arguments. No witty comebacks. How was this possible? "One of my teachers is a Knight?"

"Or a student."

"One of her teachers is a student?" Andy slapped his palms to his cheeks.

I smacked him. "This is serious!"

"The man in the skull mask knows too many details about your school. He knows when the children are vulnerable. He has to be an insider. And he is sloppy, so I feel he is inexperienced. A mature Knight would never have been seen by Munificent, or anyone else. I believe that the apprentice is the man Police Chief Munificent saw. As much as I hate the thought, you are our best hope for finding the man in the skull mask."

"So, are you saying the man in the skull mask is, or is not, Nicolaitan?"

"Yes to both," the Kilodan said.

"I am so confused." I shook my head with my mouth wide open. "How could a Knight be right under my nose without me seeing him?"

"Stealth is the nature of both Psi Fighter and Walpurgis Knight. Ours by skill, theirs by lies and deception. You are right under his nose and, as far as we know, he has not detected you, either." The Kilodan turned and pulled a dusty brown book from the massive bookshelf. He handed it to me. I took the book from the Kilodan and noticed that his hand was trembling. I glanced up into his face, though I saw nothing but the emptiness of the mask. The mask looked down at me, and the Kilodan placed his hand gently on my cheek.

"I'm always here for you, Rinnie. But I don't always know when you need help." He turned to Andy. "This goes against my better judgment. Protect her."

"You know I'd die for her," Andy whispered.

"I know. I'll probably kill you for talking me into this."

I laughed and examined the book. A silver hasp held it closed. The leather cover was badly worn, but the silver embossed letters were still readable: *The Book of Lore.*

"What's this?" I asked, opening the book.

The Kilodan folded his arms. "It will help you to understand what you're agreeing to."

Chapter Seven

The Book of Lore

The day took forever, but school finally finished. I sat with
Kathryn in the Greensburg Library, *The Book of Lore* open
on the table in front of us. The place was vacant except for the
librarian, who had sent us into a small room behind her desk.
We needed privacy, and the Greensburg Library was one of
the few safe places above ground I could discuss things with
Kathryn.

"So let me get this straight," Kathryn said. "We're having
Watusi Night at our school and that book is going to teach us
the dance steps."

"Walpurgis," I whispered.

"Gesundheit. Why are you whispering?"

"Because we're in the library. You're *supposed* to whisper."

"That's only in old libraries." Kathryn waved her hand in
dismissal. "Modern libraries are different."

"Shhhh!" the librarian hissed, shaking her finger at us.

"This place is two hundred years old," I told her.

Kathryn lowered her voice. "So is the librarian. Why don't they have a Cone of Silence or something? Now, tell me about this Wisconsin Knight dude, who apparently dwells within the very halls of learning of which we have grown so fond. And why do you think it's not a chick? Why would you assume women can't be great warriors? That's discrimination. I mean, this *is* the twenty-first century, isn't it? I actually find myself in mild shock that you are not more progressive in your thinking, Lynn Noelle."

"I don't know. I never said it was a guy. I suppose it could be a girl. You know everything about everybody at school. You tell me."

"Gotta be a dude," Kathryn said.

"But you just said—"

"Everybody knows knights are guys. Chicks don't carry swords. Too hard to accessorize."

"Joan of Arc. What about her? She carried a sword."

"And look how well that turned out for her. So this ratty old book will help you find the bad guy, huh? What is it? Combating the Forces of Evil for Dummies?"

"Something like that."

"Well, read on!" Kathryn said.

I unhooked the silver hasp and opened the worn leather cover. A musty smell filled the air. The only thing on the first page was a handwritten note. I read it to Kathryn. "This memory will be passed through time from Kilodan to Kilodan."

"Groovy. A hand-me-down. Wait, does that mean you're the next Kilodan? Or is this a loaner? Who do I have to talk to? You're a shoe-in for this promotion, girl. I'll take care of it.

I'll tell them everything I know about you."

Suddenly a soft voice spoke from the doorway. "If you can't keep your voice down, the entire world will know everything you know about her."

Kathryn jumped. "Where did you come from?"

I laid my head down on the table with a clunk.

"My mother," the librarian whispered. "Thirty-four years ago. Not two hundred."

"Kathryn, Mrs. Simmons," I said into the tabletop. "Mrs. Simmons, Kathryn."

Mrs. Simmons patted the top of my head. "Sit upright, please. I know very well who Miss Hollisburg is."

"How did you get from your desk over there to my blind spot over here without me seeing you move?" Kathryn asked.

I suppressed a giggle. It wasn't often that I saw Kathryn flustered. "It's what we do."

"We?" Kathryn looked from Mrs. Simmons to me and back. "You mean she's a—"

"I am like you," Mrs. Simmons said to Kathryn with a smile. "I help people keep their secrets. I guard friendships. We know the things we know because we are faithful and trustworthy, you and I. I know that you would never purposely reveal your friend's secrets. It is my job to make sure you don't reveal them accidentally. So please keep your voice down. Do I make myself clear?"

"Crystal," Kathryn said softly, as Mrs. Simmons returned to her desk.

Kathryn patted my hand, gazing wide-eyed at me. "So, somebody besides me knows about the Psi Fighters and all their great adventures? And you were planning to tell me this when?"

I chuckled softly. "Kathryn, she's a Whisperer."

"A Whisperer? What kind? Dog? Horse? Ghost?"

"The Whisperers sort of manage the outside world for us. Mrs. Simmons runs the library, and helps me when I need privacy. Like now. She doesn't know what I do. And you, missy, you know nothing about the Psi Fighters, except that they exist. You know my secret because you're my best friend, and the Kilodan allowed it. I mean, it took forever for him to say yes. He thinks you're good for me."

Kathryn stared off into space, slowly shaking her head. "And here I always thought I was like your Alfred, your loyal butlerish person, the only one you trusted because I had changed your diapers and raised you from an infant while your parents were off being zillionaires. I never realized I was subjected to bureaucratic approval. I suppose they had to do a background check or search my dental records?"

"No, they probably scanned your mind when you weren't looking."

"Okay, I can live with that. Now, back to this promotion. If you get to be Kilodan, do I get a raise?"

"You're not my butler."

"Good point. Could I be a Whisperer?"

"Not possible," Mrs. Simmons said from her desk.

Kathryn threw her hands in the air. "Why not?"

"Because you would need to *whisper!*"

"Oh…okay, gotcha. Tell you what, Rin, here's the plan— you start on that old book while I do my algebra. If you find anything interesting, let me know. Quietly."

"Good plan."

I read in silence for several minutes, only once allowing myself to wonder whether the book was anything more than a loaner, when I found something. "Oh, this is cool."

"What?"

I continued to read in silence.

"*What?*" Kathryn repeated.

"It's about the Knights. It says they are masters of the mistaken impression."

"We talking bad guys or politicians?"

I did a mental eye roll at her. "They're liars. They use little bits of truth to make big lies seem honest."

"Okay, they're politicians. I don't see where you're going with this." She flipped a page in her book.

Kathryn was not being as much help as I had hoped. I went back to reading in silence. Then I saw something that sent chills through me. "I think this is why the Kilodan didn't want me to be involved. Oh, this is awful."

Kathryn closed her math book and leaned toward me. "Speak."

"It says that once you defeat a Knight, he has to be destroyed. Kathryn, I can't do that."

"Tad harsh, isn't it? Why not just lock them up like normal criminals?"

"Knights aren't normal criminals. Jails can't hold them. They're too powerful."

"Send them to therapy, then. Oh, gimme that thing." She snatched the book right out of my hands. After a minute of silent reading, she jabbed a finger into the book. "See, right here's your answer. Do a Memory Lash on him!"

That got my attention. "Huh?"

"It says right here, *a Memory Lash will change a Knight in ways only someone who has experienced it can comprehend. Remorse will consume him until he is incapable of performing the dark acts of the Walpurgi*. See, there's your answer."

"Oh, joy," I mumbled.

Kathryn spread her hands wide. "The Memory Lash makes a Knight stop being a Knight. I would think that's a good thing."

"It would be, except that I hate the Memory Lash."

"That's cool. What exactly is a Walpurgi?"

"That's what the Knights call themselves."

"Awesome. And a Memory Lash would be…"

I scowled. "It is the cruelest weapon I know. It makes you remember things. The meanest things you ever did."

"Big whoop. Unless you're, like, a masochist, how's that a weapon?"

"The Lash twists your memories. Say you beat up a little kid just for the fun of it."

"That would be my brother," Kathryn said. "The little dweeb deserved it, and I have fond memories."

"You would remember the kicking and the punching and the crying exactly as it happened, but you would be the victim instead of the bully. You would feel what he felt. If he were in pain, *you* would hurt. If he were scared, *you'd* feel the terror. If he were screaming for his mommy, *you* would be screaming. The worst part isn't the pain, though."

"No?" Kathryn's eyebrows drew together. "What could be worse? I pummeled the little twerp."

"The remorse. The Lash makes you really understand how your victim felt. You just want to take it back, but you know you can't. Ever. And you're filled with such miserable regret that you want to die. One time, when I was little, I got mad at Susie for ripping the head off my doll. I smacked her little bum hard."

"So? I smack my brother all the time. It's therapeutic."

"Kathryn, I don't think you have any idea how hard even a beginning Psi Fighter hits. Every time we practice the Lash in class, I remember it." I closed my eyes. "How the tears ran down her little face. How she opened her mouth to cry, but nothing came out. How she put her tiny hands over her diaper, and started running in place because it hurt so badly. Her whole body shook. I bruised her. Kathryn, I chose a stupid doll over my own sister."

"You were little," Kathryn said. "You didn't know any better."

"I knew what I was doing," I growled, hating myself more with every word. "Every time I have to remember it, I want to hug Susie and tell her how sorry I am, and then punch myself in the face for being such a jerk."

Kathryn touched my hair. My cheeks were soaked with tears. She hugged me, and I buried my face in her shoulder, sobbing silently as she stroked my hair.

"Hey," Kathryn said softly. "I didn't do a Memory Lash on you."

I hiccuped, and we both laughed. "I know. Sorry. I'm okay now."

"You don't look okay."

"I am." I laughed again. "This is the change *The Book of Lore* is talking about. This is why I am so protective of Susie. I will never hit her again. I'm not capable of it. And the thought of anyone else touching her terrifies me. That's why I have to find this apprentice. As long as he's free, my little sister and the Psi Fighters will never be safe."

"Back to work, then?"

"Back to work."

"Okay, your Kilo-dude thinks the masked minion we're looking for is either a teacher or a student, right?"

"Masked minion?"

"Faceless fiend. Diabolical devil. Bad guy. Don't you speak Superhero? Now, let's put our astute little minds together and narrow down the options. Teachers first. After considerable consideration, we conclude it's not a teacher. End of story. Now, students—"

"Why isn't it a teacher?"

"The Kilo-dude said it was somebody inexperienced. That means kid."

I laughed. "He meant inexperienced in the Mental Arts."

Kathryn puckered her lips and squished her eyebrows together with both hands. "Okay, the problem there is that *all* of the teachers are inexperienced. Could be anyone. Except Mrs. Bagley. She's too awesome."

"True. Or Dr. Captious. He's too short."

"Maybe he's a Knight Light. Get it?"

I buried my face in my hands and moaned. Not even Andy would have tried that line.

"Don't forget, Rin, he has a connection to Mason."

"Yeah, but if Captious was a Knight, he'd brag about it along with all his other amazing talents." I shot my hand in the air. "Ooo, ooo, I know! Miss Jackson!"

"The Diva of Dodgeball? Rinnie, just because you have a personal vendetta against the woman doesn't qualify her to be a supervillain."

"Does, too. I can still feel the welts on my liver."

"Give it up, Rin. You were right all along. The Knight-in-training can't be a teacher."

"You said that, not me."

"Just trying to make you feel good about yourself. Okay, let's talk students. Tons of them have connections to Mason. Like the Red Team. Too obvious. Tammy loves the spotlight. Not exactly cloak-and-dagger, is she?"

"Art Rubric. Also too obvious. I mean, he has a nasty streak a mile long, but he's so whacked out on drugs, he could never be a Knight. What about Chuckie Cuff?"

Kathryn's face went deadpan. "Seriously?"

"Okay, that was a stretch. Leave no turn unstoned, as they say. And Chuckie is rarely unstoned. Wow, we aren't getting anywhere, are we?"

"Not yet, but riddle me this, Batman—if the apprentice just showed up at school, wouldn't his alter ego also have just shown up?"

"Not necessarily. The point of having a secret identity is that it's secret. People who have known me my whole life don't have a clue."

"That's good, because Egon is the only new kid at school."

Suddenly, the unthinkable hit me. "You said he moved here to train. Oh, Kathryn, you don't believe—"

Kathryn did a lip curl. "Only one way to find out. Fortunately, I watch plenty of crime dramas. Let's build a profile."

"I'm a Psi Fighter, not a profiler."

"Follow my lead, girl. Profile me your average Knight."

I shrugged. "Well, Knights are like Psi Fighters. They do what we do."

"Itemize, please."

"They're highly skilled martial artists."

"Strike one." Kathryn popped a finger in the air. "Not looking good for Egon."

"There are plenty of really good martial artists in the world. That doesn't make them Walpurgis Knights."

"Rinnie, when you build a profile, you don't shoot down the facts. Now, item number two."

"Knights are experts in the art of stealth. They can move without being detected."

Kathryn popped up two fingers and raised an eyebrow at me.

"What?" I asked.

"Ever notice how Egon just appears out of thin air at assemblies?"

"He didn't just appear—"

"Next."

"We make weapons from thought."

"Do Knights do that, too?"

"Yes, they can do everything we can do. Kathryn, there's no way to know if Egon can make Psi Weapons, just like there's no way to know if I can, unless he actually makes one. Knights are sneaky, and vile, and deceptive. They won't do anything that draws attention to their alter egos. The only obvious thing about them is that they've always hung out with the wrong crowd—the Huns, the Nazis, anybody who is bad news. That's their cover. Puts the attention on the crowd instead of the Knight."

Kathryn drummed her fingertips on her open algebra book. "So our profile is as follows—highly skilled martial artist, master of stealth, the ability to make weapons from thought, and totally impossible to distinguish from the lunch ladies they hang out with."

"Where did you get that?" I asked.

"It's a well-known fact that lunch ladies are nasty. Who else would serve that stuff to innocent children? They are *totally* the wrong crowd."

"Our lunch ladies are nice, and the cafeteria food is good."

"That's their cover! Add them to the list of suspects."

"Egon doesn't hang out with lunch ladies. He doesn't fit your profile, Kathryn."

Kathryn cocked her head, closed one eye, and squinted at the ceiling. "Let's examine the facts. Fact Number One—Egon is famous for being one of the youngest mixed martial artists to be undefeated. I'm sorry, a Knight wouldn't flaunt the fact that he is a world-class cage fighter. That would draw unwanted attention to his alter ego. Egon doesn't fit the profile, Rin."

I buried my face in my hands.

"Fact Number Two—the Knights are mysterious and secretive. A real Knight wouldn't stand out. He would be the last person we'd suspect."

I breathed a tiny sigh of relief. The downside to being a crime fighter is that everyone is a suspect, even guys who are totally crush-worthy. Peeking out between my fingers, I said, "So have we established that, while Egon *is* an interesting person, he's not a person of interest?"

"We have. Back to the drawing board. The *un*-obvious drawing board."

A face we hadn't talked about popped into my head. "Hey, what about Dr. Miliron?"

"Seriously? We just concluded it wasn't a teacher. Why would you make me re-conclude?" Kathryn thought about it for a second, then snapped her fingers and pointed at me. "You might just be on to something, Rinster. He's too weird to be real. Omigosh! He's the head of the Class Project. Rinnie, that means he's connected to Mason *and* the drugs. He's our man!"

Suddenly, it made perfect sense. "You're brilliant! I should have seen it. I mean, he's so completely out there that nobody would ever suspect him. He's as far from Mr. Obvious as you can get. Just the opposite of somebody who reeks of darkness and corruption, like Mason."

Kathryn's head snapped up. "Mason. What do you mean?"

"Well, Mason's a complete jerk and obviously evil, but he's not deceptive. He doesn't cover up *anything*. He knows his dad will protect him. But Dr. Miliron does absolutely nothing that would make me believe he's anything but a goofnut."

"Rinnie, I'm going out on a limb, here. Are you afraid of Egon?"

I thought about Egon sitting next to me at the assembly and got warm. "Afraid? No. I don't think it's called fear, Kathryn."

"Think about it—Egon might not be the apprentice, but he's a mixed martial arts expert. And he's not just extremely good, he's a prodigy. So let me ask you this—is a Psi Fighter, with all your Mental Arts mumbo jumbo, afraid of an amazingly tough, but otherwise completely normal kid?"

"No, of course not. He's no match for one of us. Hey, are you saying I'm not completely normal?"

"Implied it, didn't say it. Back to the question. Can Egon defeat a Knight?"

"Umm, no, he wouldn't have a chance."

"Well, Mason is scared to death of him. Why would he openly cause all that havoc and devastation, yet be a little goodie-two-shoes around Egon?" Suddenly Kathryn's eyes grew wide and she screamed like she'd just won a shopping spree. "*That's it!*"

"Shhh!" Mrs. Simmons hissed, turning toward us from her

desk. Kathryn gave her a double thumbs up.

"Apparently I missed something," I whispered.

Kathryn grabbed me by the shoulders. "You said the Knights are experts at making lies look like the truth, right?"

"So?" I gave her a looking-at-you-over-my-glasses-even-though-I-don't-wear-glasses look.

"Mason uses tiny lies to make the real truth look like a big lie. He gets away with all sorts of hinky doings right out in the open, but then pretends to be afraid of Egon. You know what that means? I know what that means! That means Mason's not who we think he is."

"But Mr. Munificent said… Are you saying Mason's not our connection to the Knight?"

Kathryn took my hand. "No, sweetheart. He's sneaky, vile, deceptive, *and* he hangs out with the wrong crowd. I'm saying Mason *is* the Knight."

Chapter Eight

The Stalker and Mr. Scallion

I got off the toilet and stepped out of the mineshaft. Having remembered to flush this time, I was happily dry and odor-free. Andy had once again strategically positioned himself under the yellow light bulb.

"If it's a brilliant mind you need," he said, pointing to the bulb glowing above his head, "I must say in all modesty that you've come to the right place."

"You're just the picture of humility." I patted Andy on the cheek.

"True, true. But enough about me. Let's talk about you. Better yet, let's talk about me. Let me summarize my amazing grasp of the situation. First, you have a vision of Amos Munificent being attacked by some guy in a skull mask and leotards. Next, you ignore my orders and let him escape."

"Actually," I said, "it was the stalker who escaped."

"Exactly! So you attack him with a weapon you can't control, see his face *and* his memories, and completely botch your first mission, crushing my high hopes for you. And now you want me to help you spy on the mayor's son because he hit you with a dodgeball. Tell me, has my uncanny mind captured the essence of the dilemma?"

"I don't remember anybody in leotards, and the entire gym class hit me with a dodgeball."

"There you have it. You don't remember. If I tell you the key to everything is your memory, will you let me go back to my Three Stooges marathon?"

I flashed an eye roll at him. "I don't think my memory is the problem here."

"Not the problem. The solution. Something sparked that vision of Amos," Andy said. "Every time we witness an event, or touch an object, we pick up memory fragments. The ones you picked up were very powerful. Strong enough to form pictures in your pretty little head without trying."

"Are you saying I actually saw someone attack Mr. Munificent?"

"Either that, or you had too many Twinkies before bedtime."

"I don't like Twinkies."

"Your life is so empty." Andy shook his head. "Tell you what. Let's project your memories and see what's in that teeny tiny brain of yours."

"I haven't learned mental projection, yet. That takes years to master."

"Yeah, yeah, yeah. So does the Mental Blast, the Psi Weapons, levitation, etcetera, etcetera, etcetera. Your point?"

"I can't levitate, either," I said. "If I knew how to project,

I could have shown you the stalker's face and he would be behind bars. What good is seeing his face if I can't describe it? I wish the Kilodan could scan me."

"You saw something nasty. Something you weren't ready for. You're suppressing those images because they are too painful. Fortunately for your emotionally clouded mind, I am a genius. Follow me, my brother, and I will lead you to enlightenment."

"I'm a girl, Andy. Girls are usually referred to as 'sister.'"

"Technicality," Andy said. "I repeat. Follow me."

Andy took me by the hand and led me through the mines, skipping and singing *The Wizard of Oz* theme song. After passing several dark corridors branching off the main tunnel, we stopped at the K-Mart sign that marked the entrance to the tech lab. We were about to enter Andy's own twisted version of the Emerald City.

Andy placed his hand on the entry panel. His hair fluffed, and the door clicked open. Inside, a man screamed as though he was in terrible pain.

"Don't worry," Andy said, entering the room. "It's just an experiment. And a very successful one, I might add. Wish I'd had it working the night you saw the stalker."

I followed, wondering what kind of experiment involved a screaming man. The room was round like the inside of an igloo, with plasma screens where walls should have been. In the center of the white floor, a white box rested on a white stand next to a white chair. At the front of the igloo, Moe was pulling Curly's tooth with a large pair of pliers, and Larry stood nearby with a mallet.

"Only you would experiment with Three Stooges movies. What are you trying to do, extract a sense of humor?"

"Not exactly." Andy glanced over his shoulder. His face was unusually serious, and the snappy comeback I expected never came. "Look behind you."

I turned toward the door we had come through. While the Stooges acted out their scene on the set in front of us, cameramen and stagehands worked at the back of the room. The director sat smiling in his tall chair, and, high above him, a boy fiddled with a huge stage light.

"Hey, I never saw that in this episode. Where did you get this footage?" I turned back toward the front of the room. Moe held a large molar victoriously in his pliers, and Curly moaned theatrically while holding his jaw.

"That's the experiment," Andy said.

"Big deal. You found some extra clips that show how they made the episode, then you projected in three-sixty."

"Not quite. You know how some civilizations won't let you take their picture, because they think you'll steal their soul?"

"Yeah."

"Well, a soul is too powerful to be captured by a camera, but thoughts can be captured by anything. Handwriting, a drawing...a movie. I have equipment that extracts memory fragments from a handwritten note. You can see who wrote it and what they were feeling at the time. So I asked myself, if it can be done with handwriting, why not film? And I answered myself—with the right combination of technology and incredible good looks, it should work. Voila! Stooges memories."

"I don't see where you're going with this."

"We have to project that memory of yours."

"I told you, I can't project. The Kilodan tried to teach me, but my mind just goes blank."

"Gasp," Andy said. "Your mind a blank! In shock, I find myself! Well, darling, maybe the Kilodan doesn't have what it takes to read a weak mind, but this baby does." He patted the white box.

"Ha ha. What's that?"

"The Psi Fighter MPU 3000."

"MPU 3000?"

"Mental Projection Unit, currently the lightest mental projector on the planet. Actually, the only one. Bright image. High resolution. Excellent color. With surround sound!" Andy pushed a button and a tray slid out of the projector. "Blu-ray, too. A complete portable cinema for a low, low price."

"Where do you come up with this stuff?"

"Well," Andy said, "it hasn't hit Walmart's shelves yet. I built it. Sit."

"I'm a person, not a DVD." Duh. "I won't fit in the Blu-ray slot."

"Better yet, you're the original memory source. We should pick up a lot of detail. Expect to see more than you remember."

"Andy, nobody can see more than they remember."

"Ever watch a movie the second time and see things you missed the first time?"

"I'll believe it when I see it." I slouched skeptically into the chair next to the projector and Andy hit a few buttons. A glaring white screen replaced the Stooges on the front wall.

"Put your hand on the electrode," Andy instructed.

I placed my fingertips on the silvery plate attached to the chair's arm. The MPU 3000 hummed with energy, and static filled the air. Psychic sparks jumped from the plate to my fingers, and my hand was drawn down like iron to a magnet.

"Okay, go ahead," Andy said expectantly. He stared at the

blank screen, bouncing on his toes, hands folded behind his back.

"And...do what?"

Andy smacked his forehead with the palm of his hand. "And our delusional Kilodan calls you his top student. Remember, silly girl. Remember, so the 3000 can see it."

"I knew that." I concentrated. The 3000 tugged on my brain, and the glaring white screen turned black, then brown and blurry. Slowly, Egon's brilliant green eyes and adorable smile came into focus and filled the screen. Oops.

"How sweet," Andy muttered. "Back to the mission. This isn't about your love life."

"Sorry." I concentrated on the stalker. The back of Elmo's head appeared on the screen with my hand snaking toward it, snatching away the mask. Instantly, anger and the stench of unwashed bad guy filled the room. I couldn't tell if my memory was that vivid, or if the odor was real, somehow extracted by Andy's gizmo. "Do you smell that?"

Andy hit a button, and the man's face froze on the screen, twisted with anger. "I do. This baby is loaded. Visual, audio, emotional, and olfactory transmitters and receivers. It will completely change the way we watch SpongeBob. Imagine, if you will, a future where you turn on the TV and the fragrance of pineapple and dead fish delights your senses."

"To think iPods used to impress me."

"Well, you know, small minds. I see why you didn't recognize Elmo. This guy is low profile."

"You know him?"

Andy walked to the screen and studied the stalker's face, completely silent for several seconds. "Name's Norman LaReau," he finally said. "His mother owns Sinclair Park. Show me the skull mask."

I tried to remember how it looked, but the memory blurred. It had flashed through my mind so quickly that night. All I could think of was the Jolly Roger on a pirate flag. Instantly, the cemetery in Sinclair Park filled the screen. The sun was setting, and I felt myself sinking into LaReau's mind. Suddenly, his hand appeared on the screen, caressing a tombstone like it was a kitten. His voice purred from the speakers.

"I love the park at dusk. It makes your grave feel so...I don't know, final. Like a real accomplishment. You shouldn't have sent me away, Daddy. On the plus side, I found some new friends while I was gone. And a hobby."

The screen flickered as though Norman had blinked. His hand came away from the tombstone and turned to reveal a watch. "Late again, are we, Mr. Scallion? I certainly hope you'll bring my package. And a bit of that freakish chemical that makes my hobby so much more interesting...la la, la-la...la la, la-la, Elmo's song."

"Having happy thoughts, are we?" a voice said.

Norman's fingers clamped together. Fear and confusion bounced from the screen. "Did you bring it, Mr. Scallion?"

The image panned slowly from Norman's clenched fist, across the graveyard to a man wearing a skull and black armor. He laughed quietly and tossed a small baggie. It sailed across the screen and Norman reached out to catch it.

"My thanks," Norman said. "Did you bring the child?"

Scallion stood motionless. "That would be reckless, wouldn't it?"

"Don't you trust me? I paid in advance."

"It's not a matter of trust. It's a matter of process. That was step one."

"Tell me about step two."

"I acquire her."

Norman's frustration filled the room. "You don't even have her? Do you understand my sense of urgency?"

"I understand it perfectly. I also understand your taste. You have very stringent requirements, do you not?"

"I do," Norman agreed.

"And I don't want to disappoint you. Meet me at the Shadow Passage. I'll contact you. She'll be gift wrapped."

"That's how I like them." Norman's eyelids came together and the screen went blank for a full second. When he opened them, he was alone with the tombstones. "But I'm not waiting."

"Got it!" Andy froze the screen again.

"Andy, I don't remember any of this. All I saw was a flash of a skull, not an entire conversation. Where did all that come from?"

"When the Memory Lash connected you to LaReau, your mind recorded everything. But the sight of the caged children traumatized you so much that you suppressed the rest of the memory. Fortunately, my equipment doesn't feel trauma. It brings up everything. Girl, this is big! Do you have any idea what this means?"

I frowned. "Norman LaReau used costumes and a creeper van to stalk kids. When the police turned up the heat, he got nervous and paid Mason, disguised as Mr. Scallion, to do his dirty work. While Scallion was setting up the next victim, LaReau got impatient, and went after someone on his own. That must be what he was doing in the Elmo mask. And I let him get away!" My mind raced off in a thousand directions. If I had only controlled the Memory Lash, LaReau would be in jail. "Andy, this is awful. We might have two kidnappers. Now we don't know whether Mason or LaReau took Christie Jasmine. Or whether another child is missing somewhere that we don't know about. Andy, this is crazy, even for Mason."

Andy looked at me blankly. "I was going to say I found the leotards, but let's go with that."

I smacked Andy. "You know something you aren't telling me."

"I know plenty of things that I don't tell you. Most of them aren't any of your business. But this particular thing may be. The hobby LaReau mentioned? Human trafficking. We never had any hard evidence against him. Just a gut feeling on the part of our glorious leader."

"The Kilodan's gut feelings are usually pretty accurate. What happened?"

"Trafficking just stopped one day. We got too close. LaReau's sly. Looks like he's back in action. Show me Munificent."

I really didn't want to. That memory frightened me. But a girl's life was at stake, so I hugged myself and concentrated. The tombstones of Sinclair Park stared down at me from the screen like giant monoliths about to topple over. In a flash they were gone, and we were spying on Mr. Munificent through a hole in a frosted glass window. He seemed positively exhausted. The floor of the dimly lit room looked like a chessboard with its black and white linoleum tile. The wall was lined with file cabinets, all black but one. It was green and battered, with an open drawer. Mr. Munificent shoved an envelope in and closed it.

Andy froze the screen. "Color me intrigued."

"What color is that?"

"The color of that off-color cabinet. Amos knows something

he hasn't told us. Let's see what it is. And...ACTION!" Andy punched the unfreeze button or something, and Mr. Munificent started to move again.

"Unbelievable," Munificent said, raking his fingers through his sweaty hair. "How could I let it happen again?"

A gauntleted hand appeared on the screen and pushed against the frosted glass, opening the office door. Mr. Munificent turned slowly as though he'd been expecting someone. A deep voice said, "You couldn't stop it the first time. Why in the name of all that is fun and exciting would you try to stop it now?"

"Didn't know who you were back then," Munificent whispered. He drew his gun. "I do now, thanks to your incredibly bad timing."

"My timing is perfect," the voice replied. "Do you believe yours is better?"

"I'd bet my life on it. Let's find out. I'll pull the trigger, and you try to take over my mind before the hammer falls."

"You say draw, cowboy."

Munificent clicked back the gun's hammer.

"Before you kill me in cold blood, officer," the voice said, "there's something you should know. Something significant."

Munificent's eyes drew narrow. "I already know. I already warned them."

Suddenly, the image on the screen shrunk and blurred and a familiar hallway came into focus. Students and teachers walked by, but it was like viewing them through a cardboard tube. Then a sea of students filled the auditorium. Suddenly, the tube narrowed, and seemed to peer around a wall, like it was spying on somebody. Dr. Miliron was talking to Mrs. Bagley. The screen blinked, and the backs of two girls appeared, one with gorgeous hair, the other, stick-straight white blond.

Kathryn and me.

Another blink, and the Kilodan's emotionless mask peered down.

The image opened up to full screen. A furious surge of emotion radiated from it for just an instant, then disappeared as quickly as it had come. The voice giggled and a gauntleted finger pointed at Munificent. "I'll remember that for future reference. Oh, by the way, I'm not the kidnapper this time."

"Of course not. And you didn't murder the Morgan family ten years ago."

"As a matter of fact, I did. But I had several excellent reasons. Can you believe they never returned the boy as I politely asked them to? Refresh my memory. Where did you send their little girl? She'd be, what, maybe fifteen, sixteen, about now?"

Munificent's anger beat down from the screen. "She's out of your reach forever."

Cackling laughter filled the room. "Don't be so sure. Now if you'll forgive me, there's a job opening I simply must create." A ghostly shadow in the shape of a hand erupted from the gauntlet, and fastened itself on Munificent's chest, translucent fingers splayed like a spider. They closed and pushed their way inside. Munificent dropped his gun, clutched his heart and struggled for breath, chopping at the misty arm that had embedded itself in his chest. His eyes rolled back. He dropped to his knees, and fell face down on the floor with a wet *thud*. His body convulsed, then lay still.

Munificent's dead face expanded to fill the screen, like the killer was kneeling down for a closer look at him. The voice said, "Naive Psi," and laughed like a jackal. Then the screen panned to the office door, and the reflection of a man wearing loose-fitting black, kneeling over Munificent's corpse, flashed on the window. He didn't wear the skull mask I had expected. He didn't wear any mask at all. In the place where his face should have been, a nearly decomposed head with rotting teeth and shriveled red eyes grinned down at me.

I screamed and pulled my hand away from the electrode plate.

The screen went blank.

Chapter Nine

Return of Nicolaitan

"This is good." Andy looked worried. "Good in a very, very bad way. It answers questions I would have rather not asked."

An involuntary spasm shook me. I was so scared I could hardly breathe. "What are you talking about?"

"Egad! What do they teach in school these days?"

"How to avoid foul-smelling things in the locker room. Are you going to explain this to me, or do I have to figure it out for myself?"

"We don't have that much time. I'll 'splain. That misty-looking hand is a Mental Arts technique. It's called Handless Death. Only the Knights use it. Leaves no mark. They'll think Amos died of a heart attack."

"Are you telling me my memory really happened?"

"That wasn't *your* memory," Andy said. "But, yes, it happened. They found Munificent's body this morning. He knew Skull Head's identity. Something had just happened that gave it away. He died before he could tell us. I have a bad feeling about this."

I was going to comment on Andy's inappropriate use of a perfectly good Star Wars line, but at that moment everything clicked. "Mr. Munificent is *dead*? Andy, that can't be right. I just saw him at the assembly. He smiled at me."

My whole body was numb with disbelief. Then another impossible thought pounded into my brain. "Mr. Munificent connected Mason to the stalker, and now he's dead. I suspected that Mason was a Knight, and knew he was a jerk. But I never thought he was a murderer."

Andy put his hand on my shoulder. "Rinnie, Mason has killed before."

Horror shot through me. My stomach heaved. I tried to talk, but didn't have words. I just stared up at Andy.

"He had a very abusive mother. He killed her with a shovel. His father covered it up. The Kilodan saw it in the mayor's mind."

"A shovel? Oh, that's— Wait, I thought she was in a mental hospital."

"Part of the cover-up," Andy said. "But you're right."

"About what? My friends at school are in more danger than I realized."

"Did you notice subtle differences in Skull Head between the two memories?" Andy asked.

"Yeah, he wore different skull masks."

"I said subtle."

"He acted like a used car salesman in one and a psychopath in the other."

Andy touched his fingertips together and made a tent.

"Can you be a tad more specific?"

I thought about it. "Mason was calm when he was with LaReau. Like he was bored. He was a lot nastier when he killed Mr. Munificent. He felt so powerful. Then he was back to normal, spying on me at school."

"You have good instincts," a voice boomed behind me, and I spun so fast I nearly broke Andy's machine.

"Where did you come from?" I said, trying to catch my breath.

"God made me," the Kilodan said. "Do you know what this means?"

"He has a sense of humor."

"Thankfully. Whose mind were you in when you projected LaReau?"

"Norman LaReau's, compliments of the Memory Lash," I said.

"Whose mind were you in when you projected Munificent?"

"Mason's, I think. But I don't know how I got that memory."

The Kilodan looked at Andy, then at the blank screen. "You believe Mason Draudimon is the man with the skull mask."

"I'm around him enough. It's possible that I picked up his memory fragments. Ooh, I remember! I saw the vision of Mr. Munificent's murder right after Mason handed me a smiley face and gave me a noogie in Algebra!"

"Memory transfer by noogie," Andy said, slamming his fist into his open palm. "Happens all the time."

I turned to the Kilodan. "Is he serious?"

"That would be a momentous occasion. No, memories do not transfer simply because someone touches us. Nor do visions pop unasked into our consciousness." The Kilodan moved in front of my chair. His expressionless mask peered down at me. "Some memories are filled with extremely dark emotions, too violent to be contained. They can force themselves into the mind of one as sensitive as you. It is unlikely that the mayor's son is the one called Scallion. However, Munificent's evidence suggests that he has connections to Scallion. LaReau has been paying Scallion for drugs and victims. I would like you to learn whether Mason can lead us to Scallion. If we find Scallion, I am certain we can convince him to lead us to LaReau."

No doubt. I would *not* want to be on the Kilodan's Naughty List.

Okay, so Mason wasn't a Knight, but he was involved with a Knight, which still meant he was a filthy marsupial.

"I'll find the other one," Andy said. "I'll stop him permanently this time."

Other one? "What other one?"

"Scallion didn't kill Amos Munificent," the Kilodan said. "You correctly sensed that the man in the skull mask felt more powerful in the second memory. If we were to replay the memories, you would notice other subtle differences. There are two Knights. The one who calls himself Scallion tries to imitate the older, more powerful Knight. But it is an unimpressive imitation. He is the apprentice we've been looking for."

Andy leaned toward the Kilodan. "Is this what Munificent knew that he didn't tell us?"

I was confused. "Okay, who is the other Knight? The one who killed Mr. Munificent?"

The Kilodan took me by the shoulders and eased me out of the chair. "Amos was murdered by Nicolaitan."

I was instantly numb. The man who murdered my parents.

"He was spying on me in that memory."

Andy shook his head. "That was a memory of several memories. Nicolaitan scanned Munificent right before he killed him. The school, the assembly. When you felt the flash of anger, that's when he saw Munificent's memory of a meeting with our beloved Kilodan. Ol' Nic doesn't like the Big K."

"Arch enemies tend to have that relationship," the Kilodan said. "We have never faced off, but someday soon, we will. On that day, one of us will have no more secrets."

"Okay, then who was spying on me in Nicolaitan's memory?"

"Nicolaitan took that memory from Scallion," Andy said. "It proves that Scallion's alter ego has been in your school. It doesn't prove who he is."

"Makes perfect sense if Scallion is Mason," I said. "I don't understand why you say Mason is not a Knight."

Andy's expression turned deadly serious. "Mason is the boy your parents rescued. We have had him under surveillance ever since. Nicolaitan never came back for him. If he had returned to train the boy as his apprentice, we would have known."

The only part of that conversation I heard was *the boy my parents rescued*. That meant… "Mason is the reason I was kidnapped?"

Andy nodded.

"If I didn't have an excuse to hate that miserable wombat before, I sure do now. My parents died because of him, and he thanks them by working for their murderer. Why didn't you ever tell me?"

"You weren't ready." The Kilodan gently took my face in his hands. "I feel your anger toward Mason. Do not let it misguide you. The only thing we know for certain is that Mason was a victim, just like you. Now, listen to me. We know that Nicolaitan has placed his apprentice in your school. What we do not know is *why*. But I fear the worst. You must learn quickly who he is and how he is connected to Mason. Your mission is more critical than we knew. There is only one way you could have absorbed a memory powerful enough to push itself into your head. You have been in contact with Nicolaitan himself."

"But how?" Kathryn wasn't totally off base, then. Mason was connected to Scallion, *and Scallion was connected to my parents' killer*. My mission just took on a whole new urgency. Hopefully that included permission to engage in wombat pummeling. "Where do I start?"

"You have to get very close to Mason," Andy said.

"I plan to," I said, punching my fist into my palm.

"And when I say close, I do *not* mean beating him to death. You have to get into his head, and you have to do it without him knowing you're in there. You can't scan him, because if he is in contact with the Knights, they can scan him as well and may see you. Mason wouldn't know that you are a Psi Fighter, but the Knight who scans him would."

"And how exactly am I supposed to do that?"

Andy grinned. "The way that women have gotten into men's heads since the days of Adam and Eve. Let him take you on a date."

I laughed. Only Andy would make such a stupid joke at such a critical time. "I know, right? *Hey, Mason, ol' buddy ol' pal, wanna take in a movie?* Seriously, what's the best way to go? Okay, how about this? I'll recon his house. Masked and armored of course, and I'll stay in Shimmer mode. Sooner or later, he has to do something to reveal his mission. Right?"

Andy and the Kilodan stared silently. Andy's face was totally blank.

"What? Am I missing something?" I looked back and forth between them. Andy slowly turned his palms up and got a slightly pained expression.

"No," I said. "You have *got* to be kidding. You actually want me to ask Mason out?"

The Kilodan sighed and said, "I believe we have just witnessed a momentous occasion."

Chapter Ten

Mission Undesirable

The next morning, I stood outside the chemistry lab wishing I'd been assigned something easy, like ending world hunger. I mean, it's not like there's not enough food on the planet. All I'd have to do is get people to share, and boom—no more world hunger.

But *my* mission was complicated. First, I had to suck up my disgust for Mason, which was considerable. Then, I had to trick him into taking me on a date. Finally, I'd have to actually show up for said date and not pound Mason's head off the tabletop. The self-control requirements were borderline unreasonable.

However, I had a duty as a Psi Fighter to take advantage of any opportunity, no matter how loudly every ounce of me screamed against it. And, I must admit, Mason had already laid the groundwork for me. After all, he *did* threaten to ask me out the day he tried to give me a new hairdo. It definitely seemed like the most straightforward approach. But it was far from a perfect plan, because I saw two gaping holes in it. First, did Mason mean it? I mean, how embarrassing would it be if I told him I'd go, and he said, "Silly girl, did you honestly think I was serious?"

The second hole was deeper. And slightly more pathetic. How does a girl actually ask a boy to go out with her? *Hey, big guy, wanna party?* Okay, that would work for Angel, but she's hot, and I'm me. Even if I figured that part out...once I got there, what would I do? I asked Kathryn for advice, but the best she could come up with was "Be yourself." Right. Myself had zero dating experience.

Heck, I had zero experience with a real social life of any kind. The Academy had been my social life for as long as I could remember. I practiced with Andy every night after school. Even my weekends began with practice. Friday night Psi Weapons, followed by Saturday morning kung fu, followed by Saturday afternoon Mind Scanning. I spent Saturday evenings hanging out with Kathryn at the movies or the mall or wherever our mood took us. Sunday was church and homework. In this single aspect of my life, I was like every other teen I knew—totally booked. Only the details were different. When would I possibly squeeze in a date? No way I was giving up Saturday with Kathryn. A girl's got to have her priorities.

Theoretically, since I had a mission, a Friday night date would count toward the assignment. I could skip out on Psi Weapons. On second thought, not a date. Hanging out. I knew how to do that. Oh, I was *so* out of my comfort zone.

"Hey," a voice said.

"YAH!" My hands flew into the air, launching my books

into the ionosphere.

"And I thought you didn't drink coffee," Mason said, his head poking out of the lab door. "Why are you out in this empty hall all by yourself when I'm alone in this dark and dreary lab? Are you stalking me? 'Cause if you are, I'm okay with it."

"No, no," I shook my head, too mortified to admit how on-target he was. "I knew you'd be here. You know, working on the Class Project. I wanted to…talk about it."

Mason raised an eyebrow. He looked up the hall, then down, then back into the lab. "To who?"

"Umm…you."

Mason seemed confused. "I'm sorry, who are you and what have you done with Miss Noelle? Hey, I have to get to class. If I see anybody you'd actually want to talk to, I'll tell him you're waiting. Toodles." Mason started walking away, then spun on his heel and bent down in one fluid motion, sweeping my scattered books together. "Here you go. Be careful. They're hot."

I took a step back.

Mason pursed his lips. "You might need these."

"What's wrong with you, Mason? You're being nice."

"I'm always nice."

"What about last week, when you tripped me coming out of the girl's bathroom? The week before that, you tossed a ketchup-covered hot dog bun at me in the cafeteria. During history, you shot gum wads at me and knocked my books out of my hands. And this week, you threatened to ask me out, then gave me a new hairdo."

"I did not give you a hairdo."

"Then you admit you asked me out?"

"Why, do you want to take me up on my offer?"

"What?"

"You want to hang out Friday after school?"

"Um. Sure." Choke! Gag! Vomit!

"You do?"

• • •

Once Mason recovered from the shock that I was willing to hang out with him (which, for the record, I was *not*—I had a mission, and not all missions are cotton candy, okay?) he said we should meet at the Shadow Passage. No surprise there. Kathryn said the gym-turned-video arcade was Mason's hangout. Most of the kids from school hung out there. I suppose it could have been worse. I could have been meeting him in a dark alley.

Walking to the Shadow Passage Friday night was torture. I felt like a mastodon dragging itself through a tar pit. Every inch of my flesh had its foot on the brakes, every nucleus of every cell dropped its anchors, every endoplasmic reticulum screamed *I do not want to do this.* By the time I arrived, I was exhausted from the struggle.

A huge baby blue awning covered the entrance. Above the mirrored front door, a sign in spidery script read THE SHADOW PASSAGE, HIDDEN GATEWAY TO ADVENTURE. I pulled the door open. Hard music and the bleeps and pings of video games blared into the street. Inside was brightly lit, and decorated like no arcade I had ever seen. Posters plastered the wall advertising free workshops on Self-esteem, Positive Self-talk, Respecting Others' Feelings, Ways to Handle Anger,

The Golden Rule, and The Benefits of a Positive Attitude. An old-fashioned pizza stand filled the center of the expansive room. Tables and booths were arranged along each sidewall. A series of monitors attached to exercise equipment occupied the majority of the room. Flashing neon signs identified each activity—Crown of Kings, Ferocious Beast Hunter, Grand Theft Bazooka, and a dozen other popular video games. Players wore visual reality headgear, wired up like patients in intensive care.

I took a seat in an unoccupied booth in the back corner where I could comfortably watch the entrance. Behind me, a long, lone table sat in front of a closed door. A sign on the door said *SSA* in bright gold letters. Across the arcade, I recognized Tish and Whatsisface. I slid down in my seat, hoping they wouldn't notice me. Several other kids from my school were at various stations, running, pedaling, battling virtual enemies… the simulators reminded me of something Andy would concoct. I watched the station closest to me in amazement. The screen character's motion mimicked the player's movements. If they had a kung fu game, I would have totally thought about blowing off Mason and hooking myself up.

While I fantasized about pitting my skills against electronic opponents, Mason came through the front door. My first instinct was to disappear out the back, but I forced myself into Psi Fighter mode. It occurred to me that this was my first time out without my mask and armor. This mission was very different from my last one. My objective was to gather intelligence about a wombat who was connected to this Scallion person. I needed to know what said wombat knew. To do that, I had to pretend to be a girl who didn't despise him. Even worse, he had to leave convinced that I enjoyed his company.

As he crossed the room, I noticed that Mason moved like a panther—disciplined, graceful—not a fighter's walk, more like a hunter. His eyes fixed on me almost immediately.

"Hey," Mason said, taking the seat across from me. A huge smile spread across his face. "You showed. Cool."

"Were you worried?"

"A little. Okay, a lot. Nobody ever asks me about the Class Project. It's usually me doing the asking."

"So I've heard."

Mason didn't respond. He just sat there staring at me. I dropped my eyes to the tabletop, my nails tapping away nervously. Say something. Insult me. Call me Peroxide. I really did not want to be there. I would have preferred a dodgeball game. Or Mummy's Magic Mix. In desperation, I asked the only thing that came to mind. "So, what's with this place?"

Mason swept his hand around the arcade. "Welcome to the twenty-first century. Some genius decided to take the old health club and turn it into a gamer's paradise. Dance games, laser tag, simulators. The controllers are built right into the exercise equipment. The longer you go, the more weapons you get. The faster you go, the more speed or power. Builds endurance and strength. The idea is to make exercising a blast. Great concept. Wish I'd invented it. I'd be rich."

Okay, Small Talk initiated. Good start. But I needed to get him pontificating on the pros and cons of hanging out with Knights. Mason continued to stare at me, an odd expression on his face. I hated awkward, and this situation was the epitome of it. I stared at the table, then the ceiling, wondering how to lead the conversation in the right direction. At one point, I made eye contact with Mason, but quickly looked away. I tried to focus on the music, or the beeping of the arcade, but the discomfort wouldn't leave. I needed my mask. I needed a hole to fall into. Suddenly Mason laughed. He was obviously enjoying this.

"What?" I asked, a bit more harshly than I intended.

"I'm sorry, it's just that…well, I never thought I'd be this nervous around you."

I gave him a 'huh?' look.

"I don't have to make fun of you to get you to notice me. You came on your own. I'm in uncharted territory."

"You pick on me to get my attention?"

Mason nodded. "So what do you want to know?"

Jerk. Where do I start? *Do you know a Knight? What's he looking for at school? Is it true that the Class Project is turning out Psychedone 10?* "Oh, I'm just curious. I mean, I've been in Dr. Miliron's chemistry class all semester, but he hasn't mentioned the Class Project yet."

Mason folded his hands and leaned toward me. "He'll only schedule one lab to do the Class Project. He wants to show each class what it's all about, and then whoever is interested can continue after school for extra credit. I'm the lab assistant. I keep the reflux condensers running until they're reacted and ready to go. It's a great program, Rinnie."

Yeah, great if you agree to do Mason's bidding. Otherwise, face the wrath. "Why is it so important to you? I mean, you *are* a little obsessed, don't you think?"

He called me Rinnie. Why did he call me Rinnie?

Mason looked off into some distant horizon that I couldn't see. "I've been studying mental illness, sort of as a hobby, since I was pretty little. Some types are curable. Others…well, it's a fascinating science. Dr. Miliron told me about this project that the mental hospital at Old Torrents sponsored. He said we would contribute to medical research and raise public awareness of a disease that affects millions of people. He convinced me to help, and here we are today. It really didn't take much. Old Torrents is cutting edge. They've been testing different versions of a new miracle drug, and have had a lot of success fighting mental illness. I'm going to get my doctorate. I'll cure it." A pained expression flashed across his face. "You asked why this is important. My mom had problems. I want to help people like her."

"I heard she lives in Old Torrents." As soon as I said it, I wished I hadn't.

Mason smiled, but I could tell he forced it. "That's the rumor, isn't it?" His eyes became moist, and he glanced away.

I was officially ashamed of myself. Mason was totally a jerk, but even he didn't deserve to be reminded about his mother. I knew she was dead, but I couldn't blow my cover. Should have just kept my mouth shut. "Mason, I'm sorry, I should have never brought that up."

"It's okay. Hey, tell me about you. What do you do with your spare time?"

The least I could do was allow him to change the subject. Maybe it would lead somewhere useful. "Me? Not much. Do homework. Hang out with Kathryn."

"I don't think she likes me."

"You beat up her boyfriend. What do you expect?"

"No, I really like Bobby."

"You have a funny way of showing it."

"He just frustrates me sometimes. He's brilliant. I really wish he'd help with the Class Project."

Crud. Mason was as annoying as ever, but I was learning

nothing. I needed to get into his head. Andy was right, I couldn't risk scanning him. My only option was to keep him talking. Maybe he'd slip and reveal something. I wasn't sure why Andy thought I could pull this off, because the Adam and Eve thing totally wasn't working for me. Maybe if I'd worn fig leaves.

I jabbed my thumb over my shoulder. "What's that door labeled *SSA*?"

Mason sighed. "Tammy Angel's dad fronted the money to build this arcade. She talked him into building a back room just for her. It's called the *Star Ship Angel*. Members only."

"How do you get to be a member?"

"Invitation only."

Like the Psi Fighters. Go figure. "And who does the inviting?" As if I didn't know.

"Angel, naturally. She rules the cool, right?"

"Right. What goes on behind the door?"

"Nothing much. Mostly storage. Angel sits at that table outside the SSA door selling her wares."

Ha! Now we were getting somewhere. School wasn't the only place Angel pushed drugs. "Wares?" I said, in my dumbest blond accent. "You mean like Tupperware?"

Mason shook his head. "No, she's into health food. Powders, natural herbs, other stuff that tastes like crap. Her dad owns Nature's Nutrients. It's a health food supplement processor in town."

Wait, did he mean... "She actually sells supplements? All natural nutrients?" Then Angel was telling the truth in the locker room. She had threatened Erica with an improved diet? That meant Tammy was just a twisted, health-conscious bully, not a Psychedone 10 pusher.

Of course, that's what a lying, corrupt friend of a Knight would want me to believe, wasn't it?

"Yeah, if you think I'm obsessed with the Class Project, Angel is *way* overboard with being healthy. She even tries to get Dr. Captious into the machines when he's here."

"I heard he hung out here with you."

"Yeah, the Capster's awesome. We have an arrangement. I let him know what goes on in the school. Who's into what. Dr. Captious is sort of a counselor." Mason pointed to the wall. "See those posters for workshops on Self-Esteem and the Golden Rule and all that? He teaches them."

"I thought he was a math teacher."

Mason nodded. "He has two doctorates. The other one is in psychology. He helps kids sort out their lives. I talk to him all the time. Helps me think through problems."

"What sort of problems could you possibly have, Mason? Your dad's the mayor. It's a well-known fact that you can get away with anything. You harass kids, treat teachers like dirt— must be nice."

"Not really. I don't see my dad much. He's always working. And when he's home, he's always preoccupied. He's really into his political career. Not so much into his son." Mason lowered his eyes. "That's why I hang out here. At least there's somebody to talk to. Somebody to eat dinner with."

If I'd had a Spider Sense, it would have been tingling all over. What normal boy would give somebody like me this type of personal information? Mason was trying to suck me in. I decided to play along to see where he was going with this. "You have dinner here? With who?"

Mason looked at me with the saddest puppy dog eyes. "Whoever."

Did he mean… "You eat alone? Every night?"

"The food's good."

Aww. His mother was gone, his father ignored him… at least I got to have supper with my family every evening before I went to the Academy. I had Mom and Dad and Susie. I had Kathryn. I even had Andy. Mason didn't have anybody. Suddenly, no matter how badly I wanted to, I couldn't hate him.

New tactic. Can the mission. "What's on the menu? I'm kind of hungry. I mean, if you are."

Mason's face lit up like a new sunrise. "I am."

After we dined on the best pizza I had ever had, I said good night to Mason. I had learned absolutely nothing useful for my mission. I was still certain that Tammy Angel was the criminal I had suspected her to be. But I saw a totally different side of Mason—sweet, caring, and lonely. He didn't say much during dinner. He just seemed content. Maybe a ruse, but it was also possible that he was not the total creep I thought he was.

That didn't mean he wasn't my main connection to Scallion, though.

Chapter Eleven

Dalrymple

Monday morning, the noise in the auditorium rose to such a crescendo I couldn't hear myself think. We were in lockdown, and the police dogs had been brought in. Last time this happened, everyone knew about it an hour before the dogs arrived. Somebody had tipped the users, and the evidence had been flushed. Probably the same story this time. According to the Kilodan, the dealers had insiders with the police. Which explained why nobody seemed worried. Basically all the students were just thrilled at the chance to get out of regular classes to attend the special assembly. I had been as well, until I saw Mason climb the balcony stairs with the Red Team in tow. He was as cocky as ever. The Mason I had pizza with Friday evening was nowhere to be seen. Which I unfortunately expected.

Over the weekend, after I debriefed Andy about my date

with Mason (I use that term in the loosest possible sense, because it was totally *not* a date, it was a critical mission), he had given me maps of the school. Ductwork and hidden corridors that only the Psi Fighters knew about crisscrossed the building like a labyrinth. Most of them were big enough to crawl through. It had never dawned on me before, but a whole other world existed inside the walls and ceilings.

Secret passageways appealed to my overactive curiosity gene. But the dust and gaggle of spiders I'd likely encounter in said secret passageways seriously pegged my yuckometer. All the same, I'd soon be sneaking through them. Surveillance had become my new priority. Friday didn't turn up anything useful, and I still needed to find out everything I could about Mason: where he hung out, who he was with, what he was up to. Fortunately, this was easy during assembly. He hung out in the balcony, with the Red Team, up to no good.

"Stu-DENTS," Mrs. Bagley's voice crackled over the microphone. "Last week, I brought in the police to help improve conditions at your school. Then tragedy struck, and we lost a great man. I believe that few of you realize what this means. I believe that fewer of you care. I pray one day you will understand, because you are all in terrible danger. Today, the Greensburg Police have sent us Police Chief Munificent's successor. He has a message for you. A message of hope. So without further ado, I give you Police Chief Dalrymple." She backed away from the microphone, clapping her hands. No one else clapped. So I did. Seeing the old Mason back had left me a tad crabby, and I wasn't in the mood for rudeness.

Some guy in full dress uniform crossed the stage to the microphone, marching like he was in a military procession. His shoulders and chest were covered in medals and badges, and he shook hands with Mrs. Bagley before facing the podium. He removed his hat, exposing a very high hairline and spiky orange hair.

"Chicken," Kathryn said, making me smile a little.

"Thank you for the kind applause from the two of you who bothered to welcome me. My name is Maximilian Dalrymple, and I have come to deliver a very important message. But first, a moment of silence." He placed his hat over his heart, and bowed his head.

After an uncomfortable yet surprisingly silent thirty seconds, he looked up while he put his hat back on. "I'd like to say a few words about Police Chief Amos Munificent. He started a program in this school that I intend to finish. Some of you knew him. He was a kind man, loyal to the city of Greensburg in a way that few men are capable of. There are rumors that he was soft, though, and let things get out of hand in our fair city. I am here, first and foremost, to squelch those rumors. Chief Munificent worked diligently, and did all his capabilities allowed him to do, to stop the drugs and violence we find ourselves forced to endure. If there was any failing, it was not one of effort. Chief Munificent, indeed all of us, find ourselves faced with an enemy who is bigger than any one of us."

"What is he talking about?" Kathryn whispered.

"No idea," I lied.

"Give me a Whopper with cheese, Ronald," Mason shouted, and laughter filled the auditorium.

Yep, back to normal. My irritationometer clicked up a notch. Any points Mason may have gained Friday night had just gone *poof*.

Police Chief Dalrymple smiled and leaned close to the

microphone. "Your simple-minded insults only prove my point, Mr. Draudimon," he said in a deep voice. The auditorium grew silent. "You don't even know your fast food facts, while I know everything about you, so be on your guard."

"I like this guy," I whispered.

"My next words are for the predators in this school," the chief said quietly. "If you continue on the path you are traveling, you will fall into the trap of drugs, crime, and death. I can't help you if you choose to be so stupid. However, I will not let you drag even one member of this fine student body down with you. You know who you are. And so, by the way, do I."

"Dude's intense," Kathryn whispered.

"I am here to declare war!" Dalrymple shouted. Feedback from the speakers echoed through the auditorium and we all jumped. "An all-out War on Drugs. And I *will* be taking prisoners. You, the fine students of Greensburg High School, have endured the business long enough. The good people of Greensburg have endured the business long enough. It is time to put an end to the business, and you have my word that I *will* put an end to the business." Dalrymple threw his hands high in the air as though everyone had given him a standing ovation.

The silence in the auditorium hummed in my ears. Dr. Captious began to clap, smirking while his hands slapped a leisurely rhythm. Dr. Miliron joined him, then everyone in the front rows applauded and cheered.

"To show you just how serious I am," Dalrymple bellowed into the microphone over the applause, "my agents and I have prepared a little demonstration for you." He turned to the left side of the stage and shouted, "Bring 'em out!"

A line of kids in handcuffs paraded across the stage. I recognized most of them. Birdie Fort, Andrea Johnson, Kent

Gable. All known drug users. All kids who had recently turned nasty. Some lanky girl I'd never seen before. The last boy in the lineup shuffled across the stage with his head down, face hidden against his shoulder. He didn't look at anyone on stage or in the audience. Must be possession charges. Guess the insider didn't get the memo. Looked like Art Rubric and Chuckie were tipped off, though.

As the line stopped, Dalrymple turned to them and barked, "I announce my mission to this fine student body. Here and now, in this hour, I am launching my War on Drugs in Greensburg. This student body is under my personal protection. Let all predators know that I will hunt them down. Let all drug dealers know that they cannot hide from Maximilian Dalrymple. I have eyes everywhere. Think of me as your own personal Santa Claus. I see you when you're sleeping. I know when you're awake. I know if you've been bad or good, so your freedom I will take."

"Poor guy just took a hard right on Batty Boulevard," Kathryn said.

"Okay, maybe he's a little off the deep end, but I like him." Andy had told me about the new police chief. He'd said he was well-meaning but totally unconcerned with political correctness. "He just wants to send a message."

"I guess so. Looks like the rumor about the informant is real. Must be how he knew to bring the dogs in. He hit the jackpot."

"When did this rumor start?" I asked.

"After the last assembly. I told you."

"Did not."

"Meant to."

Dalrymple faced the students in cuffs and drew a circle

in the air with his finger. "Turn and show your faces to the students of Greensburg High School. Show them the face of the enemy. Show them what happens when you go up against Maximilian Dalrymple."

Just like puppets, the line of captives turned and lifted their faces to the auditorium. The boy at the end of the line looked up, and I gasped.

"Bobby," Kathryn whispered.

Chapter Twelve

The Hall Monitor

"He was set up," Kathryn said. "And I'm going to find out whodunit. Deputize me. Give me one of your Psi Fighter badges."

"We don't have badges."

"Okay, a mask then. A nasty-looking mask. Something to instill fear in the hearts of the evildoers who set my Bobby up. Maybe a pink one." Every one of Dalrymple's captives had been suspended, except Bobby. Mrs. Bagley had argued that he was a model student, and that his locker had been broken into. She forced the police to pull the packet of drugs they had discovered in Bobby's locker and dust it for prints. They found Kent Gable's fingerprints, but not Bobby's.

I did a mental eyebrow raise. "What we need is surveillance. We know that Gable wasn't the brains behind this. We just have to snoop around a bit to find out who was."

"Exactly," Kathryn said. "You can't use 'brains' and 'Gable' in the same sentence." Kathryn and I had skipped out of lunch. We sat in the library huddled behind a closed door at a round table in the small, soundproof study room at the back, hidden by rows of books. I plucked the maps Andy had given me from my backpack.

"Let's get to work." I unrolled Andy's maps on the library table. "Andy says you can hear everything from the ductwork. He installed sensors. They transmit to this." I held up a small earpiece.

"Looks like the earbud for my iPhone," Kathryn said.

"Yeah, Andy has a thing for iPhones."

Kathryn pointed to the block in the center of the diagram. "Looks like the boiler room is the center of the whole school. Exits out all four sides, each into a different hallway. And look, the ventilator system is wide enough to crawl through. Takes you everywhere. Four intake vents, one on each side of the boiler. Looks like that's your way in. I wonder if it's strong enough to hold you."

"Worked on *Mission Impossible*."

"Did Andy give you cables and harnesses so you could hang from the ceiling to avoid the laser beams?"

"This is high school, Kathryn. There are no laser beams."

I didn't tell Kathryn about the mineshaft that wasn't on the drawing. Andy told me it came up under the school right smack in the middle of a hidden wall in the boiler room. I love Kathryn, but there are some things even she couldn't know.

Even if I could tell her everything, she couldn't help me. I was surrounded by jerktarts and drug dealers, and somewhere hidden in their midst, a Walpurgis Knight. All I had to do was find out who he was and what he was looking for—easy solution, if I could storm the battlefield dressed in my mask and armor, scan Mason, and see which of his nasty memories and filth-stained thoughts would lead me to Scallion. But I couldn't. That was my dilemma.

Mental Arts were completely out of the question; if Scallion were close by like the Kilodan suspected, he would sense me. I couldn't do kung fu, either: detention, fines, being grounded for fighting in school. I had trained for ten years to develop martial arts skills few others in the world had, and Mental Arts skills most of the world didn't even realize existed. But at the moment, all I could be was a sneaky kid. Where was the glamour in that?

"Rinnie, look." Kathryn pointed through the window to the library entrance. Erica and Tish walked in. Erica lumbered around like a zombie. It was heartbreaking to watch. She had made a clean break from the Red Team, and stopped taking their drugs. Or supplements. Whatever. I would look into that later. But right now, her little sister Christie was still missing.

Scallion would know where she was.

"Time to spy," I said. "Meet me back here at the end of the day."

I crept from the library and went straight to the boiler room. The halls were empty, so I tried the door. It swung open with a high-pitched squeal. Inside, a maze of pipes banged and rattled mercilessly. I eased the door closed behind me. Above the boiler, massive ductwork went in four directions like a gigantic "X" across the ceiling. Each section had a screened intake panel, hinged on one side, big enough to crawl through. According to Andy, all I had to do was pull and the screen would open like a door. Then I would be free to spy uninterrupted on the entire school.

One down.

Next, the electrical panel. It was in plain sight against the wall beside the boiler. Andy told me the electrode plate that unlocked the secret opening to the mine shaft was hidden near there. It would take me straight to the Academy. I searched, but couldn't find anything except a sign that said, "Danger! Shock Hazard! Do Not Touch!" That, and a gajillion spiderwebs. Yeah, maybe that one could wait.

As I reached to open the ductwork screen, I heard sharp voices in the hall. Curious, I stepped quietly toward the door. The bottom half was vented, so I bent down, hoping I could see through. Art Rubric and Chuckie Cuff stood across the hall, Tish's boyfriend Whatsisface trapped between them.

Kathryn never used animals to describe Chuckie and Art. She said that God wouldn't make animals that cruel or mindless. Chuckie was the oldest kid in the school, and looked like Scooby-Doo's buddy Shaggy. Rumored to be in his mid-thirties, he was massively strong and amazingly dumb. He had been a senior longer than any student in history. Art Rubric was a junior, and looked like Fred Flintstone on heroin. His whole life revolved around pleasing Mason. Rumor was that Mason could get the police to back off whenever Art needed it, and he supposedly needed it often. Mason was proud of his own drug-free lifestyle, but surprisingly tolerant of people who weren't so squeaky clean.

Art was huge, and could have played on the varsity football team, except that every time he tackled someone, he'd hold the guy down and punch his face. Which wouldn't have been so bad if he'd been on the opposing team.

"Pay the toll, dweeb," Rubric said.

Poor Whatsisface reached into his pockets.

"I told you before, I don't have any money." He turned both pockets inside out.

"No problem," Rubric said. "We'll put you on a payment plan. Chuckie, give him the bill."

Chuckie smiled and slammed his fist into Whatsisface's stomach. Whatsisface buckled to his knees, gagging, gasping for breath. I fought a terrible urge to charge through the door and use Chuckie's head as a toilet plunger. Rubric laughed and turned away. As he and Chuckie disappeared from my view, I heard Art say, "Come on, Mason's waiting."

Whatsisface dragged himself to his feet. His face was pale, and his lower lip trembled like he was trying not to cry. He turned and punched the locker. I could feel his humiliation as he waddled away, rubbing his hand. "One day," he muttered.

Guess I didn't need the ductwork. Art and Chuckie were being kind enough to take me straight to Mason. *Academy training, don't fail me now!*

I slipped silently from the boiler room and trailed Rubric and Chuckie. As they approached the chemistry lab, Mason joined them. I disappeared into a doorway.

"Mase, dude, halls are secure," Chuckie said. "Cash is flowing. Let's celebrate. I'm starving."

"You're always starving," Mason said. "Stupid people have a fast metabolism."

"Dude," Chuckie said. "That's harsh."

"Truth hurts, buddy. Go eat. I gotta make a phone call."

"The Big Chalupa?" Chuckie asked.

"He'd kill you if he heard you call him that." Mason shook his head. "I got something lined up for tonight. I'll catch up." He turned and ambled away.

How convenient. Mason might be calling Scallion. His

Friday night nice guy points had just dipped *way* below zero. A little eavesdropping should quickly tell me what Mason was up to. I let him round the corner, then started to follow. Rubric and Chuckie were ahead of me, yakking about their exciting new source of income, walking too slowly. I needed to get around them without being seen. Fortunately, Psi Fighters train for just this sort of thing.

I stepped silently, carefully positioning myself behind Rubric as he walked. It was a tricky move, but I had practiced it for years with Andy. He called it the art of invisibility. I called it being sneaky. I could sneak past *anybody* at the Academy, and they were trained to have heightened awareness.

Silent as a shadow, I moved and weaved and ducked my way around the Duncely Duo, very pleased with my mad ninja skills. I was so close I could have slapped them, and they didn't have a clue. A few more seconds, and I would be on my way to eavesdrop on Mason. Getting around these oblivious bozoids was easy sailing.

Suddenly, my neck tickled. I reached back to scratch, and pulled a prickly something off my collar. When I looked to see what it was, a monstrous spider crawled across my palm, at which time I let out the most impressive scream of my career. It echoed down the hall and into the next galaxy. I spun and shook my hand and jumped up and down until I bounced right off of Rubric and onto my butt. Anchors away.

"What have we here?" Rubric smiled down at me. "An empty hall, a very loud bleach blond, and a new source of cash."

"It's not bleached," I mumbled, pulling myself to my feet. A shudder shot down my spine as the spider disappeared under a doorway. I was *never* going in that boiler room again.

"Pay the toll to the troll, Peroxide."

I didn't have time for this. On one hand, I could easily clobber these two bozoids and escape to follow Mason. On the other hand, clobbering said bozoids would look very suspicious and would draw mundo attention. That would be mundo bad. Then a brilliant plan popped into my mind.

Run.

"TTFN," I said, and sprinted after Mason, ignoring Rubric's calls for me to stop and pay my bills. As I rounded the bend, I caught a glimpse of Mason ducking into the last place I would have ever dreamed of spying on him. Now I was faced with another dilemma, this one much more interesting than the last.

. . .

"You followed him into the boy's locker room?" Kathryn squealed when we met up at the end of the day. "You are absolutely my hero! I want to be a Psi Fighter. Where's the application?"

I grinned. The school library was empty, as usual, and Kathryn and I were back at our table in the study room with Andy's map unrolled. "Okay, I didn't actually walk in after him. I used the ductwork."

"The front door would have been a ton easier."

"True. But I'm pretty sure a girl walking into the boy's locker room would be noticed."

"Details," Kathryn demanded. "I need details. What was it like? Wait, let me guess. Boys are gross. It smelled like butt fumes and old gym socks."

"Actually, it smelled like the girl's locker room."

"Like I said, butt fumes and old gym socks. Okay, so you're hanging out in the boy's locker room. And?"

"Well, I could see everything from the main ventilator shaft opening, but I couldn't hear much. I think I broke the earbud when I bounced off Rubric."

"I assume by *see everything* you mean see *everything*. That would have been good enough for me."

"Yeah, except that I wanted to hear Mason's phone call. Anyway, I peeked out and saw him standing alone. He whipped out his cell and headed into a toilet stall. So I backed away from the opening and followed the ductwork to the stalls."

"You had to pass over the showers," Kathryn said, pointing to the map. "Speak to me."

"Umm, yeah, well…"

"Did you see any—"

"They were empty."

Kathryn shook her head. "Disappointing."

"I know." I didn't tell Kathryn, but my feelings about spying into the boys' shower had been a mixture of wild curiosity at what I might see and abject terror at the thought of my dad finding out. Or the Kilodan. Or Andy. Only Kathryn would be proud. "Anyway, I pulled open a vent cover and dropped into the stall next to Mason."

"Personally, I would have waited over the showers. But, hey, that's just me. So, which end of him was making noise?"

"The end with the mouth," I said. "It was whispering. 'Tonight, just like I told you,' he said. Then he said, 'Home. I'll bring your package. Of course, ten.' Then he hung up."

"So he's meeting somebody at ten o'clock tonight. Who?"

"I wonder if this is the delivery Scallion talked about in

LaReau's memory. Mason used the same word as LaReau—*package*." A terrible thought flipped through my head. "Does this mean Mason is involved in the kidnapping? I have to tell Andy. We need a stakeout."

"Home." Kathryn frowned and shook her head. "Not sure how anybody could call the Shadow Passage home."

"What, he meant the Shadow Passage? Not his house? Are you sure?"

"Definitely. He calls it his home-away-from-home."

Made sense. He hung out there, ate there, did who knows what else there…maybe there was more to that SSA back room than he told me. I thought for a minute. "I have to get back to the Academy. I need building plans for the Shadow Passage."

I put my map away, and we started out of the library.

"Here's the deal," I told Kathryn. "I'll go to the Academy, memorize the Shadow Passage layout, and hide myself somewhere in the building before Mason shows up. Once he arrives, I'll find out who he kidnapped, rescue her, beat him into wombat butter, and meet you for ice cream. Sound good?"

"Except for one tiny detail," Kathryn said as we stepped into the hall. Art Rubric and Chuckie blocked the path. Apparently waiting for me.

"Five small dollars." Chuckie grinned like a hyena. He spread his hands wide and gazed out onto some imaginary horizon. "Then you are free to roam these hallowed halls. Such a pittance for liberation."

"I didn't know you could use big words, Chuckie." Kathryn batted her eyes. "I'm so proud of you!"

"I saw it on a wall in town," Chuckie said. His grin grew bigger and he blushed.

Kathryn turned to Rubric. "We have someplace to be.

Touch either of us, and you'll learn what getting beat up by a girl feels like."

"We don't accept MasterCard or threats," Rubric said. "Cash only."

"I don't have any money," I told him.

"That's okay," Rubric said. "You qualify for our payment plan. Chuckles, give her the bill."

Chuckie's grin disappeared. "Dude, she's a girl."

"No exceptions!" Rubric shoved Chuckie aside and drew back his huge fist. "I'll collect."

I grimaced and tightened my stomach, hoping I was strong enough to take his punch. Suddenly, I felt a powerful arm around my waist pulling me backward.

"Maybe you'd like to collect from me," a quiet voice said. "Yeah, that's a dandy idea. Because, you know, collecting from her could really hurt your life expectancy."

"Egon." Rubric raised his hands and backed away. "What up, bro?"

Forcing me behind him, Egon pulled a huge wad of cash from his pocket. He slapped Rubric across the face with it, and tucked it away. "Oh, terribly sorry. I don't seem to have any money either." His emotionless face dared Rubric to disagree. "Whatever shall we do now, *bro*?" Egon slammed Art into the lockers. They banged like thunder.

"Dude!" Chuckie sputtered, apparently amazed that anyone could slam Rubric. He squirmed like a little girl on a candy binge. "I heard you're the secret informant!"

"Is that the rumor?" Egon crossed his arms. "If I admitted it, it wouldn't be a secret anymore, would it?"

Chuckie's eyes opened wide, like he just had an epiphany. "No, I guess not. Dude!"

Rubric stared, seemingly unsure what to do. Then he turned and grabbed Chuckie by the shoulder. "No problem, man. We gotta go."

Egon stood motionless, radiating a cloud of gorgeous.

"That's the second time you saved me," I said.

He turned toward me. His eyes became bright and he smiled. "We should make this a regular thing."

"Every girl needs a hero." And he was absolutely mine. A regular thing—the thought made me gooey.

"Are you up for anything tonight? I have a night off from practice, and thought maybe we could study together."

"Egon, we don't have any classes together."

He nodded slyly. "I know."

In my swiftly clouding mind, I saw the most beautiful fireworks display lighting the midnight sky. Alluring music played in the background. Birds and bunnies formed a circle and began singing like we were in a Disney movie.

Then Kathryn opened her big mouth.

"She'd love to, but she can't. She has *very* strict parents. Not allowed out on school nights."

I wanted to scream. "Oh, Egon, I ree-ally wish I could. Maybe another time?"

Egon's eyes narrowed, but the smile stayed in place. "My loss." He did a little wave and slipped away.

When Egon rounded the corner, I proceeded to bang my head against the locker.

"I'm asked out by the hottest boy in the galaxy, and I have to go to work. What's wrong with my life?" I looked at Kathryn and sighed. "Strict parents? That's the best you could do?"

She patted my cheeks. "I suppose I could have said you have a building to stake out and a kidnapper to capture."

Chapter Thirteen

The Shadow Passage

Ten o'clock. The air was unusually mild for a spring evening. Of course, this part of the country was used to weather patterns that stubbornly ignored the calendar.

I stood on the rooftop of the Shadow Passage, gazing out over the thriving metropolis of Greensburg like Batman overlooking Gotham City. Except he did it from buildings that were a thousand feet tall, and the Shadow Passage was, like, two floors.

Andy and the Kilodan were preoccupied with some big covert operation, so they told me to take care of Mason myself. Sweet! I waited there watching the street like a little kid on Christmas Eve. Good thing I peed before I left.

At the front of the building, a heavily traveled street went up the hill to the Court House. Behind it lay an alley. Dead End Alley, the place where my parents died. I had only a vague recollection of that alley, but knowing it was right below me left me with a very uncomfortable knot in my stomach. I instantly put it out of my mind and concentrated on the mission.

I thought it might be a long night, so I chose style over safety. Instead of armor, I wore a reversible hoodie—dark burgundy outside, light green inside, complete with secret agent pocket for storing important things like high-tech weaponry and lip gloss. I accessorized with a blunt-billed cap, also dark burgundy, complete with pull-down face mask, wafer thin night-vision lenses, and the full array of Psi Fighter psitronics. Fashionable enough for hunting bad guys, yet practical enough for a night out with Kathryn afterward.

The rooftop was flat and gritty, surrounded by a low brick wall that blocked the already dim light from the street below. A noisy air conditioner sat droning on the street side of the roof. On the alley side lay the unobtrusive trapdoor I would use to make my entrance. According to the plans, a ladder ran from the trapdoor down to the top floor of the Shadow Passage. The building layout was pretty simple. The top floor was all attic. The arcade room, with its bathrooms, utility closets, and furnace, took up most of the lower floor. The SSA was in the back corner of the building, but there was also a small room next to it, inaccessible from the main arcade. I would have to go through the SSA to get to it—or I could take a staircase that led down from the attic.

On the street below, I recognized two of my finest classmates walking into the front entrance of the Shadow Passage. Chuckie Cuff and Art Rubric.

My watch said ten-fifteen. No Mason. Must bad guys always be fashionably late? Scallion (or his slimy alter ego) would already be hidden deep in the bowels of the Shadow Passage. Since I didn't know who I was looking for, I needed Mason to lead me to him, but Mason obviously didn't care about *my* priorities. A man in a trench coat approached the front door. He kept his hat pulled low over his head. If he was trying to be inconspicuous, it wasn't working. The "Secret Agent Man" song started playing in my head, and I couldn't help but dance a little.

I continued to scan the street. The single streetlamp at the front of the Shadow Passage didn't illuminate much. By eleven o'clock, a zillion people had come and gone, and by midnight, my eyes drooped and I was bored out of my mind. There was no way I was seeing Kathryn tonight—Mason was way late and it was way past my bedtime. Real missions were just not as exciting as the ones in the movies. There should have been a boat chase by now. Or a romance scene. Egon popped into my head at the thought. He asked me out to 'study.' How hot was that? I sighed. Just as I was about to call it a night, Mason appeared in the streetlight.

How totally inconsiderate, making me wait. No more inconsiderate, I suppose, than causing my birth parents' death. I knew it was wrong to feel that way—but I felt that way. I didn't care that he was only six when it happened, a victim of Nicolaitan. So was I. But I went on to fight the Knights. He joined their fan club. Mason's Friday night bonus points plummeted even deeper into the negative digits.

Mason went straight for the door and disappeared inside.

I decided to give him a few minutes to get settled in. It seemed polite to allow him to do all the things evil villains have to do before the good guy takes them down with amazing panache. Just as I started toward the trapdoor, something caught my attention. A dark figure moved cautiously down in the alley beside the Shadow Passage. Scallion? No way! How lucky could a girl get? He kept to the shadows, right where you'd expect a vomitous mass of loathsome troglodyte to be. Not that I'm judging. Innocent until proven guilty, as they say. This was better than extra points during a pop quiz. I powered on my night-vision zoom. I *had* to see if this creep looked like he did in my memories.

Wow. Personage dressed in skull mask and black leotards. Andy would have been thrilled. Change of plan. I would still pound Mason on general principle, but first—OH MY GOSH! If I captured Scallion, he could lead me to...

Nicolaitan.

An outrage that I never knew I had coursed through my veins. I was one step closer to my parents' killer. My hands tingled as psychic energy concentrated into my fingertips.

A whole new level of determination flooded over me. I crawled to the roof's edge and crouched. Scallion stood perfectly still, seemingly at ease in the darkness. I tensed, ready to leap down to the street and take him. I had to see the face under that mask.

He hesitated, then slunk through the alley and stopped below the Shadow Passage's fire escape. I pulled back just as he tossed a line at the fire escape ladder, which ended a good fifteen feet above the ground, and swung effortlessly up to the first rung. Looked like I wouldn't have to chase my masked bud after all. He was coming to me.

I hurried to the air conditioner unit, ducked behind it, and laid flat on the gritty rooftop, my head out just enough to see, relying on the darkness to hide me. Scallion peeked over the edge of the building, then nimbly rolled his body over the low wall. Nice moves, very agile. I would have given it a ten, but the guy had no fashion sense. My taste in music was trailblazing compared to that black onesie. I had to deduct points. Haute couture he was not. I immediately felt sorry for Scallion, and considered letting him go. The shame of that getup was punishment enough.

Scallion kept to the shadows. He moved soundlessly across the roof, lifted the trapdoor, and gazed back in my direction. I crouched lower, suddenly overcome by an eerie feeling that he was looking right at me, wishing I had worn my uniform with its Shimmer mode. Then Scallion disappeared through the open door.

Relieved, I slipped across the rooftop to the trapdoor and listened.

No footsteps. No breathing.

I slowly peeked through the open trapdoor into the attic below. The attic glowed a spidery green through my night vision. Arachnophobia threatened to end my mission.

A narrow access door on the far end of the attic squeaked and moved. A shadow disappeared through it and down the stairs to the little room beside the SSA. I lowered myself silently through the roof and slid down the ladder.

The air smelled of mildew and dirt. Paper, debris, and unidentifiable glop littered the filthy wooden floor. Muffled voices and muted music floated up from the Shadow Passage below. I looked toward the narrow door Scallion had disappeared through, and thought about following him. That would be the easiest way to get into the little room. And the most dangerous. *Hi, I'm looking for a man who's dressed in Low Budget Kung Fu Movie attire. He'll likely try to kill me when he sees me. Can you tell him I'm here, please?*

I looked around the attic, searching for Plan B, when a tiny streak of light caught my eye. I moved toward it, stepping softly to keep the ratty floor from creaking under my feet.

At one time, the Shadow Passage must have had an apartment above it. In the corner of the attic stood a bathroom sink. Beneath it, a sliver of light shot through a bit of dry-rotted duct tape covering an old drainpipe. I knelt, reached under the sink, and touched the pipe. It wiggled. I tugged slightly and it moved. Slowly, quietly, I removed the pipe from the floor, leaving a two-inch hole in its place. Thick dust floated in the pale light that burst through the opening and the music got louder. I pulled a small device from my secret agent pocket and lowered it into the hole, then tapped a switch. I gasped as my mask's lens filled with a scene I was not prepared for. I wasn't looking at the arcade. I was staring into the Star Ship Angel.

Vintage video games filled the sidewall. No exercise equipment. I panned around the room. A food counter ran the length of the SSA, and a little girl sat at one of the stools with her back to me. I could put two and two together with the best of them. Mason was in the building. Scallion had just joined him. A little girl had been kidnapped and LaReau was awaiting delivery. Coincidence? Psi Fighters know that there is no such thing.

Behind the counter, an old fashioned jukebox blasted the same hard music I had heard when I was in the other room with Mason. At the end of the counter, another door. It was closed. Had to be the one that led to the back room where Scallion waited. I panned back to the little girl, and noticed that the top of the food counter was mirrored. My hunch was confirmed. Christie Jasmine's reflection stared up at me.

Christie was trembling. Her skin was nauseatingly pale.

She seemed to be talking to the mirror, but I couldn't hear her over the noise of the jukebox. "Pinpoint," I said into my mask. "Isolate." My mask's sound filters focused on Christie, and her words nearly broke my heart.

"...please, God, please bring me home. Don't let him sell me."

Sell her? What kind of psycho sells children? Then I remembered that Andy said LaReau was into human trafficking. Christie was Scallion's delivery. And Mason was helping. Anger burned in my chest as I searched desperately for a plan. Suddenly, the arcade door opened and the man in the trench coat entered the SSA. He closed the door and flipped the deadbolts, locking it behind him. Then he slithered onto an empty stool next to Christie. She tried to squirm away from him, but he snaked his arm around her, forcing her back onto the stool. I glared down at him, wishing I could reach through the hole, rip off his arm, and beat him over the head with the bloody stump. He removed his hat, and turned to talk to her. I nearly jumped out of my skin when I saw his face.

Dr. Captious.

The clues leading up to this suddenly made perfect sense. Scallion worked for Nicolaitan, but LaReau thought Scallion worked for *him*. Christie Jasmine was the "gift" that Scallion told LaReau about in the memory I absorbed. And the SSA was Scallion's distribution center, compliments of Mason. With or without Tammy Angel's knowledge, I couldn't tell.

That meant Scallion, not LaReau, took Christie Jasmine. Even though I had let LaReau escape, I saved another little girl from becoming his next victim that night. That mission wasn't a total failure after all.

So where did Captious fit in? Mr. Munificent's words at

the assembly explained it all. *Ten years ago, I hunted a masked kidnapper who terrorized the city…Now he's back…He's using you kids to do his dirty work.* Nicolaitan had both Scallion and Captious kidnapping children for LaReau. One probably didn't know about the other. And LaReau no doubt believed he was taking children for the trafficking ring, but in fact, they would be delivered to Nicolaitan. The Knights were masters of deception, and Nicolaitan was the best of the best. Munificent said he would lure kids into his scheme. It seemed that he had also lured a teacher. He was building an army of kidnapped children, just like ten years ago, but this time, he was laying a trail that couldn't be traced to him. LaReau would take the fall. Or Scallion. Or Captious.

Captious's black eyes gleamed. He tapped his finger to the beat of the blaring music, and said to Christie, "Your prayers have been answered, sweetheart. It's time to go."

Christie's face filled with panic.

Just then, the double deadbolts on the door to the arcade rattled. I heard a key scraping against the lock, and the door burst open. Mason appeared. He re-bolted the door and moved behind the counter with the sleek stride of a hunting cat.

He cranked up the already loud music, then retraced his steps and took a seat next to Captious. "Funny you should show up just when Christie does. What's the deal?"

"I was about to ask you the same thing, Mason. I thought we had no secrets between us."

Confirmed. One didn't know what the other was doing.

"Yeah, that's what I thought, too." Mason slammed his fist onto the countertop. "So what about her?"

Christie cringed.

"I'll be taking this one with me," Captious said.

Mason's face twisted in anger. "I don't think so."

"Pulling rank, are you?"

"You got it."

"Might have to fight you for it, Mason."

"Oh, get real. You're not in school. This is my world. And this is *not* how I treat little girls."

Dr. Captious stood and wrapped his coat around Christie's shoulders. He helped her to her feet. She moved like a puppet, staring with unblinking eyes.

"Have a good evening," he said, looking up at Mason. He started to lead Christie away when Mason grabbed him by the shoulder.

Captious was surprisingly fast for a fat little man. He whipped a revolver from his belt and placed the barrel against Mason's forehead in one fluid movement, hammer cocked. "It's past my bedtime, Mason. I get cranky when I'm tired."

Mason backed away, glaring. "Don't do this. You know all I have to do—"

"I know, report me to your daddy." Captious's tone said he didn't care. "I think our friendship means more to you than that. See you in class tomorrow. Don't forget, you have a test."

My stomach churned in disgust as Captious led little Christie through the door to the arcade. Mason continued to glare. The instant the arcade door closed, the door at the end of the food counter slowly opened. A skeletal face appeared, hissed the word, "Come," then pulled back inside. It took all my strength and concentration to slow my heart.

I'd been right. Scallion had been waiting in the back room. Up close, his skull face was more frightening than it was in any memory I'd absorbed. That mask was too real. And he was powerful—I could feel the fear he pushed out to control

Mason. I had to be cautious.

Mason cringed and walked to the end of the food counter. I heard him mutter, "I wonder what *he* knows about this." Then he disappeared through the door.

Bad guys were so thoughtless. The two who were my targets had gone one way, and the one who hadn't even been on my radar had gone another. With a terrified little girl, no less. Why couldn't they all stay in one place and make my life easy?

I couldn't afford distractions. My mission was practically accomplished. All I had to do was unmask Scallion and grind him into bad guy paste. Pummeling Mason would be a bonus. If I did what I had been trained to do, I could end the terror in Greensburg permanently. My town would be safe. My family would be safe. The Psi Fighters would be safe.

Time to be a hero.

I started toward the stairs.

Then poor Christie popped into my brain. Ugh! There was that distraction I was afraid of.

Andy never taught me how to handle something like this. Fortunately, I watch a lot of movies with Kathryn. *The good of the many outweighs the good of the one.* Spider-Man said that. I think. Or the Star Trek person with the ears. Whoever. Bottom line, I had to do what I came to do. Scallion was going down. I turned to leap down the stairs to the little room when an annoying thought forced itself into my head. What if "the one" wasn't a girl I barely knew? What if "the one" had been Susie?

I allowed the memory of my own kidnapping to slowly resurface from the depths of my brain. The trembling. The shallow breathing. The absolute horror.

Crud.

The problem with movie wisdom was that it was written by people who never had to decide whether to do what you're told, or save a little girl's life. Scallion was the reason the whole town was in danger. He was my link to the man who killed my parents. I would probably never have another chance to unmask him.

But Christie needed me. My eyes filled with angry tears. Another mission was about to swirl uncontrollably down the potty.

Chapter Fourteen

An Unexpected Accomplice

I flew up the ladder to the roof, my hands and feet barely touching the rungs, and sprinted to the front of the building. The night sky was like pitch. On the street below, Captious ushered Christie out of the Shadow Passage's streetlight and disappeared into the shadows. I had no idea where he was taking her, but I knew who he was taking her to: LaReau. And no way was he going without me.

I leapt to the fire escape ladder and slid down with one hand, dropping the last fifteen feet to the street, landing without a sound, and crouched in the alley on all fours like a prowling lioness. After quickly flipping my mask into a ball cap, and turning my hoodie green side out, I strolled nonchalantly into the street.

Captious and Christie were twenty yards ahead of me, marching up the hill toward Main Street, Christie wrapped in his trench coat. He had his arm around her, and acted all tender and caring. Made me want to yak. I closed the gap quickly.

"Don't worry, sweetheart," Captious said. "Everything will be all right. You're with me, now. I'm taking you to your parents."

Poor Christie's quiet little sobs echoed in the empty street. Visions of Susie popped in and out of my head. I picked up my pace, heart pounding, and drew closer to Captious. My hair fluffed. Angry psychic flames raged through my body and concentrated in my palm. I never reached for my Amplifier. Didn't need it. Only needed to touch him. I slowly extended my hand, fingers spread wide.

Suddenly, I remembered Andy's unmoving body lying against the wall, chest armor shattered. I relaxed, and disintegrated the anger. Now was not the time to lose control. There had to be another way.

What would Kathryn do?

"Hey, hey, Dr. Captious," my suddenly cheerful voice burst out. Kathryn would be proud. "Out late, aren't we?"

Captious turned quickly and looked into my eyes. He seemed terrified.

"Speaking of out late," he replied, "don't you have school tomorrow? Look, I don't have time to talk, now. I need to get this poor little girl to the police station. I found her wandering."

"Oh, I'll walk with you," I said. "It's on my way home." *Right. I just came out of the incubator yesterday. Police station. Code name for your meeting place with LaReau, where you are about to lead me. And this time, my encounter with him will end differently.*

Christie gazed up at me and the terror drained from her

face. She broke free from Captious and threw her arms around me. I hugged her tight. Scallion could wait. This was where I was supposed to be.

"You really shouldn't be in this part of town at night, Rinnie," Captious told me in his most authoritative teacherly voice. "It's dangerous. Stay close to me."

"You got it." *Close enough to give you a psionic body slam.* I held Christie's hand as Captious herded us up the steep hill toward the courthouse, a huge stone building that consumed an entire city block, beginning at the top of the hill on Main Street. It was home to numerous lawmakers, tax offices, courts, and the Greensburg Police. One small problem. This late at night, the courthouse was locked up tight. It closed at five. Other than the fact that his lips were moving, that's the reason I knew Captious was lying about where we were going. I was anxious to learn his real destination, and to hear the lame excuse he would have for not going in when we passed by the police station.

When we crested the hill, the main entrance of the courthouse was completely dark. It might as well have had a megaphone blaring *Go away, we're closed!* To my surprise, Captious didn't even attempt to go there. Instead, we crossed Main Street and walked down the hill along the north side of the courthouse. I suddenly realized where we were headed. At the end of the courthouse block sat the city parking garage. Perfect place for an exchange. That must be where LaReau waited for his delivery.

My fists clenched in anticipation. I had never even spoken rudely to a teacher before, and now I was going to have to beat one to a pulp. I was surprisingly okay with that. Although beating said teacher would totally compromise my secret identity. To beat or not to beat, that is the question.

Suddenly, Captious stopped and unlocked a windowless door on the side of the courthouse building.

"In here," he said, swishing his hand toward the open door.

The corridor was dark, but I could see light far down the hall. Normally, light at the end of a tunnel is a good thing. But there was nothing normal about a teacher leading a kidnapped child and an unsuspecting teenager into a dark building at midnight. I jumped back, shoving Christie behind me.

"I think you've had one too many power drinks." Captious reached into the doorway and hit a light switch. He patted me on the head and pointed to a brass plaque on the corridor wall.

"Greensburg Police Hall of Justice, established 1892," I read out loud. Oops. My face grew hot, and I grinned apologetically.

"Rinnie, I am one of the few people you can trust. Please. Let's get this poor child back to her parents." He smiled and led Christie down the now bright hallway. Shocked, I followed him in. This night's events had me seriously rattled.

As we approached another door at the end of the hallway, voices grew increasingly loud. No sooner did I clear the entrance when the stench of stale cigarettes and unwashed bodies made me choke. The chairs and benches were packed with more dirtbags than I had ever seen. A harmless looking man with a thin, stringy beard shifted his eyes between Christie and me. He was in handcuffs and chained to the bench. The poor man's hair was filthy, and I felt sorry for him. One side was plastered to his scalp. The other side stood straight up as though he'd been riding with his head out the car window like a dog. The kids in school worked for hours with mousse and styling gel to accomplish what I was sure this man had created by pure neglect.

He smiled at me with small brown teeth.

"Hello, girls," he said in a syrupy sweet voice as we passed him.

I gagged quietly from his stench, and decided that Mummy's Magic Mix must have scraped ingredients from him. A very uncomfortable feeling settled in my stomach, and suddenly, I didn't want to be there anymore. It wasn't the smell…there was something else. His voice was more familiar than it should have been. Christie had moved closer to me, and terror was in her eyes. Then I realized who I was looking at.

LaReau had grown a beard.

Captious turned quickly and punched his finger into LaReau's forehead. "Don't speak to them, you detestable abomination." As we continued walking, Captious wiped his finger on his pants.

"Who's he?" I asked. Did the cops have any idea who was chained to that bench?

"A dog who eats his own vomit," Captious muttered. "Not worth the air he pollutes."

Really? Captain of the Fan Club he was not. So much for my theory that Captious was in league with Mr. Smelly.

Captious stopped at the clerk's desk. "Chief in?"

The clerk slowly lifted his bloodshot eyes from a magazine. He leered at Christie and me, then rolled his eyes with disgust at Captious before returning to the magazine. "Who's asking?"

Captious just shook his head. We followed him around the counter, along a short hall, and into an open office door. Chief Dalrymple perched behind a massive desk of polished mahogany, his pale orange hair spiked perfectly. Stacks of papers cluttered the corners of the enormous desk.

"Chief, I think I have LaReau's victim," Captious said.

The night was full of surprises. How did they know? Then I realized this must have been the big mission Andy and the Kilodan were on tonight. They had arranged for LaReau's capture. But how was Captious involved?

Dalrymple's stern gaze fell on Captious, then softened when he saw Christie and me. "Hi, honey, what's your name?"

Christie squeezed closer to me and stared at the floor.

"She's Christie Jasmine," I said. "She's ten."

Dalrymple's eyes got wide, and his face became absolutely charming. "Well now, how do you know this, Miss Noelle?"

"She's my sister's friend. How do you know me?"

Dalrymple smiled. He had a surprisingly kind smile. "I know your father." Then to Christie, "Is that your name, dear?"

Christie nodded and turned her face up. "I want to go home."

"And you will, very soon." Dalrymple shuffled through the papers on his desk and pulled one out of the stack. He picked up the phone and punched some numbers. "Hello, Mrs. Jasmine? This is Police Chief Maximilian Dalrymple. My apologies for calling at such a late hour, but I have some very good news for you."

After he hung up, Dalrymple turned to Captious. "Our source never mentioned this one. How did you find her?"

"Right place, right time." Captious smiled his smug little poodle smile.

Dalrymple's eyes narrowed. "Good work, Ben. You'll have to fill me in. In the meantime, why don't you take the girls into the file room to wait for Christie's parents? The lobby is crowded, and Christie has seen enough slime, I think, to last her a lifetime."

I followed Captious as he led Christie down the hall. He opened the door to a dark room, felt for the light switch, and motioned us in. A desk and some chairs were crammed against one wall. Filing cabinets squished together on the other. In between was cramped and dingy and packed with cardboard boxes, dusty old newspapers, broken furniture...and spider webs everywhere.

Captious sat on the desk and motioned us toward the chairs. I sat beside Christie and caressed her hair. She leaned against me and smiled, like she was coming out of a trance. Captious was back to his old self, talking incessantly, but I didn't pay attention. I needed to figure out what was up with him, but not tonight. I relaxed, content that my mission wasn't a total failure. LaReau was in chains. Scallion was still out there, but Christie was safe. The night had begun to catch up with me, and I was ready for bed. I surveyed the room, wondering how long we'd be stuck waiting.

Suddenly, I caught my breath. The floor! Black and white squares of linoleum tile, like a massive chess board...I tore my gaze to the door, and there, in the frosted window, was a hole, just the right size to spy through from the other side. Fear flooded my mind.

I was sitting in the room where Amos Munificent was murdered.

Chapter Fifteen

Captious's Secret

While Captious blabbed to Christie about how everything would be okay, I desperately tried to remember what I saw in my vision of Mr. Munificent's murder. There was something important in this room. Where was Andy and his MPU 3000 when I needed him? I studied the tiny room, looking for anything that might spark recognition. Spider-filled corners, chairs stacked on chairs, tile, door with a spy-hole, an old typewriter. Nothing clicked.

Then I saw it. There in the midst of five black, shiny new filing cabinets sat a dull green one, battered, out of place— instantly, Mr. Munificent's image, soggy with sweat, zipped through my mind. He leaned beside the ugly cabinet, his hand clutching the drawer, second from the top. He forced it closed, when a shadow appeared outside the frosted glass window.

Suddenly, the office door opened and I nearly jumped out

of my chair.

"There's someone here to see you, Christie," Dalrymple said as he strolled through the doorway.

I definitely needed sleep.

"Christie," a woman sobbed, shouldering her way past Dalrymple. She scooped Christie out of the chair. "Christie, thank you, God, thank you. Everything is all right, now, honey. It's all right."

Christie simply nodded and buried her face in her mother's neck. "Momma."

"Ma'am." Dalrymple placed his hand on her shoulder. "I want to get you out of here as quickly as possible, but I need to ask a few questions, and we'll have to examine Christie. The doctor is on her way."

Christie's mother shuddered and managed a weak "Yes, anything." Then, "Is it true, officer? You found the man who took her?"

Dalrymple smiled. "Yes, ma'am. An anonymous informant tipped us off. We have the kidnapper in custody."

An anonymous informant with an angelic mask and electronically altered voice. This was good. I sighed as the frightened images I saw in LaReau's mind dissolved. Being a Psi Fighter was definitely worth the headache.

Mrs. Jasmine hugged her daughter tightly. Christie picked her head off her mother's shoulder as Dalrymple led them out of the room. The eyes that had prayed for help in the SSA's mirrored countertop now looked content and tired. She smiled at me.

Definitely worth it.

"Make sure she gets home safely," Dalrymple said, pointing to me.

"I'll handle it personally," Captious promised.

Dalrymple closed the door.

"Now it's time to take care of you, young lady." Captious held up a finger. "But first, I have to make a phone call. Wait here. I'll be right back."

I wondered what he meant by taking care of me…was it only because I was tired that it sounded like something the mob does to people who get in their way? Before the door had completely closed, I bounded to the battered green cabinet and jerked open the second drawer. It screeched like a zombie rising from the grave. I froze, expecting the whole police force to come running, but the only thing I heard was the murmur of crabby voices down the hall. Slowly, carefully, I opened the drawer the rest of the way, cringing as the frozen steel wheels grated against the track. Did these people not understand the concept of oil?

The drawer was packed tighter than the little room. I tugged at a folder, but it was wedged. Delirious from lack of sleep and determined not to be outmuscled by an inanimate object, I pulled hard. The contemptible thing shot out like a Pop-Tart, spraying papers everywhere. I fired a quick glance at the door, then back to the papers strewn across the tile.

A picture of a woman in a dark blue business suit. The same woman in a bright orange jump suit. The words *grand larceny, embezzlement, fraud.*

I had evidently stumbled onto criminal records or something. I jammed the papers back in the folder, and forced it into the drawer in frustration. I would need hours to go through those files. I didn't have hours. I didn't even know what I was looking for. I pushed through the remaining folders. They were packed in so tightly they barely budged.

"This can't be right," I whispered, and closed the drawer. I opened the top drawer. It was packed even tighter. I opened every drawer in the cabinet, but each was crammed. A spider scurried down the wall and disappeared behind the cabinets. Wonderful.

I concentrated on my vision of Munificent again. His image flashed and disappeared. Then he was back, about to close the file cabinet drawer. He held something in his hand, then forced it into the drawer, slamming it shut.

Suddenly, I heard Captious's voice in the hall. "Yeah, what do you need? I'm in the middle of life and death here."

I was out of time, so I reopened the second drawer in frustration and tore out a handful of folders, hoping against hope that nothing would crawl on me. If I could transport the folders from the building, Andy would have some sort of thingamabob to scan them in the comfort of his spider-free tech lab, instead of this arachnophobe's nightmare of an office. The remaining folders expanded and pushed themselves neatly together to fill the open space. As the gap closed, I noticed something lying on the bottom of the drawer, hiding. I reached in and plucked out a yellowing envelope.

As soon as I touched it, fear gripped my heart. An image of Scallion danced in front of my eyes, searching, sniffing like a wolf, hunting for— Suddenly I heard the click of a doorknob and I pushed the vision out of my head. Just as the file room door opened, I shoved the envelope inside my secret agent pocket and forced the folders back into the drawer.

Leaning against the cabinet, I smiled at Captious.

"Stay out of there," he snapped. "Those are police records, not fashion magazines."

The jerk. "Is Christie okay?"

"She will be," Captious said. "Now, let's get you home."

Yeah, right. "I know the way."

"This isn't the friendliest part of town. Come on. I called your father. He knows I'm walking you home."

Lovely. Not tonight, Bucko. I was about to throw a carefully calculated hissy fit and escape through the back door, when I noticed how awful Captious looked. His eyes were sunken as though he hadn't slept for days. His comb-over had flopped to the side like a gigantic earmuff. Must have been a rough phone call. If I hadn't been so tired myself, it would have been hilarious. I suddenly felt sorry for the little round man, so I followed.

As we moved down the hall, panicked voices reverberated from the holding area. "Get an ambulance! He's in cardiac arrest!" A uniformed policeman rushed past us. "I need a bus!" he shouted into an open office door.

The holding area had been cleared of prisoners. There on the floor, eyes glazed and wide, greasy hair askew, lay Norman LaReau, his face a gruesome shade of gray. Dalrymple knelt over him, his thick arms stiffened and his back hunched as he compressed LaReau's chest again and again, counting softly.

"What happened?" I asked.

"Justice," Captious said, shielding me from the grisly sight with his little round body.

I grudgingly followed him out into the street. The night air was cool but refreshing after the stench of the police station. Captious appeared to be lost in smug thought. We walked for a few minutes in silence. Then I asked again, "What happened to that guy?"

"I'd like to think a slow, agonizing death, caused by implements you only read about in *Tortured Weekly*, but I'm afraid it was just a heart attack. I'm surprised Dalrymple tried to save him. He hates child slavers."

"Child slavers?"

"Criminals who kidnap children and sell them into the overseas child labor industry as farm workers."

Human traffickers. So he knew. "I take it you're not fond of them, either."

"If there is a Hell, I would like to personally send every one of them there."

Okay, things were getting weird. An hour ago, I wanted to batter Captious, because I was certain he was taking Christie to LaReau. Then he rescues her right out from under me, and almost dances the Macarena when LaReau goes belly-up in the police station. Now, he was walking me home like he was my nanny. If I could say, "Curiouser and curiouser" without sounding like a complete dweeb, I would.

What was up with this guy? I wasn't surprised that Dalrymple knew him, because of his war on drugs at the high school. But it was like everybody at the police station knew him, too. And showing up at the Shadow Passage just when Christie was there? That was no coincidence. Dalrymple even seemed perplexed about it. Lack of sleep had made me cranky, and I revisited the idea of beating Captious to a pulp. Purely for informational purposes.

"Out of curiosity," he asked, "why were you out on a school night in this part of town?"

"Studying with Kathryn. Don't we have a test tomorrow? Why were you out?"

"Rinnie, I'm being honest with you tonight. Please show me the same respect."

"You want to talk about honest?" I spun to face Captious,

my patience suddenly gone. "You told me you found Christie wandering the streets. I saw you come out of that arcade with her."

"I'm sorry I lied to you," Captious said simply. "Things are getting very dangerous."

"Huh?" An honest liar. The man was a living oxymoron. Beating him to a pulp was definitely sounding attractive.

"Mason Draudimon knew about the Jasmine girl's disappearance before we told anyone at school. That made me very suspicious. I knew he would be at the Shadow Passage, so I stopped in to talk to him. When I got there, I found Christie. We got lucky."

"Who is *we* and what does Mason have to do with this?"

"You heard Dalrymple's announcement at the assembly."

"Yeah."

"He's keeping tabs on Mason. Everybody knows Mason is bad news, but he's the mayor's precious son, and we have to be careful."

"If he broke the law, they should arrest him. Arrest his dad, too. And his dog."

"It's not that simple. This town is completely corrupt. I don't know whom to trust, even on the police force," Captious admitted. "Rinnie, I know your father consults with the police, so I want to tell you something…in case anything happens to me."

How did he know Dad helped the police? I never talked about it to anyone. Not even Kathryn. "How do you know these things? What do you have to do with the cops?"

Captious drew a deep breath and gazed up at the full moon as though it was the last time he'd ever see it. His eyes glistened with tears. "They already got to Munificent. After the stunt I pulled tonight, they'll be after me. I upset some very powerful people in the Shadow Passage when I left with Christie."

"I don't get it."

"Mason is backed by a group called the Walpurgi. They're behind the corruption. Their leader is…" He shuddered. "Things happen in the Shadow Passage that nobody sees. Munificent was right when he said the drug ring is just a cover-up for something much more significant. He stuck his nose where it didn't belong. Once he learned of the man in the skull mask, well, look what happened. With him dead, I'm not sure how much time I have. Munificent assigned me to watch Mason and his gang from the inside. My job is to gather evidence against him so even his father can't save him. But now, my cover's blown. There are police involved in the cover-up. I don't know which side Dalrymple is on."

"You're the police informant?"

"Please make sure you tell your father everything I've told you."

The police force was corrupt. No news there. Captious was an informant. I could deal with that. *But the Knights are backing Mason!* How did Captious know about them? He even knew they called themselves *The Walpurgi*. I wasn't prepared for that. The Knights were as covert as we were. Munificent was the only non Psi Fighter with that knowledge. The Kilodan trusted him. Did he tell Captious? Did he also tell him about the Psi Fighters?

This was way beyond curiouser and curiouser. This was terribler and terribler. And that isn't even a word, which was how bad the situation had become in my tired little brain.

Chapter Sixteen

The Class Project

I woke up tired. Mostly because I couldn't stop dreaming about Walpurgis Knights sneaking through my house, capturing my family, and making us eat egg drop soup. Don't ask. Exhaustion makes my brain malfunction. Fortunately, I had chemistry the next morning, and that particular class didn't require a functioning brain. We were getting our introduction to the Class Project.

I have to say, chem lab always disappointed me. I kept wanting it to look like a mad scientist's laboratory. But alas, there were no flasks spewing green smoke. No body parts in jars. No brains labeled *Abnormal*. Nothing freakish at all. Instead, sparkling glassware neatly lined the polished shelves, and petri dishes, stacked and dusted like fine china, rested on the bench tops. Major yawn. If linen tablecloths and candles had covered the lab benches, we could have been learning chemistry in Rachael Ray's kitchen. Okay, *that* was freakish.

Kathryn and I had strategically placed ourselves at the smallest bench in the lab, off to the side, where we could discuss life without being overheard.

"Let me get this straight," Kathryn whispered as she plopped her chemistry book open on the bench. "Short-Fat-and-Squatty-All-Butt-and-No-Body saved Christie Jasmine? The man is not exactly a poster boy for fitness. I thought cops had to be in better shape."

"Kathryn! If you say a word, I'll never tell you anything again."

"Dude, open the dictionary to the word 'clandestine' and there's my picture. By the way, you look like poodle poo. Why don't you nap through class? Miliron'll never notice. I sleep in Math Club all the time."

"Not a bad idea."

Just as I was about to lay my head on a test tube, the lab door opened and Dr. Miliron, resident mad scientist, promenaded in. He stopped at the front of the room, grinning as though he had won a prize.

"For those of you who may be a tad curious," he said, bouncing on his toes and making his fingers do pushups against each other, "today we'll get a taste of the chemistry Class Project. I know you've all been waiting for it. I haven't mentioned it to you yet, but I hear about it all over the school. I must say, the excitement is contagious!"

I sighed. Dr. Miliron was one of the most likable teachers in the school. And one of the most clueless.

"The Project includes many captivating experiments, but today you are especially lucky! We're making an absolutely fascinating sixteen-carbon structure of fashionable hexagons.

Technically, it's 6-Methyl-9,10-didehydro-ergoline-8-carboxylic acid, with a molecular mass 268.31 grams per mole." Dr. Miliron laughed quietly and shook his head as he passed around a lab handout. "Of course, in everyday language, it's simply $C_{16}H_{16}N_2O_2$. So, slap on your goggliers and let's get cooking, gang!"

Dr. Miliron held the title for spewing the incomprehensible. He spoke in long, chemically abundant phrases that apparently excited him, but completely confazzled those of us who only spoke English. I put on goggles and measured out some odd-colored powder labeled ERGOT.

"Okay, so about Egon," Kathryn whispered. She shot a sly glance at me. "Did he ask you to the Spring Fling yet?"

"How did that come up?" I felt my face getting warm.

"Well, he *did* offer to be your bodyguard, and the Spring Fling is next week. It's the perfect place for guarding." She did a finger quote around "guarding." "Two and two, Rinster."

The Spring Fling. Biggest event of the school year. And Kathryn's area of expertise, not mine. She'd been on a gajillion dates. I had a grand total of one under my belt, and it was technically a fact-finding mission. "Must have slipped his mind. You should probably check your math. You going?"

"Not sure." Kathryn blushed. "Mark and John and Matt and Luke and Hank and Jeremy asked. But, you know, I'm not sure I'm right for them. They're such sweethearts, but I told them I probably wouldn't be able to go."

"All four Gospels *and* the captains of the football and track teams? Amazing. Holding out for Bobby, are we?"

"Could be. However, Ms. Noelle, it seems to me that *you* have two major hitters at the moment."

"What are you talking about?"

"Did you, or did you not turn your bodyguard down so you could go out with Mason?"

"No, *you* told Egon I wasn't allowed out on school nights. And I didn't go out with Mason. I spied on him."

"And learned that the evil wombat hangs out with the wrong crowd as suspected. Correct?"

"He does. And let me tell you, Scallion is *super* creepy."

"Like the Sith, they are," Kathryn said in a first-rate Yoda voice. "Two there should be— no more, no less. Master and apprentice."

I shook my head. "Not exactly. You don't get an army with two." I pulled an envelope from my backpack and took a piece of paper from inside. "I found a sort of…something…at the police station. I think it may be information Andy's looking for. It's from Mr. Munificent." I had tried to pull the image of Scallion from it again, but that required mundo concentration, and I was just too out of it.

"The dead dude?" Kathryn's eyes widened. She snatched the paper from me. "Did he write to you from the Great Beyond?"

"No, from the police station."

"That is just weird." Kathryn turned the page upside down. "What is it?"

"I don't know. A sketch, I guess. He wasn't a very good artist."

Dr. Miliron clapped his hands and I nearly sullied my undies. "Okay, let's continue! This is really an intriguing project, class. Those of you who can produce a successful chemical reaction will not only get an A, you will be helping medical research. Our work will benefit the production of an experimental drug used at the Old Torrents Mental Facility."

"Look at all the pretty colors," Kathryn squealed, pointing to a group of glass bottles. "Hey, what's this?" She plucked a bottle labeled DMSO off the workstation shelf and popped the glass stopper. The powerful stench of rotten eggs wafted out. Kathryn touched two fingers to her lips and said in a giggly voice, "Excuse me, I fluffed."

I choked back a laugh.

"I see you have discovered an important dipolar aprotic solvent from another experiment!" Dr. Miliron sniffed at the air. "It appears our last class failed to put away their dimethyl sulfoxide, or DMSO, also known as methylsulfinylmethane, an all-natural substance derived from the normal decomposition of plants. This wonderful, colorless liquid is readily miscible in water *and* a wide range of organic compounds, making it extremely useful. Isn't that exciting? The disadvantage, as you may have guessed, is a rather foul odor, likely due to catabolic processes which reduce DMSO to dimethyl sulfide."

"What did he say?" Kathryn asked me.

"It stinks."

Kathryn held the bottle up to the light. "Do we have to use it in the Class Project, Dr. M? It clashes with my Bath and Body Works."

"Heavens, no, dear," Dr. Miliron said, prancing across the lab to plant himself at Kathryn's shoulder. "A single drop of DMSO would contaminate our compounds, rendering them completely useless for the medical field."

"Our ergot is ready to be boiled," I whispered to Kathryn. "What's ergot?"

"Ergot," Dr. Miliron whispered back, "is the common name of a saprophyte in the genus Claviceps. This particular saprophyte is parasitic on certain grains and grasses. It is, in fact, a sclerotium! This small structure is usually referred to as ergot, although," he put his hand over his mouth and laughed quietly, "referring to *any* member of the Claviceps genus as ergot is also correct. Claviceps can affect a number of cereals including rye, wheat, barley, and triticale. It affects oats only rarely."

"I see," I said, although I didn't.

"What did he say?" Kathryn asked when Dr. Miliron had moved on to the next group.

"We're boiling gookem puckey."

"I prefer lobster. But I'm flexible."

As our gookem puckey boiled happily away, Dr. Miliron sprang from group to group explaining in extremely long words how the gunk we were making would be taken to Old Torrents Labs for final processing, then used to help the mentally ill. I personally didn't see how it would help them do anything but smell like mildew. After what seemed like hours, the bubbling glop at our workstation turned reddish and became thick, like syrup.

"Nice work, Miss Noelle," a charming voice said from over my shoulder. Mason stood right next to me, staring intently at my beaker. "I had hoped you were this talented."

"How did you get in here?" My first instinct was to tackle him and tactfully beat out a confession about what happened in the little room beside the SSA after I left. Then I remembered my cover. I needed to be friendly and caring so I could stay close to the filthy wombat.

"I'm the lab assistant. I told you. I thought you knew."

"Oh, that's right," I said, smiling. "I knew."

"I knew you were an egotistical megalomaniac," Kathryn said.

"I don't know what that means, but I like the sound of it." Mason glanced at me out of the corner of his eye. "Dr. Miliron, I think we have a successful experiment."

Dr. Miliron danced his way across the lab and planted himself between Kathryn and me. Rubbing his hands together, he said, "Now observe the reflux condenser. That's the key to this experiment. You'll notice that the condensate progresses up the inner cylinder, then cascades back into the elixir, which, of course, is home to a chemical reaction that will alter the carbon chain." He smiled and shook his head. "Once again, I get carried away." He turned to me and winked. "We're really only hydrolyzing lysergamides. A simple process, actually. Fascinating. Absolutely fascinating. Go ahead and analyze this one, Mr. Draudimon."

Dr. Miliron pranced over to the next experiment, whistling the Star Wars theme song.

"What did he say?" Kathryn asked me.

"We're done boiling gookem puckey."

"Ladies," Mason said, "if you don't mind, I'd like to show you the analytical tests we use."

I faked a sweet smile and handed Mason my beaker.

Kathryn and I followed him to the other end of the lab where a heap of equipment sat blinking and flashing. I'm sure Dr. Miliron had a techno term for it, but to me, it was a silver and black doohickey with curly metal tubes. Next to it were shelves with sealed bottles labeled PASS and REWORK. Much more mad scientist lab-ish.

"This," Mason said, swishing his hand like a game show host, "is a gas chromatograph."

"It has a name," I said.

"It does."

"Just a sec." Kathryn stepped close to Mason, took him by the face and tilted his head up, then sideways, like she was checking him for fleas.

"What are you doing?" Mason asked quietly.

Kathryn released his face. "You're confusing me, Mason. You're being nice. I thought maybe you had been replaced by an alien."

"Sorry, it's the real me." Mason opened a drawer under the chromatohickey, pulled out a thin glass syringe with a long needle, and filled it with solution from my beaker.

His eye caught mine, and he smiled. "I fake being nice pretty well, don't I?"

Half truthfully, I said, "You have your moments."

"Do you like it?"

"Maybe."

"Careful, it might become a habit."

I'll believe that when I see it.

Mason's deep blue eyes sparkled, but behind them lay the pain I saw Friday night, and a tenderness I had never noticed before.

"It's you, all right." Kathryn suddenly shoved me behind her and dropped into what I could only assume was a fighting stance, although it looked more like SpongeBob doing the Jellyfish Jam. "Come near us with that needle and I'll kick you so hard your mother will feel it."

Mason looked hurt. "Hey, it's me."

"Hence my defensive posture," Kathryn said.

"I told you she doesn't like me," Mason said to me.

"What's to like?" Kathryn said, shuffling her feet, apparently adjusting her fighting stance. "You pick on skinny blonds who don't stand a chance against you, you're nasty to any teacher who hasn't had the benefit of a doctoral dissertation, and you abuse smaller boys who are too polite to slam you into oblivion."

Mason dropped his eyes to the floor. "I'm sorry. Sometimes

I get carried away when my friends let me down. I'll talk to Bobby. And for the record? My mother's dead. But she had no feelings when she was alive."

For the first time since I had known Kathryn, she was totally speechless. She just shook her head slowly and stared at Mason. "I'm so sorry," she finally whispered. "I didn't know."

"Nobody does," Mason said. "Don't worry about it. Hey, do you want to see how the chromatograph works? Watch, this is cool!" He stuck the syringe into the front of the machine, pushed a button, and it started to hum quietly. A narrow strip of paper with a jaggedy line emerged. Something beeped, and Mason ripped off the printout.

"Another good one, Dr. Miliron. Chromatogram looks excellent. These two ladies have perfect peaks." He poured my experiment into a new bottle, sealed it and placed it on the shelf labeled PASS.

Mason grinned at Kathryn, but the twinkle in his eye was gone. "It was a long time ago, and I've moved on." He turned to me and the twinkle reappeared. "Rinnie, I would like you to consider donating some time after school to help continue this project. It would mean a lot to me, and it's for a very good cause. Please think about it. For me." Then he nudged me gently with his shoulder and went to the front of the lab. I stood in a mild state of shock, gaping at Mason as he glided to the next finished experiment.

Then I turned toward Kathryn. "Hey, what's with the skinny blond crack?"

"Just covering your trail, girl. When he pulled the needle, I was afraid you might kick his wombat butt with one chromatogram tied behind your back." Kathryn smiled. "I'm practicing to be a Whisperer."

Chapter Seventeen

The Strange Nature of Gookem Puckey

"Absolutely not," Kathryn said as we exited the lab.

"You don't think it's weird that I noticed Mason has a nice side?"

"Weird, no. Blind, definitely. Mason only has one side, and nice it's not."

"Maybe he just had a bad childhood. Maybe he's trying to change."

"Maybe he's an evil wombat. Be afraid. Be very—" Kathryn must have sensed a disturbance in the Force or something, because she suddenly spun on her heels. Bobby rounded the corner down the hall.

And I was supposed to be the psychic one.

"Okay, Bobby," Kathryn sang as he approached. "What's your secret? You're smiling!"

I didn't see any smile.

"S-s-secret?" he stammered.

"You know, Bobby, the Spring Fling is coming. I think you're out here deciding who to ask."

Bobby turned a morbid shade of purple. His scalp glowed under his buzz cut. His eyes went wide with fear.

"You are as subtle as a pipe bomb," I told her.

"Hey, I was simply inquiring as to what was on Bobby's brilliant mind while we were in chemistry boiling gookem puckey. I mean, it's not like he's *only* an awe-inspiring specimen of virility. He has a mind, too, Rinnie. I utter a gasp of dismay that you only see his outward hunkness. That's just shallow."

Bobby scowled. His eyes narrowed. "Gookem puckey? They're making lysergic acid in that lab!"

"May I inquire as to what your brilliant hunkness means?" I asked. Kathryn elbowed me.

Bobby shook his head. "I wasn't certain before, but now I know. You hydrolyze ergot to make lysergic acid. That's what Miliron sends to Old Torrents. He's too harebrained to realize what they're doing. Lysergic acid is only one step away from LSD, which was originally developed to treat mental patients. But in the lab at the Old Torrents Mental Facility, they change the chemical structure to make it do things LSD was never meant to do."

"And you know this how?"

"Plenty of research. And I overheard Tammy Angel bragging about how she made Kent Gable stash it in my locker for the cops to find. The real thing, not the harmless stuff from the Class Project. Angel is smart. She knows somebody at the Old Torrents lab. Now she has Chuckie and Art pushing this poison on us. It turns people nasty. Look at what it did to Erica

Jasmine before she quit. And Agatha Chew. Chuckie Cuff has always been weird, but now he's just mean. And it's not because he hangs out with Rubric."

Suddenly a light went on in my head, and my stomach knotted. I remembered Andy's words. *The Walpurgis Knights kidnap children and train them to be Knights. They use mutated hallucinogens to change their personalities. Nice people can't be Knights.*

"See?" Kathryn said. "I told you he's brilliant."

Yes, Bobby was brilliant. How could I have missed it? The Knights were making Psychedone 10 right under our noses. And Mason had just invited me to help, although I wasn't convinced that he knew what he was asking.

· · ·

The next morning, lost in thought, I drifted down the hall to meet Kathryn for language arts. I was pretty sure I finally understood, and I didn't like it at all. The Knights were manufacturing Psychedone 10. The Class Project was the precursor. And, if what Bobby said about Angel was true, the Red Team was in charge of distribution. Angel's stash in the SSA was actual vitamin supplements, a nice ruse to cover her if anyone questioned the garbage she was pushing in school. But judging from Mason's sincerity when he talked about helping the mentally ill, it was unlikely that he knew anything about the Class Project other than what he had told me. He really believed he was producing the first stages of a miracle cure.

According to the *Book of Lore*, the real truth about Psychedone was frightening—after extended use, it caused physical addiction and altered the users' personalities, breaking down their mental defenses. They couldn't think for themselves, and became almost totally unable to disobey the commands of a stronger personality. It was a very powerful mind-control drug. And the formula had advanced over the years.

When I was kidnapped, it was called Psychedone 5. Each version became more deadly. The Knights forced their victims to take the drug, then trained the strongest to become Knights. The rest were used as scapegoats for the Knights' crimes.

I also now understood how Captious knew of the Walpurgi. I was worried that Munificent had let secrets slip, so I asked during practice. Andy assured me it wasn't so. Apparently Munificent had told the police force that the Knights were a powerful street gang called 'The Walpurgi.' And even if Captious had knowledge of the Psi Fighters' existence like I feared, that didn't automatically guarantee our destruction. The Whisperers spread rumors about us on purpose. That's how we let the Knights and the rest of Greensburg's underworld know that they were being watched. By the time we were done talking, Andy had confirmed what I already knew. In my exhausted state, I let my real fear surface—the fear that I would lose my family. Again. Andy told me that the time would come, probably sooner than I wanted, when I would have to stop suppressing my past. All well and good, Dr. Phil, but first, I needed to figure out Mason's part in all this.

My assumptions had been totally wrong. I assumed Mason and Captious were in this together. But when Captious took Christie, Mason was angry. It seemed that Mason was as surprised by Christie's kidnapping as he was clueless about the Class Project.

A strained voice around the corner broke into my thoughts.

I flattened myself against the lockers and listened.

"No, it's illegal and I'm not doing it."

"It's not. I think you should reconsider, little guy. You are the best we've ever had."

"You never had me. Did you make Gable plant that stuff in my locker? Angel said it wouldn't have happened if I had listened."

"I don't know what you're talking about."

"You're a liar. I'm outa here. Leave me alone."

"Please, Bobby, this is important. The work we do here is completed at Old Torrents. They have equipment we don't. They use our product to make medicine that helps the mentally ill. I doubt that you can understand it, but this means a lot to me. My mother was mentally ill. If I can help people like her, I will do whatever is necessary. Please reconsider. We really need you."

"No, *you* don't understand. Talk to Angel. She'll tell you. I'm done."

A dull clang, like the striking of a gong with a stale loaf of bread, echoed down the hall. I sprinted around the corner. Bobby crouched on the floor in front of a dented locker, holding his forehead, Mason towering over him. Mason turned at the sound of my footsteps.

"Lucky you, Bobbykins," he said, smiling at me. "It appears that it's time for me to go to class. We'll have to reschedule. Have a lovely day."

As Mason turned to leave, Bobby leapt to his feet, grabbed him by the shoulder and shoved him. Mason's face brightened with an admiring expression that said, *You are extremely cool for a four-eyed dweeb, but I can't honestly believe you did that and expect to live!*

"Touch me again and I'll knock your teeth out," Bobby

growled. He looked tiny next to Mason, but I had never seen such fire in his eyes. He was shaking with the force of his anger, both hands tightly clenched, and his chin raised, daring Mason to hit him.

"Ooh," Mason said, reaching out with his pinky. "How tempting. But I think I'll have to decline for now. I have other duties at the moment."

"Like pushing drugs?" Bobby snarled.

Mason cocked his head like a bird and looked sideways at me. "Wherever does Roberto get his imagination, Miss Noelle?"

Mason was acting like a jerk, but Bobby was off base. I thought maybe this one time Mason deserved the benefit of the doubt. "I'll talk to him." Then I pointed at Mason, not in a mean way, but so he would know I meant it. "But you'd better stop hurting him. There is no excuse for it. You told me you liked Bobby. You told me that being nice would become a habit. I'd like to see it. Please?"

Mason bit his lower lip. He looked right into my eyes, and said, "For you." He turned to Bobby and extended his hand. "I'm sorry. I shouldn't have done that. Can you forgive me?"

Bobby glared at Mason, but didn't say a word.

Mason's eyes flashed sadness, but he smiled, dropped his hand, and walked away. As he rounded the corner, I heard him mumble, "Everybody deserves a second chance. Even me."

"I'll give him a second chance. Next time he touches me, I'll knock his teeth out," Bobby whispered, still glaring as Mason disappeared. "Twice." Then he turned to me and smiled. I noticed the swelling redness on his forehead. "Kathryn says you do kung fu. I've been researching on the Internet and already know a little. I need you to teach me a little more. Just one punch? Or a death ray. That's all I need. Pretty please?"

"Hey, hey, hey!" Kathryn waltzed down the hall toward us. "What did I miss? Fill me in!"

"Hi, Kitty," Bobby whispered. Except for the red bump on his forehead, his face had lost all color. He appeared to have forgotten Mason and acted like he was about to barf.

"Hi," Kathryn said quietly, looking at the floor, smiling like a Barbie who had just discovered she was a real girl. She shuffled her feet and slouched slightly, like she was trying not to be taller than Bobby. For the second time since I had known her, Kathryn appeared speechless. Something was up, and she had not told me about it.

To my complete astonishment, Bobby turned to me, and looked straight into my eyes. He tried to speak, then stopped. He tried again, and this time succeeded with all the grace of a person in mid-vomit.

"Ummm, would you…ga…ga…ack!…go-to-the-Spring-Fling-with-me?"

"Huh?" I said. I felt my face flush. I turned to Kathryn. She stared dreamily at Bobby like I wasn't even there.

"I mean, if you don't want to, that's okay." Bobby continued to stare right at me.

"But—" I desperately needed my armor's Shimmer mode, or someone to beam me up.

"It's just that, well, you mentioned that the Spring Fling is coming, and you thought I was deciding who to ask, and I *was*, deciding I mean, so I was wondering, you know…"

Oh. Relief flooded me like a long overdue bathroom break. I reached out, took Bobby by the chin, and turned his head. "She's over there."

Kathryn squealed like a hamster who had run too many

circles on its exercise wheel. "Oh, Bobby! Oh, Bobby! Oh, Bobby!"

"I believe you can take that as a yes," I said.

Bobby suddenly appeared very calm. Color returned to his face and one corner of his mouth smiled slightly at Kathryn. "Cool. Umm, would it be okay to meet you there?"

"No driver's license?" I asked.

"Can't afford insurance."

"I feel your pain." Same reason I didn't have one. Fortunately for me, Kathryn did.

The bell rang, and people popped out of nowhere like cockroaches.

"Seven-thirty?" Bobby asked.

"She'll be there!" I took Kathryn by the hand. "Come on, we'll be late for class."

Kathryn squealed again as we skipped along the hall. "Bobby asked me! Bobby asked me! I'm going to the Spring Fling with Bobbyyyyyy! Rinnie, I didn't think I would get to go at all."

"You turned down six other guys."

Kathryn giggled.

"You're obsessed."

"I am," she sighed. "Isn't he beautiful?"

Suddenly the crowd of students parted, and a blond head made its way toward us.

"Rinnie, wait up!"

Egon waded through the pack and stopped right in front of me. Breathing suddenly became difficult, and everything started to fog up.

"Hi," he said, smiling.

My legs turned to noodles. "Hi."

The late bell rang. Egon looked at the clock, then at me. "You. Me. Spring Fling. You in?"

My tongue suddenly became a mass of stupid. "Blahr," I said.

Kathryn burst out laughing. I punched her in the arm, blushed, and smiled at Egon.

Chapter Eighteen

Attack in the Park

I walked home from school that afternoon, totally elated. Kathryn was overjoyed too, but she took the bus. Go figure. She lived closer to the school than I did. Each of us handles our bucket of bliss differently, I suppose. Strolling through the park made my life seem like a fairy tale. The flowers, the trees, the tombstones—well, maybe not the tombstones.

I was going to the Spring Fling! Everyone would talk. Tammy Angel would be outraged. Boot Milner would be jealous. And I would be oblivious to it all. I would only see Egon. I couldn't believe it! Bobby said Egon had approached him and asked if I was going with anyone. He and Bobby knew we would be headed for language arts. It was a setup! A wonderful setup!

I imagined Egon and me sitting on the chairs lining the walls of the gym floor. Everyone else would be dancing, but we would be sitting. Sitting, staring, thinking… Then he would reach over and touch my hand. I would smile. A slow song would come on, and Egon would look into my eyes. *May I have this dance?* he would ask. *I'd love to*, I would say. Then he would lead me to the center of the dance floor, taking me in his arms. His arms would be strong, his embrace overwhelming. He wouldn't notice my shaking, because he would be looking so deeply into my eyes. We wouldn't talk. There would be no words to express what we felt…he would lean down, bring his lips close to mine…

"Get away!" a voice screamed. I was jerked from my fantasy like a bad act from *America's Got Talent*. Directly ahead of me, Mason and Rubric had Bobby pinned against a tree. Mason leaned on a baseball bat. Rubric was empty-handed, but he swayed unsteadily, and had a dazed, angry look in his eyes. He was definitely high. This was so not good.

"Leave me alone," Bobby snapped. Blood ran from his nose, but there was no fear in his voice.

"I wanted to be ladylike and give you another chance," Mason said. "You were the best we ever had. Almost as good as me."

"If I were only as good as you, I wouldn't have figured out that your wonderful Class Project was part of a drug ring." Bobby stepped toward Mason, fists clenched. "I guess you never talk to Angel."

"*Au contraire, mon Frère*," Mason said, wagging a finger, his speech almost imperceptibly slurred. "I asked her. She said you were a *dweeb!*" Mason suddenly became furious, like he'd lost his mind. "She gave me the stuff you're all girly frightened of, and I tested it. *It's nothing, Bobby! Nothing!*"

Bobby jumped back. "I see that," he snapped.

"Do him," Rubric muttered. "He deserves it."

"Don't tell me what to do," Mason growled. He shoved Rubric, staggered, then turned to Bobby and said softly, "You don't trust me. You won't give me a second chance. Everybody deserves a second chance, Bobby."

"Earn it," Bobby said. "Fight me without the bat, coward."

"This is for the greater good, Bobby," Rubric said. "He doesn't want to fight you. He wants to make an example of you. He wants to show people how serious we are about the Class Project. Right, Mase?"

Mason turned to Rubric, the pain in his face unmistakable. "Shut up, Art. Just shut up." He gripped the bat in both hands and stepped toward Bobby.

Suddenly, Andy's words flashed through my mind. *Mason has killed before.* I had no idea what was wrong with Mason, but it was time to move. I sprinted toward him. My mind quickly calmed. I would take him out first. A few pressure points, and nighty, night, little Mason. Once he was down, Rubric would probably take off. If not, so much the better.

Just then, Mason noticed me. "Rinnie," he whispered. He suddenly looked like he would cry. "Bobby was wrong. I tried it, Rinnie. Why won't he believe me?"

Understanding slammed me in the gut. Mason was high on Psychedone 10.

"Howdy there, Peroxide." Rubric grinned and blew me a kiss.

I scowled. "I'd rather kiss a rhino."

Rubric made a grunting sound that I can only assume was meant to be a rhinoceros, but sounded like a heifer with four upset stomachs. He puckered his blubbery lips at me. "Come get some!"

"Don't make me sick."

"Why don't you rush on home, now, Peroxide?" Rubric slurred. "Your mommy's calling, and you might get hurt here. Oh, did I say 'might'?"

"Yo, babe," Chuckie's voice boomed in my ear from behind. Suddenly, I was in his powerful grip, jerked off my feet.

Rubric grinned. "By the way, your bodyguard isn't around to protect you, so you might want to watch your back."

"Put me down," I yelled, totally miffed that I'd let Chuckie take me by surprise. His cheek felt like a cactus against mine, and his breath was horrible. "Don't you people use toothpaste?"

"I don't like the taste," Chuckie said.

Obviously.

"Chuckie!" Mason roared. "Don't touch her!"

Chuckie inhaled sharply, and his grip loosened, which I totally took advantage of. I shifted so that my arms were partly free. Chuckie would soon be in for an unpleasant surprise.

"It's okay, Mase," Rubric said. "Remember, we have to set an example."

Mason gritted his teeth. "If you hurt her, I'll kill you."

Rubric staggered to Mason and put his hand on his shoulder. "For the greater good. She's not the problem."

"Leave him alone!" Bobby shoved Rubric. "Let him think for himself. Is this what that garbage does?

"Mase," Rubric said, ignoring Bobby. "For the greater good."

Mason glared fiercely at Rubric, then stepped into Bobby's path. "Why did you lie to me?" Mason poked Bobby hard in the chest. "Why won't you give me another chance?"

Bobby's fist moved like lightning. He punched Mason

square in the teeth with a sharp crack. Mason's head snapped backward, and he stumbled, blood trickling down his chin.

"I told you not to touch me!" Bobby yelled. His fists clenched, his knees bent, he looked like a small tiger ready to spring. "And I told you the truth. You just didn't want to hear it."

"Do him," Rubric said.

Mason raised his bat.

"Do him," Rubric repeated.

Mason wiped the blood from his lips and lowered the bat. "No."

Bobby held his fists ready to strike again, so tiny next to Mason, like a mouse defending itself against a lion. Just then, Rubric stumbled forward. I screamed, but it was too late. He punched Bobby right between the shoulder blades. Bobby's knees buckled, and Rubric grabbed him from behind, pinning his arms against his sides.

"Do him, Mason." Rubric's voice was low, intimidating. "For the greater good. Do him. He lied to you."

"Don't talk to me, Art." Mason stood holding the bat in both hands, trembling. "Just shut up."

I was officially fed up with Art Rubric. "Chuckie, if you don't put me down right this second, I will embarrass you more than you can possibly imagine."

"I have an excellent imagination, babe," Chuckie said. "And I can't possibly imagine anything you could do to embarrass me."

"Don't call me babe."

"Look, babe." Chuckie tightened his grip. "Be good so you don't get hurt. I am *very* strong. And you are small and *oh* so much weaker—"

I slammed both elbows into Chuckie's ribs, snapped my head backward into his face, and stomped on his shin. He gasped, then whimpered, then dropped me to the ground. I spun to the right and cracked my elbow into the side of his head, then spun to the left and blasted a spinning back kick into his jaw. Chuckie's eyes rolled and he dropped like he'd been hit by a bus. "I told you not to call me babe."

"Do him!" Rubric yelled. *"Now!"*

Mason suddenly looked so helpless, so defeated. He raised the bat over his head and took aim at Bobby. Bobby tried to lift his arms to cover his head, but Rubric held him tight. I was too far away to stop him without doing something drastic. So I did.

Chapter Nineteen

Mason's Memories

Sorrow, I thought as I drew my Amplifier. Mental fire flashed from my fingertips. I flicked my wrist and the psychic whip closed the distance between Mason and me, snapping around his arm. I jerked hard. The bat flew from his hand, and he fell to the ground, screaming.

I took my Amplifier in both hands and glared at him. He screamed and writhed in pain. I held tight as Mason struggled to pull free. This time, I would control the Lash. I would *make* Mason feel remorse. Suddenly, my mind filled with horrible memories that I knew weren't my own.

Mommy glared down at me while she tied the dog's leash around my neck. This time, she attached it to the tree. I trembled with fear. I had done it again, and Mommy was mad. Her eyes scared me. They looked dead. Mommy wasn't the same anymore. She grimaced, lit a match, and tossed it in my hair.

I whimpered and slapped it out, but it burned. She lit another one and flicked it. It stuck to my forehead, singeing a massive blister before I pulled it off. I screamed, "I'm sorry, Mommy, I'm sorry!" I wanted badly to stop wetting the bed, but she made me drink so much before I went to sleep. Another match! The pain on my scalp was agonizing. "It hurts, it hurts, it hurts!" I shrieked and slapped at my head to stop the torture, but my hands blistered. The smell of burnt hair and skin filled my nostrils.

"You were always the stupid one, Mason," she said. She lumbered over to the tall pine tree I was tied to. A can of gasoline and a shovel sat next to it. She picked up the can. "You should have died. Not your brother." She unscrewed the cap slowly, a demented smile cracking her face, and poured gasoline in a circle around me, drenching my shoes and splashing my legs. "He was such a good boy. Why don't you ever listen to me? Why can't you just do what you're told?" Then she lit another match.

I wailed. "Please, give me another chance!"

"You don't deserve a second chance."

Suddenly, I heard a metallic ring and Mommy was sitting on the ground, glaring up at me. Her poor head was covered in blood. A man stood behind her, holding the shovel. Rotting flesh hung in strips from his face, and white bone shone through. A bolt of fear shot through me.

He swung the shovel hard. It made a dull clang against Mommy's head. He hit her again and again, and every time he hit her, his jawbones clacked together. Then he handed me the shovel and said, "I'll come back for you."

The front door burst open and Daddy ran out. "Mason, no!" He stared at me in horror, then his eyes shot to Mommy. "Why couldn't she just leave you alone?" he whispered. "Don't worry, buddy. I'll take care of everything."

Then I felt older. I looked down from the balcony of the high school auditorium. Munificent pointed up at us. He talked about a man who wore a skull mask. The familiar terror filled my chest. The cop was wrong. It wasn't a mask. It was him. He had come back for me. Just like he said he would.

I was in the SSA with Angel. "Is it true what Bobby said?"

Angel smiled and caressed my cheek. "Bobby's a dweeb. Why would you listen to him? Mason, I can get the stuff he's talking about. Trust me. It's harmless."

I pushed her hand away from my cheek. Tammy Angel was beginning to annoy me. She had changed. "Give me some. I want to prove that Bobby is wrong."

Angel smiled and reached into her purse.

Mason moaned loudly. I screamed and released him from the Memory Lash. My knees gave way and I fell, shaking violently, tears streaming down my face. My scalp burned from the memory of the matches, and the smell of gasoline was everywhere. Mason's memories still surged in my mind. They boiled, forcing themselves to the surface, but I pushed them back.

I shook my head, my mind cleared, and I stayed in control. I had finally mastered the Lash. Then my eyes focused, and my moment of triumph dissolved. Mason was on the ground curled up in a ball, whimpering like a savagely beaten animal, sobbing and hiccuping, and I realized that the Lash still sucked.

"What'd you do, you freak!" Rubric had dropped Bobby. He pointed at me, terror in his eyes. "You killed him! You killed him!" He turned, slammed into a tree, and fell on his butt. Then he picked himself up to stagger off through the park, disappearing into the woods.

Bobby limped toward me and helped me to my feet. I

leaned on him. He felt surprisingly strong for someone so small. "Are you okay, Rinnie?"

"Yeah," I said with no confidence.

"Was that the Memory Lash?"

I lurched, and must have given poor Bobby a pretty nasty look, because his eyes got huge and his jaw dropped.

"K-Kitty told me," he stammered.

What? The one person I trusted! Kathryn's hopes of ever being a Whisperer had totally crashed and burned. I would deal with her later. I pulled away from Bobby. "Come on, we have to get out of here."

"I don't think it'll work on him."

I looked down at Mason. He was babbling, sobbing softly, and every so often he mumbled, "Mommy, Mommy, I'm so sorry," then started whimpering again.

Bobby was wrong. I had never seen the Lash have that effect on anyone. Not even Mason Draudimon deserved the agony of that nasty weapon. I knew too well what it felt like. And I finally understood Mason. He looked up at me with huge, soft eyes, and for a moment, seemed to know what I was thinking.

"He'll be all right," Bobby said. "Kathryn told me it wears off quickly. Especially when you aren't capable of remorse. And I can't imagine anyone less capable. Let's go."

"We can't just leave him here like this," I objected. A low moan made me spin around.

Chuckie was regaining consciousness. He pushed upright slowly, his face distorted with confusion, an enormous bruise already showing on his cheek. He shook his head, then his eyes grew wide like he had just realized why he was facedown in the dirt. "Whoa, babe, you are a major butt-kicker!" He struggled to his feet and tottered toward me. "I'm impressed."

Before he knew what had happened, I grabbed his thumb, twisting his hand into a wrist lock. Chuckie yelped. "Babe, like, I meant what I said. I'm on your side, now, 'cause I don't want nobody to know a girl kicked my butt. You won't tell, will ya?"

"I told you not to call me babe," I said softly.

"Hey, that's cool…Rinnie."

I released Chuckie from the wrist lock. "Take Mason home."

"The Shadow Passage isn't open yet."

"Were you born this stupid, or did you take supplements?" I looked down at Mason and shuddered. "Take him to his dad's house."

Chapter Twenty

Hunter Becomes Hunted

"Oh, boy." Andy rubbed his forehead with both hands. "Here we go."

"What? Was I wrong?"

"You did what you had to do. Under the influence of Psychedone 10, Mason might have killed your friend. I'm just afraid. The past has a nasty way of repeating itself."

"Why would he be so stupid, Andy? Mason wasn't into drugs of any kind. Why would he take something so nasty?"

Andy shrugged. "Like you saw in his memory, he wanted to prove that Bobby was wrong. Mason so badly wanted the Class Project to be what he needed it to be that he took a stupid chance."

"What did he need it to be?"

"A miracle. A cure for his past. His second chance."

I felt so bad for Mason. "He didn't even realize he was

under its influence. He tried so hard to disobey Rubric."

"On the plus side, we know Mason didn't kill his mother like we all believed. *And* you kicked some major butt in that park. Three at a time!"

"Two," I said, feeling my face turn red. "Art ran into a tree."

"The forest is our friend. Okay, hand over the papers you stole from the police station. Let's see what Amos didn't tell us."

"I didn't steal them."

Andy raised one eyebrow and cocked his head sideways. "My apologies. I meant to say *purloined*."

"Isn't that the same thing?"

"Yes." He held his hand out. "Give."

I opened my backpack and dug around for the envelope. "Andy, does the Memory Lash ever get easier? I can't stop thinking about what happened to Mason."

"You controlled it this time." He pursed his lips. "An obvious result of my brilliant instruction."

"Have you been hanging out with Dr. Captious?"

"No, he's too self-absorbed. He'd rather talk about himself than about me. Can you imagine?" Andy suddenly became serious and cupped my face in both hands. "The Lash...was never intended to be easy. Just powerful. Rinnie, it's the only weapon known that can change a person's heart. Do you understand how difficult that is?"

"Do you think it changed Mason?"

Andy shook his head. "Maybe. Only God knows that. You can't always tell if a person is changed. But you can be certain when he isn't."

I nodded, remembering LaReau. He had no remorse at all. "LaReau was dead inside. The only emotions I felt were dark, empty. Mason was dark, too, but it was more like a little boy trying to dig free from layers of pain."

"I believe Mason suffered through too many repressed memories not to be affected. From what you described, his remorse is deep. He'll never stop remembering. The change is going to be slow and painful."

"I don't get it. Mason didn't *do* anything. In the memory I saw, he was the victim."

"Of course."

"What does that mean? That's not how the Memory Lash works."

"Think about it. What did Mason say after you released him?"

"He curled up in a ball and told his mother he was sorry."

"Yep."

"What, yep?"

"From what you described, Mason believes he caused his mother's death. That was the most painful thing he ever witnessed, and he blames himself. That's why the Memory Lash showed you that memory."

"And the man with a decaying skull for a head? He didn't feel like Scallion." I knew the answer before I asked, but I was really hoping to be wrong.

"Nicolaitan. He's very powerful. He made Mason see him as death. Hence, the skull."

"Did he also make Mason believe it was, hence, his fault?"

"No. Mason really believes it. Just like you really believe your parents died because of you. No matter how often we tell you it wasn't your fault. Because it wasn't, in case I haven't told you. You were six. Six-year-olds are innocent, even bratty ones like you."

"Hey!"

"Now, where were we? Oh, yes." Andy smiled and snapped his fingers. "Papers, please."

I pulled the envelope from my backpack and took out the drawing. "See, it's just some sort of doodle. No words, no real picture. I can't make anything out of it."

Andy looked at the paper, turning it in all directions, then rubbed his finger across the scribbles.

"Wow!" he hollered, nearly dropping the paper. His face got totally serious and he gaped at me like I was a burn victim. "I prayed this would never happen."

"What's wrong?"

Andy shook his head. "Be right back." He turned and disappeared into a closet at the far end of his tech lab. He returned wheeling a flatbed scanner with the words *Andy-Scan 1000* molded into its shining cover.

"Why are you scanning the doodle?" I asked. "You gonna Photoshop your face onto it?"

"Lemme 'splain." Andy shook his head. "You know how, when you're trying to think of something to draw, you start out by doodling, then ideas crystallize in your head, and you eventually end up with some very intricate artwork?"

"Uh…no. I doodle when I'm bored. Like in language arts when they talk about subjunctives and conjugation and big words that real people never use."

"You should try doodling when you need to think," Andy said. "Because the thought is in the doodle."

"Sounds like drivel."

"Doodles only drivel when the ink is wet. That's why Munificent used pencil."

"Okay, I'm lost. What are you trying to tell me with your

twaddle?"

"Munificent was writing to the Psi Fighters. This is how he communicated with us."

"By doodling? Andy, that is weird, even for you. Why don't you just build them a Bat Signal?"

"I'm working on it," Andy said, smiling down at me. "Now, follow me, if your tired brain can stay awake. How do you put thoughts on paper?"

I folded my hands, placed them daintily under my chin, and batted my eyes. "You...write them?"

"Good, good...and what do you do in language arts *while* you're doodling?"

"Daydream, because paying attention would cause me to fall asleep, then I'd get detention."

"And daydreaming would be the same as..."

"Thinking?"

"She shoots! She scores!" Andy shouted, and moonwalked around the room.

"So you're saying my thoughts are in my doodle?"

"Keep your doodle out of this. We're talking about Munificent's communication to us, which we would have already known about if he had not been so inconveniently murdered. You need to hear it."

I smacked myself in the forehead and sighed. "Where is this going?"

"Right there," Andy said, slapping the paper into the scanner's auto-feeder.

"So," I said slowly, "you're going to scan it..."

"I thought we already established that." He pressed a key and the scanner started to hum.

"All we established is that you are a Looney Tune," I said,

ready to bang my head off the wall. "What does—"

"This is the Andy-Scan 1000, a clever device invented by— need I even say it?—my own pretty little self. It does for the written word what the MPU 3000 does for memories."

"You can scan the thoughts out of a scribble?"

"Or a doodle, even if it's drivel." Andy punched another button on the scanner.

"Psi Fighters," a voice boomed over the sound system hidden somewhere in Andy's tech room walls. "I have—"

Andy hit the button again, and the voice stopped.

"Why did you stop it?" I looked around for speakers I knew I'd never find.

"Honey." Andy put his arm around me, growing unusually serious again. "There's something you have to know. If we had gotten this message from Amos Munificent in time, we may have been able to save him. But he wasn't trying to warn us about a danger to himself. He was telling us that Scallion's mission isn't what we believed."

"How do you know what's in the scribble?" I was beginning to feel very uneasy.

"I scanned it when I touched it. You'll learn how. It's a lot like scanning minds, and you know how to do that."

"I hate scanning minds. It hurts."

"This won't be a field of daisies, either." Andy punched the button.

"—new information," Munificent's voice boomed out. "Nicolaitan has infiltrated the high school more deeply than we believed. I've confirmed that the apprentice who goes by the name of Scallion is a student there. I have also learned that he's searching for the Morgan girl. Nicolaitan knows she is back. He believes she attends the high school."

"You okay?" Andy asked.

"What?" I had a bad feeling that I was missing something very obvious. "Wait, the Morgan girl…he means *me*?"

Andy nodded. "After we rescued you, we put you in hiding. All traces of your existence evaporated. It was like six-year-old Lynn Morgan never existed. With your parents dead, it was the best way to protect you. Nicolaitan had assumed that we sent you far away. But he must have seen something in Munificent's mind."

"What sort of something?" I asked.

"If you hadn't brought me this memory, I couldn't have pieced it together, but it makes sense now. Remember the memory of Munificent's murder, when Nicolaitan asked him about the Morgan girl? He kidnapped you ten years ago. He should have given up and moved on by now. I underestimated how much he hates us. He wants you because you are the only Psi Fighter ever taken alive."

"I was six. How hard could it have been?"

"That's not the point. He believes he can unlock your mind and learn the location of the Academy. Then he'll send his Knights to destroy us. That's always been his goal. Something caused him to resurface. He must have pulled a fragment from Munificent's mind somehow. A fragment with you in it."

"Mr. Munificent acted like he knew me at the assembly," I said, suddenly in terrible fear. "If Nicolaitan read Mr. Munificent's mind, he knows who I am. I have to get home. Andy, we have to protect my family!"

Andy took me by the shoulders. "We don't know whether he knows your identity. Munificent only knows Rinnie Noelle because your dad consults with the police force. He doesn't know you're the Morgan girl. He thinks she disappeared."

"She is correct," a voice barked from behind me. I jumped into Andy's arms and nearly knocked him over. The Kilodan stood only feet from me.

"Why would you sneak up on me when I'm already frightened out of my skin?" I snapped.

The Kilodan let loose with an electronically altered laugh that made the Joker sound sane. "I'm training you to control your emotions."

"Not doing a very good job of it," Andy said as he peeled my arms from around his neck and sat me on the floor.

"Munificent may not have had knowledge of your true identity, but Nicolaitan does," the Kilodan said. "He has a long memory, and will have retained fragments from the kidnapping. What he does not know is your current identity. He knows the Morgan girl has Psi Fighter abilities, but he has not yet linked her to you. We must be cautious. He has eyes everywhere. But as long as you don't use the Mental Arts while unmasked, he'll never make the connection."

My heart was in my throat. "I just did."

Chapter Twenty-one

The Spring Fling

The next day I was a bundle of nerves. The anxiety of being discovered by Nicolaitan was awful. If he found me, he'd unlock my mind, learn the identities of the Psi Fighters, and the location of our secret Academy. Then we would all be vulnerable. As frightening as that reality was, it was marshmallows and chocolate pudding compared to the sheer terror of choosing an outfit. The Spring Fling was that night, and I had nothing to wear. Fortunately, Kathryn was skilled at all things soirée. She invited me to her house to get ready. I seriously wanted to murder her for telling Bobby things I trusted her with, but I decided to wait. The last thing I needed at the moment was a fight with my BFF. And, to tell the truth, I was terrified to hear her reasons, especially if they confirmed that my most trusted friend in the entire cosmos was untrustworthy. I didn't know if I could live with that.

"Powder blue," she said, plucking a dress from her closet. "It brings out your eyes. This is perfect. Delicate, feminine, petite. Asymmetrical hemline to make you appear taller, show a little leg…then just a touch of blush, a hint of eyeliner, a very light eye shadow, and matching lip gloss. Oh, Rin, the poor boy won't know what hit him."

By the time we got to the school, my anxiety had subsided a bit. Kathryn had a comfortable confidence with social events that was very calming. Unfortunately, I didn't. The minute we walked through the double doors, my nerves took over again.

The poorly lit gymnasium was packed, people dancing everywhere. We had arrived fashionably late, although I would have preferred being fashionably later, by, say, a year. As I scanned the gym, searching for signs of Egon, Kathryn began dancing happily beside me, oblivious to my pain, singing along with the music. "…you don't know you're BEAUTIFULLLLLLL… Hey, Rin, our men will find us soon!"

I nodded. My mouth was dry. "I don't feel so good."

Kathryn laughed. "Oh, you'll be fine. Such a worrywart. What's the worst thing that can happen? Oh, never mind…it just did."

The double doors slammed open. Rubric, Chuckie, and the Red Team sauntered into the gym.

"A meeting of the minds," Kathryn said. "Don't they look precious?"

Art Rubric and Chuckie Cuff looked like hit men in their stupid trench coats, but the Red Team looked amazing. Gorgeous hair, expensive jewelry, high heels—Tammy had a low-cut gown with a slit up the side that made her look like a runway model. I was officially jealous. Any black-hearted person who looked that good deserved my wrath.

"What's Angel wearing?" I asked. "Sleaze Bag by Gucci?"

"Meow, Rin."

Teachers had positioned themselves around the gym, just like they did during assembly, to feel like they were in control. But we all knew better. It was common knowledge that the teachers hated chaperoning (I can't imagine why with such model students). Consequently, only the ones with low seniority had to attend, and they were too busy chatting to each other to notice anything the students were doing. Unless there was a nuclear explosion, it was unlikely that they would leave the safety of their seats.

Suddenly, my heart stopped. My lungs seized. "Kathryn, I'm seriously gonna upchuck."

"Oh, you lucky girl!" Kathryn chirped. "Yours came first!"

Framed by the door, all alone and absolutely beautiful, Egon shimmered in the light like an archangel. Dressed in a blue button-up shirt, he glided into the gym.

The instant Egon crossed the threshold, cretins surrounded him. Tammy Angel flung her beefy arms around his neck. A sudden urge to dismember her filled my kind and loving heart. Egon smiled politely, but didn't appear to be talking much.

"Ignore her, Rin," Kathryn said. "She knows he's with you. She's being the Alpha, as usual."

"Are you saying I shouldn't give away my secret by destroying her in public?"

"I'm saying Egon is a gentleman, and you have nothing to worry about."

Kathryn was right. Egon scanned the gym as he pried Tammy's monkey arms from his neck. Then our eyes met, and he broke into the most adorable smile I had ever seen on a human. While Tammy flapped her never-ending jaw, fake-laughing hysterically, Egon brushed by her, his gaze never leaving mine. I chuckled quietly at Tammy's blank stare when she realized she had been deserted.

"Hi, Rinnie. Hi, Kathryn."

"Hi, Egon," Kathryn sang. "Oh, look! Bobby's here! I'll leave you two alone."

"Kathryn, wa—" Panic suddenly bodyslammed every other emotion I owned.

"Hi," Egon repeated.

"Hi."

"You look amazing," Egon said, taking a step back, eying me from head to toe.

"Thank you. I brushed my hair."

Oh, wow! I had officially destroyed every contender in the Stupidest Response to a Compliment contest. We stood in silence for a few very awkward moments. I decided I was wrong about there being no words to describe how I felt. Discomfort, nausea, regurgitation…those words did a fine job.

"So…I guess you saw Tammy Angel attack me," Egon said. "I'm sorry, she's just hard to control. We went out one time, and now I can't get rid of her."

"Try flea and tick medicine."

"Maybe *I* need a bodyguard." Egon did a double eyebrow-raise. "Are you interested? I hear you're better than you admitted."

"You did?"

"Yeah, Chuckie said he saw you kick some dude's butt in the park."

"He…umm…yeah…" Chuckie was officially dead. "Sometimes we do Tai Chi in the park. That's probably what he saw. It's very relaxing." Oh, Chuckie was so very dead.

I looked out across the gym, searching for something clever to say, when I found Mason on the other side. He was dressed in a classy Diesel jean jacket and T-shirt, but he looked like I felt—lost, completely out of his element, like he didn't belong. Then his eyes connected with mine. He opened his mouth like he wanted to say something, but shook his head as though he were arguing with himself. His eyes closed, and he turned, disappearing into the crowd. I wondered what was going through his mind.

All at once, the music changed, and a slow song echoed through the gym. "Hey, I like this one." Egon smiled and gently took my hand. "May I have this dance?"

Warmth rose in my face. My first instinct was to run, but he slipped his arm around my waist. That did it. I was a goner. I was about to melt right at his feet. Which I was totally okay with.

Egon pulled me close, and his thigh brushed against mine. Little shivers ran through me. When his feet moved, mine followed. We swayed slowly to the music, bodies in total sync. Dancing with Egon was like—okay, this will sound slightly abnormal, but it was more relaxing than sparring. It was more exciting than wearing my mask and armor. When I laid my head on his shoulder, I utterly disappeared. It was even better than Shimmer mode! If you were a Psi Fighter, you'd totally understand how awesome it felt.

Sometime during the song, Kathryn and Bobby were dancing beside us. I glanced over and saw Kathryn kissing Bobby. His eyes were wide with fear, pleading with me. I shook my head, smiling. Poor Bobby never had a chance.

Egon leaned down and gently pressed his forehead to

mine. I laid my head back on his shoulder until the song was over, then found myself being led by the hand away from the dance area. Without warning, he turned me toward him, a mischievous glimmer in his eye. "Bobby hasn't learned defense against lip locks, has he?"

I smiled and glanced at the floor.

Egon took my hand and said, "Have *you*?"

In the darkened room, I was sure he couldn't see how red my face had just turned. I closed my eyes, took a deep breath, and tilted my chin up. Just as I felt his breath on my lips, Egon grunted and crashed into me, knocking me off my feet. I landed hard on the gym floor and heard the thump of a large, soft something beside me. Tammy Angel, butt down and glassy-eyed, the contents of her purse on the floor beside her. She harrumphed and scooped everything back inside. Then she looked up. Her pupils dilated and slowly focused on me. A smirk crossed her face, and she hauled herself to her feet.

"Watch where you're going, Peroxide," she slurred. "You shouldn't embarrass Egon like that."

Egon helped me up, the concern in his eyes barely hiding something darker. He turned to Tammy. "She's not the embarrassment," he whispered.

Tammy jabbed her finger at me. "Stay out of my way, Peroxide. I'm not in a good mood tonight."

"And that's different from when?" I asked sweetly.

Mason suddenly appeared, shouldering his way through the crowd. He took Tammy roughly by the arm, jerking her finger out of my face. "Sorry, no harm done. Right this way, Tam." He smiled at me and slipped away, dragging her behind him.

"Mason, let me go!" Tammy struggled against him, but he

towed her along like a puppy on a leash. Before disappearing into the mass of dancing kids, he glanced back at me. Sadness filled his eyes. I sighed, overcome by an unexplainable longing. For just an instant, I forgot where I was.

"What's going on with him?" Egon asked.

Oops. "What do you mean?" I pushed Mason out of my mind.

"Something's up." Egon's eyes narrowed. "Mason's not causing trouble."

I touched Egon's arm. "He's not himself. Maybe he's afraid of you."

Egon laughed and took my hand.

"Let's get something to drink," I said. Before we started toward the punch table, I noticed a slim object lying on the floor at my feet. "Tammy didn't clean up her mess too well." I bent down to pick it up—a fountain pen, red and silver barrel with a white rectangle in the center. Just as my hand touched it, mental sparks jumped from my fingertips and I jerked back. I reached out again, carefully closing my mind, and picked it up. My heart raced, and I scanned the room, searching.

Tammy Angel was Scallion?

No. Way.

I watched the creep disappear into the crowd, but now that I understood who I had let get away at the Shadow Passage, I found myself giggling inside. Early on, Kathryn and I had decided that Angel couldn't possibly be the face behind that mask.

Which was the signature of a Knight.

"I'm not thirsty anymore," I said to Egon. "Come on, let's dance." I took him by the hand and towed him back to Kathryn and Bobby.

"But, I am," Egon said quietly.

Kathryn was not going to be pleased with me, because I was leaving. Unfortunately, neither was Egon. But I needed to tell Andy and the Kilodan what I had learned, and I had to do it quickly. What a relief. Now, the Psi Fighters could protect my family. The kidnapping would be ended permanently. And we could force Scallion to lead us to Nicolaitan.

I led Egon across the gym floor, stopping in front of Kathryn and Bobby. "Could you excuse us for just a sec? C'mon, Kathryn." I yanked her away from Bobby and glanced back at Egon. "She has to potty."

Egon had that expressionless expression, but he didn't object, so I made a beeline for the bathroom. There was no more time for interruptions. I could worry about what he was thinking later.

"This had better be good," Kathryn snipped. "Bobby and I were getting very, very friendly."

"I noticed," I said. "And don't worry, it's extremely good." As we approached the girl's bathroom, the door banged open and a cloud of smoke rolled out, followed by a swarm of people. Laughter echoed inside. I grunted, led Kathryn down the hall, whipped open the boiler room door, and shoved her through.

"Will you please tell me why you dragged me from a hot guy to a hot boiler room where, by the way, we will get detention if we're caught?" Kathryn growled.

"I found something!" I proudly plucked Scallion's Amplifier from my purse and brandished it over my head.

"I have a pen, Rinnie. If you wanted a pen, you should have asked. Tonight is the night for *having* romance, not writing about it."

"Kathryn, if this is what I think it is, I found Scallion."

"And what, I ask in an irritated tone, *is* it?"

"It's an Amplifier."

Kathryn stared blankly at me. "I thought you weren't supposed to show them to anybody."

"It's not mine."

"Well, whose is it?"

"Scallion's. It all makes perfect sense now."

Kathryn grabbed me by the shoulders. "I will give you two more seconds that rightfully belong to my Bobby. Now tell me…who…is…Scallion?"

"The head of the drug ring. Tammy Angel."

"Oh. Unexpected."

"Tell me about it."

Chapter Twenty-two

A Bad Ending

"How do you know it's her pen?" Kathryn asked.

"Amplifier. It fell out of her purse when she crashed into us."

"Tammy Angel is the kidnapper?" Kathryn shook her head. "We already ruled her out. Too obvious. Drugs, grand theft auto, being stupid without a license, definitely. But kidnapping? Never."

"I know. That's why it makes perfect sense. Nobody would have noticed her hanging around the elementary school or the playground. To the outside world, she's just an extremely hot cheerleader. But we know better. And as soon as you can get me out of here, I'm taking the Amplifier to Andy. He'll analyze the memory fragments. Then we have her."

"Okay, here's the plan." Kathryn took my hands. "I am going to the bathroom…and you are coming with me, because that's what girls do. Then I'll get back to my romantic moment, and make an excuse for you to leave."

"How about if you go potty, and I find Egon and Bobby?"

"That works, too. Tell my Bobby I'll be right there." Kathryn opened the boiler room door and the Red Team stood waiting. Tammy's eyes were still glazed, but she seemed to be in control.

"Lose something?" I asked, wondering if Tammy knew I had her Amplifier.

"Hi, Kathryn, beautiful gown," Tammy sang. "You really should hang with us tonight, you know. The Red Team always needs women of your caliber."

"Thanks," Kathryn said, "but I'm planning on hanging with my boyfriend. TTFN."

Tammy sneered at me. "Speaking of boyfriends, Peroxide, Egon was mine first. Thought you should know."

Liar. "I do believe," I said, batting my eyes and forcing the sweetest smile I could fake, "that *was* is the key word here. Don't you agree?"

Tammy huffed and led the Red Team into the girl's bathroom.

"Good one," Kathryn said. "Okay, you find our dates while I do my thing."

"I'm on it."

As Kathryn disappeared through the bathroom door, I headed toward the gym, last known location of two very hot boys. I approached the crowded dance floor, but Bobby was standing alone.

"Where's Egon?"

"I don't know. He disappeared right after you did. Where's Kitty?"

"Girl's room."

"Rubric's going around badmouthing her. I'm probably going to have to erase him."

"Erase?" I giggled at Bobby's attempt at being cool.

"Less clichéd than 'end' or 'destroy.' I'm working on my tough guy vocabulary."

"That's where clichés were invented." We stood in silence for several minutes, me wondering how Andy would handle Scallion once we verified that he was a she, Bobby apparently making up new superhero sayings.

"What are they doing?" Bobby finally asked. "Did they leave without us?"

Suddenly, someone grabbed me by the shoulder. I spun without thinking, twirled my arm up and around, and forced an arm lock on whoever it was that shouldn't have been grabbing me.

"Hey. That hurts."

I gasped. Poor Egon was all doubled over, his arm twisted in my grip. I let loose, and he stood up slowly. "Nice move." He smiled, rubbing his shoulder. "We should spar some time."

The very thought filled my head with pictures that I never knew I was capable of imagining…Kathryn would have been proud. I opened my mouth to say something witty, but just sort of gurgled.

Egon peeked at me out of the corner of his eye. "On second thought, maybe I'll keep my distance. I don't wanna be damaged."

"Oh, Egon, I'd never damage you. I am so sorry. Are you okay?"

He continued to rub his poor shoulder. "I've had meaner opponents. But if you'd like to make it up to me, we could dance."

I nodded happily. One quick dance before telling Andy about Scallion couldn't hurt. Scallion wasn't going anywhere.

"No more nose powdering?"

"I promise."

"Can you retrieve my date first?" Bobby asked.

"She said she'd be right back." I looked up at Egon.

"Go ahead. I'll be right here. Then you're all mine."

What a sweet thought. When this kidnapper thing was over and Tammy was doing time, I would be free to be all his. As I worked my way through the crowd back to the bathroom, I thought about Tammy's Amplifier. It would help us locate the other Knights. Maybe even their training ground. With Andy's gadgets, he could trace it to wherever it had been. Like he always said, *Memories...better than DNA.*

Just as I reached for the bathroom door, it crashed open. Boot Milner burst through and pushed me aside with one arm, a wild look in her eyes. Agatha Chew rushed after her.

"You're excused," I said.

"Rinnie." Agatha stopped in front of me, blocking the bathroom entrance.

"Look," I said. "I don't want trouble." Then I noticed the terrified expression on Agatha's face.

"It was him."

Suddenly, I was frightened out of my mind. "Who? What happened? *What did you do?*"

Boot yelled, "Shut up!" and ran.

Agatha followed, disappearing into the crowd, and I shoved the bathroom door open. Thick cigarette smoke rolled out, burning my eyes. The bathroom looked empty through the haze.

"Kathryn?" I whispered.

No answer. No sound, not even breathing. Suddenly, my heart pounded. My breath came in rasping gulps. Strands of luxurious, blond hair protruded from under the closed stall door, stuck to the grimy tiled floor and soaked in blood.

"Kathryn!" I slowly lowered myself to my knees to look under the door. My whole body shook. Kathryn lay unmoving on her side, facing away from me, her head in a puddle of blood. I knew I had to get to her, but couldn't force myself to crawl into the stall. Pushing aside my fear, I put my hand under the door, but stopped short, afraid to touch her, afraid of what I might feel. I had never touched a dead body before.

"Kathryn," I sobbed. I reached for her throat to check for a pulse that I knew wasn't there. As my quivering fingers touched her skin, Kathryn moaned.

"Kathryn!" I jumped up and tried to pull the stall door open. It was locked from the inside. Without thinking, my hair fluffed and I released a Mental Blast. The door crumpled, burst off its hinges, and landed upright on the toilet against the stall wall.

Instantly, I was inside. I rolled Kathryn on her back. Her forehead was gashed open. A tiny rivulet of blood ran from the crook of her elbow, and a hypodermic needle lay on the stall floor.

Suddenly the bathroom door was flung open. Egon and Bobby rushed in.

"What's wrong?" Bobby yelled. "Egon heard you scream— *Kitty!*"

"I don't know what happened. The needle…"

"Kitty?" Bobby's mouth hung open. "Egon, gimme your cell!"

"I'm on it," Egon said with less than his normal coolness. I listened as Egon called for an ambulance. I shivered when I heard him say, "Overdosed and hit her head." That wasn't right. Kathryn didn't use drugs. But the needle…

It felt like hours before the paramedics arrived. I watched helplessly as they bandaged Kathryn's head, strapped her to a gurney, and loaded her into the ambulance. Bobby grabbed the door as they were about to close it. The paramedic put his hand on Bobby's chest.

"Sorry, we can't—"

"She's my girlfriend." Bobby swiped the man's hand from his chest. "I took her to this dance. I'll bring her home."

"I wish I could let you."

"I didn't ask permission." Bobby forced his way into the ambulance. He squatted next to Kathryn and held her hand.

"I want to go, too," I said, but I could see there was no room. The paramedic looked at me apologetically as he closed the ambulance door.

• • •

Back in the gym, I stood in a daze. Whatsisface and Tish leaned against the wall close by me, holding hands, Tish looking lost, Whatsisface looking protective. Egon had gone outside to bring his car around to take me home. The teachers had shut the dance down early. They were out in the hall, probably planning for the massive police investigation that would be coming. The students who drove had been allowed to leave. The couple dozen who didn't had called home, and waited in the gym for their rides. All around me, I heard them whispering, shocked at what had happened.

"Did you hear about Hollisburg?"

"I can't believe it."

"I never expected this from Kathryn."

"She seemed so decent."

Whatsisface said, loud enough for everyone to hear, "It's a lie. Kathryn would never do this. She is the most decent person I know."

Art Rubric staggered out of nowhere, pushing his way through the crowd. "Decent, shmee-sent," he slurred. "I told you she's a user! Not the goodie-two-shoes she pretends to be, is she? I should know. I sold it to her."

Helpless tears burned my eyes. The filthy liar.

"Shut up!" I screamed. "Just shut up!"

Art tottered toward me, stopping just inches away. His body weaved, his crossed eyes worked to focus as he grinned down at me. Rancid breath rolled out of his foul mouth across my face as he spoke. "Truth hurts, huh, Peroxide? She never even offered you any, did she? Kept it all to herself. Some friend."

"Let me show you what hurts." My purse slid from my shoulder. My hand curled into a fist. My arm drew back. As Rubric's bloodshot eyes grew wide, I fired off the most devastating haymaker I had ever unleashed, right at his ugly, slimy nose. Just before impact, something incredibly strong stopped my fist dead. A huge hand had caught me by the crook of the elbow.

Mason's hand.

The gym went silent.

Mason's face was drawn like a lost little boy. He tried to smile at me, but couldn't. He released my arm and turned to the crowd.

"What's wrong with you people?" Mason asked quietly, placing himself between Rubric and me. "Why do you believe Art's lies so easily? Can't you think for yourself? Aren't you upset that this would happen to someone like Kathryn?" He paused to look around the room, and let out a loud sigh. He held his hands wide as though he were praying, and stared up at the ceiling for an instant. Then he dropped them to his sides and shook his head. "Doesn't anyone stand up for friends anymore?"

The group moved to the other side of the gym without a word. A few of them looked back, anger in their eyes. I heard Whatsisface say, "He's right. It's time."

Mason turned to Art. "You disappoint me. But you always have. Next time, I won't stop her from punching your face in. I might even do it for her. Go home."

Art's eyes bugged wide, his mouth opened just a bit, and his lower lip quivered. Without a word, he spun clumsily and staggered across the gym.

Mason turned to me. The pain on his face was heartbreaking. He reached for my cheek, jerked his hand back like he had made a mistake, then wiped my tears away. He leaned down until our foreheads were nearly touching, and whispered, "Rinnie, I'm sorry about Kathryn. I'll find out who did this."

How could I tell him I already knew who did it? How could I tell anybody? Mason's breath was warm and soft. The touch of his fingers on my cheek comforted me, and for the smallest instant, I felt like everything would be all right.

"I have to call Bobby," Mason whispered. Then he left. Just like that. As quickly as he had come, he was gone.

I leaned against a stack of folded wrestling mats. I needed

to sit down, but the floor was too low, and the mats were too high. I heard footsteps. A hand gripped my shoulder.

"Hey, mystery girl." Egon turned me to face him. "Your chariot awaits. Ready to go?"

"Hey," I said.

"You dropped this." He held out my purse. "I'm a little worried. Are you and Kathryn involved in something? Something dangerous? If you need to talk about it, I'm a pretty good listener."

"Oh, Egon." Yeah, I was involved. Deeper than I had ever imagined. This was what it meant to be a Psi Fighter. It wasn't just people I hardly knew getting hurt anymore. It was people I loved. But I couldn't talk about it, not to Egon. Not to anybody, now. Kathryn was the only one outside the Academy I could ever talk to. "She's my best friend."

"Kathryn is in good hands." Egon put his arms around me. "Bobby will take care of her. Let's get you home."

I buried my face in Egon's shoulder and sobbed uncontrollably.

• • •

It had been hours since Egon dropped me off, and I still hadn't heard from Kathryn's parents. I felt like lying in bed and crying myself to sleep. But I couldn't. I had to do something. Then I remembered Tammy's Amplifier. Maybe it had answers to this whole mess.

I got up and dug through my purse, but I only found one Amplifier. Mine, in the hidden pocket. I searched my gown—nothing. I grabbed my purse again, ripped it open, and dumped it on my comforter.

"Where is it?" I screamed, sitting angrily on my bed. Just then, I heard my phone ring. I had left it in the kitchen when I came up to my room. I looked at the clock. One-thirty in the morning. I heard footsteps coming toward my room and my heart froze.

"Baby?" Dad stuck his head into my room, holding out my cell. "It's Bobby." He sat down beside me and put his arm around me.

"Bobby, how is she?" I asked, terrified of what I might hear.

"Kitty overdosed. Psychedone 10." Bobby's voice was thick. "She fractured her skull when she fell. They aren't sure she's going to make it."

My chest seized, and a single loud sob escaped my mouth. "Bobby, no!"

I leaned against my dad and felt him trembling, but quickly realized it was me. My whole body fluttered with helplessness. With rage. Images of Kathryn's bloody head hung in my mind. I felt like an invisible blanket had separated me from everything that's fair in the world. My dad pulled me close. "You okay, baby?"

"No, Daddy." I looked up into my dad's eyes, then buried myself in his arms and totally fell apart.

Chapter Twenty-three

Justice League Move Over

I strode down the hall, alone without Kathryn, and feeling very dangerous. I hadn't made it to the Academy all weekend, and I needed exercise. Something strenuous, like slamming an evil bozoid into the wall hard enough to leave a moosh mark.

Tammy Angel.

Chew said it was *him*. Meaning Scallion. Of course she wouldn't know a Knight's true identity. She would assume Scallion was a guy. But I knew otherwise. I would find Angel and force her to reveal her identity to the whole school. And maybe learn something about Nicolaitan, so I could pluck off his arms and legs like a bug.

Yeah, I was feeling pretty nasty. PMS would have been a major improvement to the mood I was in.

"Hey, Peroxide."

The disgustingly familiar voice broke my concentration. I

228

really hated that voice. What an unexpected stroke of luck. I turned and glared.

Tammy Angel and the Red Team surrounded me. How thoughtful. An early practice session. Suddenly my day was just a little cheerier.

"Ooh," Tammy said, "Peroxide's an unhappy girl. I understand your best friend overdosed and busted her head on, of all things, a *toilet*? You know how shocked we all are. And just so you know, we think that Kathryn being a user is, well, uncool."

A powerful mental surge whipped uncontrollably through my body. A fireball of psychic force rocketed down my arm, but I quenched it. As much as I knew I'd enjoy it, sending the Red Team into oblivion with a Mental Blast would be considered bad form by the Kilodan.

Tammy was as cool and beautiful as ever. So was Boot. But Agatha was visibly on edge. Maybe I could push her over it. "You should be proud, if what Rubric said is true," I lied. "He told everybody you sold it to her."

"Oh, Art Rubric!" Tammy started to laugh. "Give me a break. Everyone knows he's the dealer. He doesn't have the brains to blame somebody else."

"He doesn't need brains. We all saw you fall on your butt last night. Bloodshot eyes. Talking like your mouth was full of marshmallows."

Tammy looked confused. "What are you talking about? I never fell."

"Too high to remember? What happened to 'Users are Losers'? I suppose you don't remember stumbling out of the bathroom while Kathryn was in there unconscious." Agatha's face became a mask of fear. That was all I needed.

"Stop the lies, Peroxide." Tammy faked a yawn. "You're

boring me."

"I'm not boring Agatha, though, am I? Tell me what you saw last night, Chew. What happened to Kathryn?"

"I can't. He'll kill me!"

"That's a merry-go-round ride compared to what I'm planning."

"Shut up," Tammy snapped.

"Did I strike a nerve?" Time to see what was on their minds. I couldn't scan Tammy. She would sense the psychic energy and know I was a Psi Fighter. But someone without Mental Arts skills wouldn't notice anything but a totally lame assault. "Let me strike another one."

I grabbed Agatha by the arm and was jolted as though I had clamped onto a hot wire. Scanning minds was like touching a high voltage electric fence. As I pulled on Agatha's memories, frightful visions of a skull-faced figure flashed across my mind. I released her arm. She was stupid enough to be fooled by Angel's disguise, but I wasn't.

Boot squealed mockingly, "Oh, please, no! Don't squeeze my arm, too, you big bully."

"Was that supposed to scare me?" Agatha snapped, obviously as a show for Tammy and Boot. "Because it didn't."

"Go to class, Peroxide," Tammy said quietly. She got nose to nose with me. "Or do you need another lesson in the social graces?"

Partly because she was a Knight, but mostly because I felt like it, I decided to try a different tactic with Ms. Angel. "No, Tammy, what I really need is some answers. I'm feeling a little impatient today. I think I'll beat them out of you."

Tammy smiled smugly, but backed up a step. "You and what mob of lowlife geeks?"

"That would be us," a voice said from down the hall.

Bobby approached quickly with Erica, Tish, Whatsisface, and a group of people I recognized as the usual victims of the goons. They forced themselves between the Red Team and me.

"Well, well, well, if it isn't the Dweeb League." Tammy raised her nose in the air.

"You touch her," Bobby warned, "you touch all of us."

"As unappealing as that sounds, I think I'll pass. Come on, Red Team. Let's leave the superzeroes to their fantasies."

I continued to glare at Tammy. *Go ahead*, I thought. *Bump into me.*

Tammy, Boot, and Agatha made their way past everyone without a foul word or nasty deed. When they disappeared around the corner, Bobby and his squadron began to cheer.

"One for Kitty," Bobby said.

"The Dweeb League," Whatsisface remarked quietly. "I like it."

"It's us," Tish said. "Definitely."

Whatsisface puffed out his meager chest, placed one fist on his hip, and pointed to the sky. "The Dweeb League!" His voice fell miles short of manly. "Mild-mannered reporters by day, purveyors of justice by night. Violently handsome crime fighters, we possess abilities far beyond those of mere mortals. When the sun sets, we unite to protect the noble metropolis of Greensburg High School."

I wasn't sure whether to laugh or gag, so I just said, "Thanks, guys."

Whatsisface exhaled loudly and resumed his abnormal shape. "At your service, ma'am," he said, and gave me a quick two-fingered salute.

"Rinnie." Bobby's voice was somber. "We came to ask you

a favor. We got together and decided we want to fight back. We want you to train us. They might be bigger and stronger—"

"And faster and meaner and more likely to win," I interrupted. "They'll fight dirty, and most of them carry weapons. Not a good argument for fighting back."

"But you, Miss Kung Fu Master, can teach us to use that against them. We want vengeance."

I studied the kids standing behind Bobby. Tish continued to dress like a zombie, but she'd stopped slouching. She even smiled. Whatsisface apparently felt like Captain America, but his hairdo made him look like Major Mushroom. Erica Jasmine's entire demeanor had changed—she looked whole again. The entire group glowed with something I had never seen in them before. I only hoped it wasn't contagious.

"I don't do vengeance," I said. "Bobby, you just stopped them without my help. All you have to do is stick together. Nobody will ever bother you again."

I turned and walked down the hall.

"Wait up." Bobby hurried after me. "We gotta talk."

"Not now, Bobby. I'm going after Angel. Don't try to stop me."

"Stop you? I want to hold her while you pound her."

Robbed of my chance to bludgeon a poor excuse for a Walpurgis Knight, I suddenly felt irrational. "You're right. We *do* need to talk. And you won't like the subject." I grabbed Bobby by the backpack and dragged him backward into the library, straight to the little study room Kathryn and I always used. I closed the door, pushed Bobby into a chair, and began laying my schoolbooks out on the table.

"What are you doing? I didn't follow you in here to do homework."

"We have to look like we're studying." I glared at the poor boy. "And you didn't follow me. I dragged you."

"What's the matter with you?" Bobby held up his hands. "I didn't do anything."

"You wanna know what's the matter? Let me tell you what's the matter. Kathryn told you things about me she shouldn't have. *That's* what's the matter."

"And that's my fault...*how*?"

"You're here to yell at and she's not. Being yelled at for things you have no control over is in the boyfriend job description."

"Oh. I didn't know there was fine print."

"Duh."

"Umm, what did she tell me?"

"Memory Lash," I whispered. "Ring a bell? What else did she tell you?"

"Oh, yeah, well, that. And that you're a Psi Fighter and—"

I pressed my history book against my forehead. "Wonderful. Do you have any idea what that means?"

"Yeah, you're part of a secret society that fights bad guys. You're the people they call when there's real trouble. Kind of like Spider-Man without the cape. Secret identity and all that—"

I slammed the book on the table. "And because she told you, my secret identity is *not* secret, which means that my family is in danger, and we'll all be murdered in our sleep. Happy? And Spider-Man does *not* wear a cape! Who else knows?"

"The whole school will if you don't yell at me a little quieter," Bobby said. "Jeez, I thought superheroes were discreet."

My throat tightened. I wondered how upset Kathryn would be if I murdered her boyfriend. "Who. Knows?"

"Nobody. What do you think, your best friend is a moron?

She never said a word. I brought it up. Don't forget, Rinnie, I was there. I saw what you did."

"You knew about the Memory Lash before that day in the park. I suppose you found that on the Internet?"

Bobby blushed. "Well, to tell the truth, Kitty talks in her sleep."

"WHAT?"

"No, nothing like that. She always falls asleep during Math Club. I was going to wake her to leave, and she mumbled something about a Memory Lash changing hearts. I thought she was dreaming until I saw what you did to Mason. After you saved me in the park, I asked her about it, and she totally flipped out on me. Believe me, you do not want to be on the wrong side of Kitty. She swore she'd cut off body parts that I'd really prefer to keep if I ever spoke a word to anyone. She is *extremely* protective of you, and made it painfully clear that I will be, too, if I want to remain alive and unharmed. We did everything we could to cover up what happened that afternoon. You're just lucky Rubric was so whacked out on drugs he doesn't remember anything. He doesn't even know he was there. You knocked Chuckie out, so he didn't see anything. It's Mason I'm worried about."

So Kathryn didn't give away my secret after all. She was totally trustworthy. I sighed silently. "I'm not worried about Mason anymore. I want Angel."

"Rinnie, I have an idea."

"Put all my secrets on Facebook? You mean you haven't already?"

"I brought you an army. Train them."

"Your army can't help me. It's too dangerous. This is something I have to do alone. In case Kathryn left out any other details about my personal life, I fight very ruthless people. My birth parents were murdered. I'm going after their killer as soon as I stop this kidnapper."

"They…" Bobby's mouth hung open. "You're adopted? That part must've slipped her mind."

"They kidnapped me and used me as bait. If it weren't for me, my parents would still be alive. I want Angel. She's one of them."

Bobby looked down at the floor, then back at me. "Are you telling me that Tammy Angel is the Walpurgis Knight called Scallion? So…she is the kidnapper. She attacked Kitty. Makes perfect sense." Bobby touched my shoulder. "The Knights do all these nasty things to lure you out, right? They beat people up, they run drugs, just to get you to try to stop them. Just to find out who you are."

I mentally smashed my head repeatedly against the tabletop.

"Is there anything Kathryn *didn't* tell you?" I mumbled. On the plus side, she had obviously instilled a healthy fear of giving away my secret. I had no doubt Bobby would keep his mouth shut. "Look, I'm positive Tammy is Scallion, but I lost her Amplifier, so I can't prove it. I have to get her to come out of hiding."

"Let's give them a taste of their own medicine." Bobby leaned toward me and slammed his fist into his palm. "Let's kick Angel's butt right here. We'll stop the Psychedone 10 production. We'll put her and her goons in jail. If that doesn't make her show herself, I don't know what will. Leave it to the Dweeb League. We'll give the school its dignity back."

I smiled, struggling only a little with the idea of restoring dignity to someone with a Three Stooges hairdo. "That might actually work."

Chapter Twenty-four

Psychedone 10

I went to the hospital the next day after school. I've never seen a corpse up close, but if I ever do, I can't imagine how it could look more frightening than Kathryn.

Her room in the Greensburg Hospital ICU smelled very septic, like they had embalmed her, but waited a little too long. It seemed like her body was already decomposing. Her eyes were sunken into deep pits. The dark purple surrounding them was the only color on her face, except for her dry, cracked lips. They were the same bluish hue as her fingernails. Her shallow, forced breathing terrified me.

Suddenly, Kathryn inhaled sharply and sat up. Her pupils were so tiny, it was like they weren't even there. Sweat poured down her forehead. She shivered uncontrollably.

"Fight it, fight it, fight it," she whispered, drawing her knees up to her chest and squeezing her arms around them.

"Kathryn." I touched her sweat-soaked hair.

She turned slowly, her gaze unfocused. A weak smile cracked her face. "This sucks." Then her eyes squeezed shut in a horrible grimace, and her whole body tensed.

I threw my arms around her, ignoring the cold stickiness of her skin. Kathryn moaned quietly and leaned into me. I could tell she was in terrible pain. Suddenly she gasped and pulled away, straightening her legs. They quivered, and she began to massage them. "Oh, it hurts, it hurts." She gagged and reached for the bedpan. She tried to vomit, heaving and retching, but nothing came out. "So cold."

I covered her with a blanket, and she curled up in a ball, moaning and shaking.

"Do you want me to come back later?" I asked. My voice cracked, but I bit back the sobs as best I could. Kathryn didn't need to know how this was killing me.

She reached out, took my hand, and tried unconvincingly to sound like nothing was wrong. "So, how have you been? How's Egon? Did you have a good time at the dance?"

"Worried. We're all worried."

Kathryn seemed to relax. She pulled herself to a sitting position, never letting go of my hand. "Rin, Munificent was so wrong when he said the drugs were poison. I'd take poison over Psychedone 10 in a heartbeat. Poison only kills you. But this stuff…I fractured my skull, Rin…that's a pinprick compared to this. I can't even describe how terrible—it's like my whole body is tearing itself apart. Like the worst flu I ever had, the aches and fever and nausea, and the nastiest cramps, but spread it everywhere, even my toes. Multiply that by a thousand and it still wouldn't be as awful as this. But the pain isn't the worst part. You know what I want more than anything?"

I patted her hand. "What? I'll get it for you."

Kathryn's face became bright for an instant. "Out. I have to get out of this hospital."

"You're sick. You can't leave."

"That's just it. All I can think about is escaping so I can get more. It's *all* I think about. It's awful. See that window? It's calling to me. It's saying, 'Open me and you're free.' Rin, I know I'm on the seventeenth floor, but if I did what this stuff is trying to make me do, I'd go right through that window. I want that high again, that awful, wonderful high."

I just stared at her, shaking my head, speechless.

"It spread like cancer. It's trying to take over my mind. It's making me stupid. It wants me to do things I would never do. I have to fight it. I have to beat it so I can come to my senses. It's hard, Rinnie." She broke down in tears and curled up in a ball. After a few minutes, her breathing steadied, and she fell asleep.

Seeing Kathryn confirmed my worst fears. She was suffering through the most horrible withdrawal imaginable. If she didn't have such incredible self-control, she would have broken out of the hospital by now to find more of that murderous drug. What I didn't understand was how she could become physically addicted after one use. According to *The Book of Lore*, Kathryn shouldn't have been dependent at all yet. It was extended use that led to addiction and a changed personality.

Kathryn must have been a guinea pig, a test case for a new version of Psychedone 10, because nobody else had been affected the way she had. Rubric was a long-time user, and no doubt addicted. But Erica Jasmine quit after a few weeks of use. And Mason. Even he had used it once. But poor Kathryn was physically addicted immediately after the attack. According to Bobby's research, the base chemical—the chemical they made in the Class Project—would have had to be altered for that to happen. I suddenly wondered whether Miliron's goof-nut act was a deception.

"She's strong," a familiar voice said. I felt a gentle hand on my shoulder, and turned to see Mason gazing at Kathryn as though he were viewing a body in a coffin, his face twisted with grief, his eyes wet and red. He reached out and caressed Kathryn's hand.

"I didn't know," he whispered. "I would have stopped it."

"What do you mean?"

"I should have listened to Bobby," Mason said. "I thought I was doing the right thing. I even changed the formula. They lied to me, Rinnie. This is my fault."

There it was. "Lied about what?"

"The Class Project. The formula. Everything. They turn it into Psychedone 10, just like Bobby said."

"Who lied, Mason?" My fist clenched, but I forced myself to stay calm.

Mason shook his head. "I saw Mrs. Bagley today. She told me to give you a message if I saw you here."

I looked into his eyes. Sadness stared back at me.

"She said, 'Events of the sort in which you are involved can be misleading, but you know right from wrong. Trust your heart.'" Mason chuckled softly.

"Was that all she said?"

Mason nodded. "I used to trust my heart, but I don't know what's right anymore. I have to go. There's something I need to do."

Mason touched my hair delicately. He looked at Kathryn

out of the corner of his eye.

"Where do you have to go?" I asked.

"Back to the beginning." His eyes snapped to mine. His lip quivered for just an instant. "Rinnie, what if she dies? How can you ever look at me again if I killed your best friend?"

Mason held my gaze, struggling for words. "If I could go back in time, things would be so different right now."

Mason looked up at the ceiling and mouthed the words, *Please, God.* Then he turned and walked away. Just like at the dance. I reached for him, but pulled my hand back.

As I watched him disappear through the door, I struggled to stay quiet. I could see he was in the deep stages of remorse caused by the Memory Lash. The pain of his past would never go away. I wanted to tell him, but those details seemed irrelevant. Mason's heart had changed. I was certain of it, and I felt sorry for him.

But I also wanted the information he had. Someone tricked him into changing the formula, and I had the distinct impression he wasn't talking about Scallion. I needed to know if *back to the beginning* meant Dr. Miliron.

Mrs. Bagley's message popped into my head. *Events of the sort in which I was involved.* I almost laughed at how formally she put things. I assumed she was trying to say that I was a teenager in a very dysfunctional high school, and that this sort of thing was just a normal part of growing up under those conditions.

So why did I have the feeling she meant something else, something much closer to the truth?

Soft footsteps caught my attention. Egon walked through the door and shouldered up to me.

"Hi," he said, smiling. "How's my mystery girl?"

I smiled back, leaning against him. "I've been better."

Egon took my hand. "And how is your best friend holding up?"

"She's been way better."

"Rinnie, you know the rumors around school. You don't believe them, do you?"

I pulled my hand away and glared. "Angel had better watch her back. I'm done with her."

Egon slowly turned his gaze toward Kathryn, the smile still on his lips. "I wouldn't want to be on *your* bad side."

I elbowed his ribs gently. "I can't believe you went out with her, even once."

A dark, almost frightening laugh erupted from Egon's throat. "Neither can I. Speaking of going out, do you want to do something tonight? You know, maybe just hang out?"

I shot him a look that said, *Are you serious?* "I'm not really up for anything, Egon. I want to be with Kathryn. I'm sorry."

Egon turned to Kathryn and touched her hand. "I meant here. I could keep you two company. You never know when you might need a bodyguard."

I touched Egon's shoulder. "I'd like that."

Chapter Twenty-five

Enough is Enough

"Time to cross over the border from Loserville," Tammy Angel said.

The locker room was empty except for the Red Team, a ninth grader named Jessie, and my contingent of spies. Tammy held a small plastic bag. Jessie took it, her hand shaking. I pictured Kathryn's face, and it took all my strength to keep from force-feeding the bag to Angel.

"You getting this?" Erica whispered.

"Uh huh." I watched Tammy and her latest victim from behind the bank of lockers through Andy's tiny high-tech video camera. It had a cool zoom microphone that was so sensitive it could record a person's breath from across the room. "Make your move."

Erica shuffled toward the Red Team and stopped beside Angel. "Hi, Tam."

I zoomed on Tammy Angel's face.

"Hey, hey, Erica! How's Christie? Change your mind about quitting, did you? Gimme a sec, I have to take care of Jessie here." Tammy turned toward the ninth grader. "Do one of those before gym class. These are the best supplements available. You'll jump off the Loser Express and onto the Star Ship Angel, where the Cool Rule. You'll be one of us. If you like it, bring a couple of your buds. I'll fix them up, too. Remember, this one's free. Next time there's a nominal fee."

Jessie nodded quickly and then walked away. I zoomed in on Tammy's backpack. Tammy pulled out a plastic bag and dangled it in front of Erica's face, holding it between two fingers. "I knew you'd be back, Erica. This stuff always brings 'em back. And you can be among the first to sample our new, improved blend. Cash first, of course. House rules."

"I didn't come for your drugs," Erica said.

"Supplements, Erica. Hugs, not drugs, as they say. I hope your little sister is being good."

Erica's expression turned to fear. "I gotta go." She quickly left the locker room.

Tammy laughed. "Price just went up."

Boot Milner sneered. "Maybe we'll put some pressure on her."

Tammy shook her head. "No, we'll just take her out. It's time to set an example."

Boot's eyes grew wide. "Take her out? Seriously?"

"That's what he says is next for the nonbelievers," Tammy said. "He's the boss."

Agatha Chew said nothing, but from the look on her face, I was pretty sure she didn't like what she had just heard. The police would, though.

I turned off the camera and crept into the hall. When I reached the boiler room door, I opened it and slipped inside. Jessie and Erica waited beside Bobby.

"Nice work, Jess," I said.

The ninth grader nodded. "Will this really stop them?"

Bobby held up the bag of Psychedone 10 Angel had given Jessie and scowled. "We're just getting started." For such a nice boy, I noticed that he had a real mean streak.

I was okay with that.

• • •

The next morning, I marched down the hall surrounded by Bobby, Tish, and Whatsisface.

"The Dweeb League on patrol," Whatsisface said quietly.

"We stick together no matter what, got it?" Bobby punched his fist into his palm.

"Okay, but this one is mine." Whatsisface had fire in his eyes. I prayed he wasn't about to have it doused. We walked toward an oblivious Chuckie Cuff, who had a tenth-grader pinned against a locker.

"What'd your mom pack for me today, Dougie?" Chuckie held the boy's lunch bag above his head.

"C-c-come on, Chuckie, n-n-not aga-in," Dougie said. He reached up, trying to get at his lunch bag, but Chuckie pulled it away.

"When you learn to t-t-t-talk right," Chuckie said, "you can eat. This is for my own g-g-g-g-good."

"My m-m-mom said you should get your own lunch. I'm not allowed to f-f-f-fuh-heed you anym-more."

"Your mom's not very nice."

"Let him alone, Chuckie," Whatsisface said. Tish and Bobby stood at his shoulder. I stood right behind them, hoping that once Chuckie noticed me, my services wouldn't be needed.

Chuckie looked a little irritated at the interruption. "You come to dance again, babe?" He held his hand out to Tish.

"I did." Whatsisface knocked Chuckie's hand away. "On your face. Give him back his lunch."

"You ladies gonna make me?"

"You think we can't?" Whatsisface grinned. "Wouldn't look good to have your butt kicked by a lady, huh?"

Chuckie stared at Whatsisface, then Bobby, then Tish.

Then he noticed me. "You promised not to tell," he muttered.

"I didn't say a word." I shrugged.

Chuckie looked thoughtfully at Dougie. "Okay, no problemo, I wasn't hungry today anyway." He tossed Dougie his lunch, and poked him in the chest. "But tomorrow, bring me something good, got it?"

I tapped Chuckie on the shoulder and whispered, "You stop picking on him and everyone else, or I *will* tell. Got it?"

Chuckie's face puckered. "Hey, Rinnie, I was teasin'. Dougie and me, we're buds."

"No more, Chuckie. Okay?"

"Hmmm…okay." Chuckie turned and walked away. Then he stopped. "Hey, Rinnie."

"Yeah?"

"I started brushing my teeth. I'm minty fresh!" He blew into the air in my direction.

"I'm so proud of you." I smiled as Chuckie disappeared down the hall.

"Thanks," Dougie said.

"Our pleasure." Whatsisface put his hand on Dougie's shoulder. "How 'bout we do lunch and chat about membership in our exclusive club? I'll have my people call your people."

Chapter Twenty-six

The School's New Groove

I was amazed at the faces sitting around the lunch table as the week progressed. Bobby smiled quietly. Tish, Erica, Jessie, and Dougie, however, were doing happy dances. The plan had worked better than expected. Even students I didn't know had begun rebelling against the bullies. The Dweeb League was growing.

"Did you see their faces?" Tish asked.

"Angel's face was blurred out on Greensburg Action News that night, but you couldn't mistake her squawky voice," Bobby said. "The video we made was awesome. We nailed her."

Erica clapped her hand on the tabletop. "Angel's dad wouldn't even come out of the house when the reporter wanted to interview him. How cool is that?"

Whatsisface jumped to his feet. Holding a pencil to his mouth like a microphone, he pretended to knock on a door.

"Toby James, reporting on what appears to be a drug bust at the high school. Mr. Angel, how do you respond to these allegations? Mr. Angel? Mr. Angel? Hello? Is anybody home?"

Tish laughed and shook her head. "No, I mean today. I saw them this morning in the hall. Talk about your new attitude! Everybody is talking about it. Something is finally being done. The whole school is different today."

The school was different, but some things never changed. Tammy's father had pulled strings, as expected. He said that the evidence was circumstantial, that Tammy was set up, and that he would personally sue the school district for allowing his innocent daughter to be exposed to dangerous drug dealers. Mrs. Bagley was livid that the school board wouldn't let her expel Angel. But like Tish said, Angel had a new attitude. Which I saw right through. She was a Knight, and the personality change was part of the deception. She was still going down.

"Yeah, even Mason is acting weird," Bobby said. "He hasn't hit anybody or stuffed them in a locker…nothing. He even apologized to me. But I'm not falling for it."

I hadn't discussed Mason with Bobby. I hadn't told him that the Memory Lash did what it was supposed to do. Bobby was a smart kid. He'd figure it out on his own. Mason was changed, and the change felt deep.

"Hey, what's up with you and Egon?" Bobby said.

"What do you mean?" My heart sped up.

"He says he asked you out, but you're too busy."

"Busy? That's not what I told him." He hadn't asked me out since the day we hung out at the hospital. Of course, I hadn't really been still long enough for him to ask. As soon as my mission was complete, I had to make time.

The bell rang and everyone headed for class. I followed the Dweeb League out of the cafeteria and right into a traffic jam of ninth and tenth graders. Rubric was twisting a girl's arm and had her in tears.

"Please, stop, it hurts!" the girl pleaded.

"I said five dollars," Rubric bellowed. "Are you people deaf?"

"Air a little thin up there in the bozone layer?" It took all my self-control to not rip Rubric's arm out of the socket. But I didn't want detention, so I speared my fingertips into his elbow joint instead.

Rubric's eyes grew wide. He let out a little yelp and released the girl, then started jumping around holding his arm. His hand opened and closed involuntarily. "What'ja do ta me?"

"Not what I wanted." I helped the girl to her feet and wiped her tears away. "Are you okay?"

"No!" The girl glared at me, rubbing her arm, then turned and kicked Rubric hard in the shin. "Now I am."

"Hey!" Rubric shouted, switching his grip to his shin. "What is with you people? This is my hall. You want to pass, you gotta pay."

"I'm surprised your brain has enough voltage to make your lungs work," I said.

Rubric stopped jumping and glared, holding out his open palm. "Pay the toll to the troll."

"Too stupid to realize he just insulted himself," Bobby said under his breath. "This is scary."

"Be careful," Whatsisface whispered. "He's as strong as he is stupid."

"I'm the strongest in this school," Rubric said, smiling. "Except for Chuckie."

I burst out laughing. "Let's go, it might be contagious."

Rubric held out his hand. "Five bucks. Each."

"No," Bobby said.

Rubric reached out to smack Bobby on top of the head. Bobby slapped his arm away. "Don't touch me."

"Are you and your girlfriends gonna stop me?"

Dougie stepped forward. "N-n-now that you mention it, we are, D-d-d-umbelina."

"Die, Dweeb." Rubric pushed past Bobby and dove at Dougie. Whatsisface stuck out his foot and Rubric landed flat on his face. The ninth grader whose arm he had twisted jumped on his back and began beating his head with her book bag. Then the other kids joined in. Before Rubric could get up, he was buried beneath a stomping, punching, laughing mob.

"Get off me," his muffled voice screamed.

I almost felt sorry for Rubric as he lay under the pummeling heap of kids, all former victims of the school's bullies, finally able to release years of pent-up frustration. Almost.

Heads popped out of doors all the way down the hall. One of them belonged to Mrs. Bagley. She stepped out and came toward us, walking like a gunslinger at high noon. In place of a six-shooter, she carried a yardstick.

"Students!" she barked. The bell rang and the hall became silent.

The pile of bodies got to its feet. All except Rubric, who lay there unmoving.

"Mr. Rubric," Mrs. Bagley snapped. "Arthur! Please get up off that filthy floor."

Rubric stirred and looked up. "Get lost, Old Bag, before you get hurt like the rest—"

"Mr. Rubric!" She broke her yardstick over his head. "I

asked you to get up. Don't make me ask again."

Rubric mumbled a filthy word that only people with deflated brains use. He dragged himself to his feet, raised his fist and took a step toward Mrs. Bagley. Before I could stop him, the mob of kids swarmed, forcing themselves between him and Mrs. Bagley.

"You touch her, you touch us."

Rubric lowered his fist. His face became bright red. "I'm outta here."

"Just a minute." Mrs. Bagley pulled a pad from her pocket. She scribbled something and handed the paper to Rubric.

He slowly reached out. "What's that?"

"That is your detention slip, Mr. Rubric. Fighting is forbidden. I would like to expel you, but then I couldn't keep an eye on you. Instead, you will serve two hours after school for the rest of the school year. If you refuse, I will turn you in to the police, and your parents will be fined. I know they don't care about money, but they certainly won't like the publicity when the story is in all the newspapers. Now go to the office."

Rubric turned and walked away. "Don't think I won't get even."

"Yeah," Tish said. "Even more of what you just got."

The hall remained silent. We all looked at Mrs. Bagley.

"Students." Mrs. Bagley shook her pad of slips at us. "The bell rang, and you are late. You are aware, I am sure, of the rules against tardiness."

Wonderful. I didn't have time for detention.

Mrs. Bagley wrote quickly and tore off a slip, handing it to me, the slightest hint of a smile cracking across her face. "You'll all need late passes to get into class."

• • •

I took a little detour before meeting Bobby in study hall. With everything that had happened since the Spring Fling, I needed to regroup. Normally, I would have talked with Kathryn. Thanks to Tammy Angel, I didn't have that option. So Plan B. I snuck into the girl's bathroom, opened a stall, and plopped down on the closed lid.

See, here's the thing. The kids at school were pulling together, which was good, and Angel had been arrested, which was also good. But her father had connections. Which stunk. Tammy was acting all proper, but that's just what it was, an act. I knew she was a Knight, but without her Amplifier, I couldn't prove it. I had to get into her head without letting her know that I was the Morgan girl she was hunting. A life without secrets would have been so much easier.

Then there was Egon. He'd been such a sweetheart through this whole thing, but apparently felt like I was neglecting him. I really needed to spend time with Egon if our relationship was to go anywhere. Maybe it was time to rethink my priorities.

Speaking of time, I peeked at my watch and panicked. My late pass couldn't buy me enough to sort this out, so I rushed out of the bathroom and into an empty hall. Or so I thought.

"Hey."

Mason's voice sent such a fright through me that I let out a tiny shriek. He sat on the floor, cross-armed against the wall, like he had been waiting for me. I shot a quick glance over my shoulder to see if we were alone. Terrifyingly, we were.

"Got a sec?"

No. I didn't. Not even part of one. Between planning the

downfall of the forces of evil and wallowing in self-pity, I was booked. But I was actually glad to see him. Maybe I could learn something about Miliron. "Always."

Mason smiled. "I just wanted say I'm sorry for…you know, for that day in the park. I didn't know what I was doing. And the hundred years before that. Everything is different now. I want you to know." Then he gazed up at me with sad eyes and patted the floor. Before all this happened, my Bad Guy Meter would have seriously pegged, but the batteries must have been dead. I sat down beside him.

Mason stared blankly and shook his head, like he was totally lost. "I can't stop thinking about the things I've done. About my mother. She had problems. But I loved her." He leaned a little closer, and gazed right into my eyes. His breath warmed my cheek. "I just wanted her to love me back, but all she ever did was tell me what was wrong with me. When I came home from a friend's, she never said hi, or asked me if I had fun. She'd show me the toy I didn't put away, or tell me my socks didn't match. Or ask me why I didn't wear a different shirt. I was never good enough for her. She always compared me to my brother." Mason's eyes filled with tears. "Rinnie, I never had a brother. My mother was sick."

I wanted to tell him I knew, that I saw it.

"Everybody thinks my mom is being treated at the asylum. She's not. What I told you and Kathryn that day in the lab is true. She was murdered. I watched it happen."

"That's awful." I had only vague memories of my parents' murder, and they scared the pants off me. From what the Memory Lash had showed me, Mason's recollection was completely clear. "That had to be a horrible thing to see."

"It was. But it's not what I saw that bothers me. It's what I felt."

"Shock? Grief? Mason, that's normal."

"No." He shook his head and took my hand in both of his. "Liberation. It was like this big iron chain I had been carrying around my neck all my life just fell off. I watched a man beat her to death with a shovel, and all it made me feel was relief. My mother was right. There's something wrong with me."

What I had felt in Mason's memory was sheer terror, not relief. I noticed he didn't mention that the murderer had a rotting skull for a head.

"Dad thought I'd killed her, and I couldn't convince him it was somebody else. So he covered it up. That's when I knew I could get away with anything. My poor father. What I put him through. But that day in the park... I see things differently now. What did you do to me?"

Uh oh. This was why he wanted to talk. "I, uh...maybe you hit your head. You were high, weren't you?"

Mason raised an eyebrow. "I guess we both have secrets." Then his face softened. "I tried to apologize to Bobby, but he won't talk to me."

"You tried to bash his head in with a baseball bat. That probably put a strain on your relationship."

"Maybe." Mason closed his eyes. "But I never meant for you to be hurt. I'm sorry for the way I treated you since, like, forever ago. You never did anything to deserve it. I've been a total idiot. I was hoping that maybe you could give me a sec— Maybe we could start over. Be friends. Or something. I mean, I understand if you can't."

"We've been arch enemies for how long? Do we even know how to be friends?" Before the Memory Lash, I had only heard rumors of the horrible childhood that made him a total bonehead. Now I knew the truth in a way that nobody but Mason could appreciate. And I understood why the Lash had brought up that memory. Not because Mason blamed himself for his mother's death, but because he felt like a monster for being glad she was gone. I understood. It was like we had gained a special connection that day. Like our souls had touched. And now he was being all sweet. Maybe the Memory Lash wasn't such a nasty weapon.

Forgiveness was supposed to be heavenly, so I could only assume that I had suddenly been zapped by divine intervention. After the abuse I had tolerated, after the nights spent crying on my bed because he picked on me so relentlessly, after that nasty nickname that had spread like thorns because of him. After all that, my heart wanted desperately to forgive him. Being friends would be so…strange. But what the heck? "Everybody deserves a second chance. Especially you."

Mason's entire face smiled, like the Grinch when his small heart grew three sizes. "Cool."

"But why me, Mason? Why were you always so mean to me?"

His cheeks turned pink. "I thought you were pretty."

I think mine turned pinker. "You had a funny way of showing it."

"I knew you'd never want to be with somebody like me. I did whatever I could to get your attention. You only noticed me when I knocked your books down." He smiled. "Rinnie, I have a hole in my heart the size of you. It's always been there."

A meteor could not have flattened me more completely. The situation had suddenly spun a one-eighty from the "friend" direction, and was speeding toward "awkward."

He brushed his fingers across the back of my hand. "I know you're with Egon, but I was hoping that, maybe, you know, if that doesn't work…maybe we could hang out? I know a good pizza place."

Suddenly his cell phone buzzed.

I leaned back, feeling a smile pull across my lips. Saved by the mobile communication device ringtone. "Hey, I gotta get to class. This pass is gonna expire soon."

We both jumped to our feet.

Mason's cell buzzed again, and he dug it out of his pocket, blushing even worse than I was. "Okay. See you around?"

"Definitely." I turned toward my next class in a state of perplexification while Mason took his call.

"Hey, no problemo," I heard Mason say. "Delivery tomorrow. It's finished. Yeah. Old Torrents will be pleased."

I spun and glared at him. I couldn't believe what I had just heard.

"One day, I hope I understand how I can be so stupid!" I shoved past him and stomped down the hall, not caring that I was headed in the wrong direction, trying hard to keep from destroying the universe with a stray thought. Not that I could actually do it, but I was mad enough to maybe knock down a loose ceiling tile or something.

"Rinnie, what's wrong?" he called after me.

I ignored him and kept going. What was wrong was that I was a complete bozoid. I always had to see the good in people, even when they obviously had none. I really wanted to believe that the Memory Lash had changed him. But facts were facts. He had gotten high on Psychedone 10 and attacked Bobby. He was connected to the Knights, the nastiest people the world had ever seen. And now he was about to help Old Torrents make more of that garbage that put Kathryn in the hospital. He was so *not* helping the mentally ill. Either he still didn't have a clue about the Class Project, or his change of heart was a total hoax.

Time to sabotage a high school science project and find out the truth about Mason Draudimon.

Chapter Twenty-seven

Excuse Me, I Fluffed

Bobby and I walked out of study hall with a plan.

"We have four minutes between classes. That leaves us three in here." Bobby ducked into the chemistry lab with me on his heels. The shelves at the back were full. That had to be the shipment Mason was setting up.

"It's in the cabinet," Bobby whispered as I followed him across the lab.

He tried the double doors of the supply cabinet, but they were locked. "Crud, now what?"

"Got it covered." I pulled my Amplifier out of my belt.

"What are you gonna do with that?"

"Kathryn told you everything else about me." I focused and a smoky blue blade of pure psychic energy exploded from the end of my Amplifier. "Didn't she mention my favorite weapon?"

"Cool!" Bobby reached out toward the Thought Saber.

"Don't." I put my hand out to stop him.

"Doesn't look like it'll cut me."

"It won't. It'll short-circuit your brain." I spun the Saber in a short arc and slashed between the cabinet doors. They swung open with a click, and I extinguished the Saber. "But it'll cut steel. We're in."

Bobby examined the lock. "Wow. Looks like it was cut by a laser."

"Gotta have a sharp mind in this business." I giggled. I always wanted to use that line. Andy would have been so proud.

"Ha ha." Bobby pulled out the bottle of DMSO and handed it to me.

I uncorked it and poured a drop into the first bottle on the shelf labeled PASS. A stench like an open sewer filled the air. Memories of Kathryn flashed through my mind, and I burst out laughing. "Excuse me, I fluffed."

"Right in Angel's face," Bobby said.

We worked swiftly, contaminating the entire PASS rack before moving on to the REWORK rack. Finally, we contaminated all the remaining flasks of ergot.

"This place smells like the boy's bathroom after Rubric leaves," Bobby said.

"The Knights' Psychedone 10 production is officially in the potty. And we have a whole minute to spare. Let's get to class."

"What a week. We got Angel arrested, shut down Chuckie and Rubric, ruined their drug production…"

"Only one more thing to do," I said.

· · ·

Masked and hoodied, I squinted through the air vent into the empty lab. School had ended an hour earlier. The halls buzzed with the news that the Class Project had been vandalized, and I knew Mason would stay late to investigate. After that phone call, I thought a bit of espionage might be in order. I wanted to watch his meltdown when he saw what we had done. Justice for making me want to be friends with a filthy wombat.

The lab door opened and a dumpy-looking figure in a lab coat came in…Dr. Miliron…and close on his heels, Captious.

No Mason.

"Ruined." Dr. Miliron had no lightness in his voice, no goofiness. He was angry. Which led me to believe he was more than just a featherbrained science teacher.

"Can't you decontaminate it?" Captious asked, arrogant as ever. "You *are* the resident chemist."

Miliron shook his head. "DMSO is totally miscible. No way to remove it without altering the chemical structure. The Class Project is a loss, Ben."

Totally miscible. Wow. That was so cool. I had no idea what the word meant, but it sounded awesome. One for the Dweeb League.

"Six months of planning down the tubes." Miliron banged his fist on the lab bench.

"But, Martin," Captious said, "we have plenty of evidence against Mason Draudimon without the Class Project."

I nearly smacked my head against the steel ductwork when I heard Mason's name.

"Draudimon's your target, Ben. It's his boss I want. Keep

this between us. Before Munificent died, he assigned me to find the man who gives Mason his orders."

"How interesting," Captious said. "I didn't know."

"Munificent liked it that way. He kept us all in the dark. So much corruption in the police force. I don't trust any of them. Present company excepted." Miliron shook his head. "Dalrymple is going to have a fit when he hears about this."

I was shocked. Dr. Miliron was an informant, too?

"Why?" Captious asked. "What does Dalrymple care about the Class Project?"

"Dalrymple didn't start the war on drugs, Munificent did. We designed the Class Project as part of his Old Torrents sting operation. Munificent believed that the entire drug ring operates from inside the mental hospital. They have a very advanced laboratory. He also believed that Mason has a connection there. The Class Project was meant to lead us to that connection."

"So the Class Project is a setup. It has nothing to do with helping the mentally ill, like you've been telling the faculty."

Miliron was quiet for a moment. "I needed some way to bring Mason in on the project so I could follow his movements. We know his mother has issues, so we concocted a story about providing Old Torrents with experimental chemicals for their mentally ill program. It caught his attention."

"Enlighten me," Captious said. "How can we possibly use a high school science project to stop the drug cartel? With the exception of the chromatograph, the school's equipment is very unsophisticated."

"We don't need sophistication. Munificent leaked information that the simple experiments we do in our lab would produce the base chemicals Old Torrents needs to make

Psychedone 10. The base chemicals themselves are completely harmless. Old Torrents' problem is that these chemicals aren't normally used in a mental hospital. If they bought them openly, they would draw attention from the Feds. The Class Project is the perfect setup. Glassware and heaters are all we need. I included the chromatograph to keep Mason interested. With Munificent gone, Dalrymple is the only one on the police force who knows that the Class Project is part of a much bigger plan. The teachers think it's just community service."

"And now that I know, I suppose you'll have to kill me."

Miliron laughed. "Something like that. Ben, this is big, and you're the only one left I can trust. I don't know where Dalrymple stands."

"I don't trust the man."

"There you have it. I need help to finish what Munificent started. Look, you know Mason. I know the drug ring. Maybe the two of us should work together instead of keeping secrets."

"A bit dangerous, don't you think, using our classroom and students to trap a drug cartel? Look at what just happened to Kathryn Hollister."

"That was a shock. No one thought she was a user. But Kathryn overdosed on the real thing. I don't know where she got it. Like you said, the Class Project is a setup. Even though what we make here is harmless, the advanced equipment at Old Torrents can make it deadly, so I added a time-released reagent that would decompose the drug after the final chemical reaction at Old Torrents. It still would have looked like Psychedone 10 to the drug boss, but by the time it reached the users, it would be no more potent than salt water."

Captious put his hands behind his back like a little kid who had just stolen a cookie. "Who exactly is this drug boss, and what makes you think he doesn't already know he's been set up?"

"Nobody knows who he is. The guy's too slippery. We know he's behind the drug ring. We suspect he has something to do with the kidnappings. We don't have a clue about his identity. The Class Project would have helped us to trace drug traffic from Mason to him, but now that it's polluted with DMSO, we can't pass it off as anything but toxic waste. Without the shipment to Old Torrents, we're dead in the water. We have no other links. I think Munificent got close, though. Too close."

Looks like I messed things up for the Knights *and* the police. Oops.

"Mason was kidnapping children for the recently defunct Norman LaReau," Captious said. "What about that link? Not that it matters. The mayor already tossed it."

Miliron's eyes narrowed. "I read your report on that, but it never felt right. How do you know?"

Captious laughed. "I know everything about Mason."

You wish, mister. Captious was obviously not as all-knowing as he thought. He sees Christie with Mason at the Shadow Passage, puts two and two together, and comes up with goose poop. Mason is linked to Scallion, not LaReau.

"Well, Ben, that's your case, not mine," Miliron said. "Hey, how convenient is it that LaReau died from a heart attack right at the station? Don't get me wrong, it couldn't have happened to a more deserving guy."

"Yeah, I was there. It was beautiful. LaReau flopped like a fish. Dalrymple tried to resuscitate him. Don't know why. I wouldn't have."

"He knew LaReau could lead us to Draudimon's boss. What's up with heart disease at the police station? Munificent died the same way. I hope it isn't contagious."

Captious laughed again. "Mason has to be pretty mad right now. Maybe he'll do something stupid and lead you to his boss."

"He doesn't know anything about the contamination. He went home sick earlier today."

Home sick? I needed to see what that was all about. Maybe a trip to Mason's house would be worthwhile, since eavesdropping on the undercover brothers had led nowhere.

I crawled back through the ductwork and dropped into the boiler room. As expected, it was empty. I quickly removed my mask and hoodie and stuffed them in my backpack. There was no noise out in the hall, so I quietly left the boiler room. I thought about popping over to the Greensburg Library before paying Mason a visit, when a voice stopped me in my tracks.

"Hey, Rinnie, I didn't know you were still here."

I spun around. Egon was coming down the hall behind me.

"Hi," I said, wondering if he saw me come out of the boiler room. "What are you doing here?"

"Aikido practice. Gotta get ready for a match. Wanna head to Mickey-D's with me? I'm buying! Got four entire dollars to squander."

My heart went into overdrive. "Oh, Egon, I wish I could…"

"C'mon, it'll take twenty minutes. Then you can rush off with a full stomach to do whatever it is that you'd rather be doing instead of being with me."

I recoiled at Egon's keen ability to fold kindness and a nasty helping of guilt all into one badly timed request. "I reeally, really want to, but I'm already late. I am so sorry." I reeally, really meant it, too.

"Last time you didn't feel like it. Okay, your friend was

hurt. I got it. So I gave you some time. Now you're too busy." Egon looked away. "Rinnie, it's okay if you don't want to hang out with me. Just say so."

"No, that's not it! It's just—"

"It's that kung fu school of yours, isn't it? Look, I understand dedication. I practice a lot, too. But you're a little… overboard, aren't you?"

Overboard? Practicing every night wasn't overboard. Putting on a mask and chasing bad guys might be… "No," I said, hugging myself, rocking back and forth. "I just have something I need to do tonight."

"It's okay. Look, I thought we had something—"

"We do, Egon, we do!" I took Egon's hands and pulled him toward me. "I like you, Egon. A lot. I never had a real boyfriend before."

"Then tell me what you're into." Egon's face was turning red. His hands quivered in mine. "What are you and Kathryn doing? I'm worried about you. I think you're involved in something dangero—umm…" Egon got a really weird look on his face. "Boyfriend? Really?"

I felt like I had been kicked in the stomach. "Really."

"Cool." He squeezed my hand. "Mickey-D's?"

I blushed, and gazed at my feet. I suddenly hated being a Psi Fighter. "Look, maybe we can go out tomorrow night? I promise, I won't make any plans."

Egon's mouth hung slightly open, and the deepest sadness I had ever seen filled his eyes. He shook his head and slowly pulled his hands away. "Sure, whatever. If you don't have something else you'd rather do."

"Egon…"

He turned and disappeared down the hall.

I stared, unsure of what had just happened. I suddenly lost all desire to go after Mason.

It was time to go home.

Time to wonder how a day that had started out so sweet had ended up smelling like the Class Project. Time to brood about how my secret life was ruining my real life.

Chapter Twenty-eight

Psi Fighter No More

The smell of bacon filled the kitchen. I sat at the table watching my dad cook, hoping breakfast would help perk me up from my sleepless night. Even during the few minutes I did sleep, I dreamt of kidnappers with decomposing skulls, and Egon saying he didn't have time for me.

"What's wrong?" Susie took my hand in both of hers and hugged it. "You just look so sad today."

"I'm sleepy." I pulled Susie in close. Susie always knew.

"I love you, Rinnie."

"I love you, too." I felt my eyes fill with tears. So I didn't have Egon. Big hairy deal. I didn't need a stupid boyfriend. I'd always have my family. They would never leave me.

"Can you walk me to school today?" Susie asked.

"That would be fun."

"That would be wet and muddy," Dad said. "Been storming

all night. Hurricanes, lightning, earthquakes, devastation. I think the end of the world is near. Better take the bus."

"Dad."

"Rinnie could ride the bus with me," Susie said.

"Rinnie hasn't even showered yet." Dad gazed at me with concern. "She'll never make the bus."

I knew the look. Dad didn't argue when I had said I didn't feel good enough to go to school that morning, but he knew it wasn't because I was ill.

"I have a meeting this morning. I'll drop you off on the way if you're feeling better."

I watched Susie get on the bus. Two hours later, I got in the car with Dad. He rarely dropped me off at school. It was a short ride, but it was nice. The Monkees blasted away on the stereo, and Dad was singing "I'm a Believer" at the top of his lungs. Seriously, he didn't help my taste in music any more than Andy did. Maybe it was time for a change.

"Dad, I don't think I want to be a Psi Fighter anymore."

Dad choked and turned off the music. "What, tired of practicing every night?"

"Oh, no." I shook my head. Fond memories of kicking Andy's butt flashed through my mind. "I love practicing. It's fun. It's the…other stuff."

"First Kathryn, now Egon. I know how you feel."

"First my birth parents. I mean, I don't really remember them, but it still leaves a hole in me."

"I have a hole, too, sweetheart." He took my hand and gave it a gentle squeeze. "I remember them. I was there that night. No six-year-old should see what you saw. Your mom and dad were our best friends. We filled the hole a little when we adopted you. Filled it a lot, actually."

I kissed my dad's hand. "You stopped being a Psi Fighter after you and Mom found us, didn't you?"

"I don't know if you ever really stop being a Psi Fighter. The world can't afford to lose them. But your mother and I changed our relationship with them that night."

"Egon and I changed our relationship yesterday. I guess I'm not a very good girlfriend."

"It's tough hiding your secret. Especially when you have feelings for someone. Sometimes you have to choose. Whatever you decide, you know I'm with you."

"Thanks, Dad."

We pulled into the school parking lot. Suddenly the day didn't seem so bad. My dad was right. Sometimes you have to choose. After school, I would see the Kilodan. He would understand my reasons for leaving, and would wish me well. Surely I wasn't the first Psi Fighter to want out. Today's plan was simple—find Egon, reinstate the girlfriend clause, live happily ever after. Next time Egon asked me to do something, I'd say *no problemo, dude*.

I felt relieved, like a huge burden had gone away. Kathryn was getting better and would be out of the hospital soon. The Red Team was running scared, and Mason was…well, I didn't need that distraction.

Students and teachers filled the halls, but I didn't feel any tension as I walked toward my locker. Kids were laughing, nobody was swiping lunches, Mrs. Bagley had a shiny new yardstick…then I noticed something odd.

My locker's door was twisted as though it had been pried open and forced shut again. None of the other kids' lockers had been touched. I opened it slowly, not knowing what to expect.

Nothing seemed to be missing. I couldn't imagine what anyone wanted in my locker. My homework was intact. If they stole it to copy it, they had put it back right where I'd left it. That was weird. My Amplifier was in my purse. I never left anything remotely Psi Fighterish in my locker, so I wasn't worried about that. What were they after?

The broken lock looked like something had been jammed into it, gouging the steel. That was just mean. The thief should have at least had the courtesy to pick the lock. I swung the door wide to examine it and found a note taped inside. I unfolded it and my heart stopped.

Inside was a picture of Susie, bound and gagged, on her knees, and the handwritten words *Meet me in Dead End Alley at noon.*

I stared at the note again, but the words refused to change. Susie looked so scared in the picture. I fought the urge to cry, then anger started to burn inside me.

How could I have been so stupid? After what I did in the park, I might as well have painted a sign on my back: *I'm a Psi Fighter.* My birth parents had been murdered for the same carelessness, and now Susie was in danger.

"Rinnie, what's wrong?"

I jumped. Bobby had magically appeared next to me.

"I think they have Susie," I said.

But that couldn't have been right. I watched her get on the bus that morning. I stared at the picture, but couldn't tell if it had been tampered with—Susie was so tiny, so helpless. "This has to be a psychotic joke. I have to get over to the elementary school and see if she's there."

"Why not check the school office computer? It shows everything that goes on at all the schools."

"How can I get on the office computer? I can't wait until school's out to break in. I need to know now." I pushed back the panic that threatened to strangle me.

"To the Bat Cave," Bobby said, taking me by the hand. I followed him into the boiler room. He opened his backpack, pulled out a gleaming silver laptop, and put it on a table. "Welcome to the wonderful world of WiFi," he said.

"You have a password?"

"We don't need no stinking passwords," Bobby said in a really bad cyberpunk accent.

I clenched the table. I was in no mood for joking.

"Lucky thing I skipped my Hackers Anonymous meetings this month." Bobby tapped at the keyboard, talking quietly to the screen. "We're…connecting. Hello…yes, I am the System Administrator, thank you very much. Never question me, you simple-minded machine. Yes, I want complete access…good! Okay, let's take a peek at Student Attendance…here we are." Bobby looked up at me and smiled. "I think we're okay, Rinnie. Your mom reported her home with the flu this morning."

Bobby's words stabbed into my heart. Panic gripped me like a bear trap. My chest tightened, my legs threatened to buckle. A metallic taste coated my thickening tongue as my salivary glands kicked into overdrive. I tried with all my strength to keep breakfast down. I leaned against Bobby, breathing hard. Then the nausea passed, and I began sobbing uncontrollably. "Oh, Bobby, it's happening again—no no no no…"

I barely noticed that Bobby was hugging me, patting my hair, speaking…his words grew more distant as vague memories of my long-dead birth parents became crystal clear. Forgotten funerals flashed into my mind, and the scalding pain of loss ripped at my breaking heart. My birth parents lying on the street, a monstrous figure standing above them, ripping a ghost-like hand from the chest of one of their prone bodies— then turning to me as I attacked with a rage I had never felt before. Just before everything went black, the monster spoke.

You poor, helpless child. How does it feel to cause your parents' deaths?

The memories brought back deeply hidden pain, then suddenly uncovered something more, something ten years had smothered but not squelched—ravenous, unavenged fury.

I didn't cause my parents' death. *He* did.

My hair fluffed and I snapped into the present. I pushed away from Bobby. "I'm not helpless anymore. I am a Psi Fighter."

"Huh?" Poor Bobby looked very confused.

Suddenly, I understood what my birth parents felt when they learned I had been kidnapped by the Knights. They knew they'd be walking into a trap in Dead End Alley, but they were going anyway. Just like me.

Then it occurred to me that I didn't have to stumble into this blindly. The note was bait, meant to lead me to Dead End Alley, not to Susie. Susie was being held somewhere else. All I had to do was find out where. Andy could scan the note for memory fragments. The answer would be there.

Suddenly I heard voices in the hall. Rubric and the Red Team.

Tammy Angel.

The answer might also be there.

Chapter Twenty-nine

Rinnie Unchained

"Bobby, get Rubric and Angel to follow you in here."

"What are you doing?"

"Please, Bobby, before they get away. They can't know I'm in here. Hurry."

Bobby's face became grim. "I'm all over it." He rushed from the boiler room.

I opened my backpack and pulled on my mask and hoodie.

Bobby's muffled voice came through the boiler room door. "Hey, the Idiot's Convention came to town! They want you for mascots!"

Confident that Bobby had gotten their attention, I moved behind the boiler pipes, thinking he just might be Psi Fighter material one day. The boiler room door burst open and Bobby shot in. He flew around the boiler and out the other side.

Agatha Chew stomped in, followed by Tammy Angel and

Rubric.

"Hey, pretty boy. We're coming for you."

I closed in behind them like a shadow, striking hard at a pressure point on Angel's neck, then Rubric's. They both dropped to the floor.

I concentrated, imagining my face to be a naked skull with burning eyes. I tapped my mask's voice button and stepped into the light. Agatha's eyes and mouth opened wide in silent fear. She gaped at Rubric and Angel unmoving on the floor, then at me. Her knees shook, and she covered her mouth with both hands.

"Don't scream." My electronically altered voice was haunting in that dark boiler room as I pounded delusions into her mind.

"I know," Agatha whispered. "I saw what you did to Hollisburg when she screamed."

"Who took the little girl this morning?"

"What g-girl?"

I drew my Amplifier and a Thought Saber burst out. I pushed the point slowly toward Agatha's heart.

"I don't know anything," Agatha pleaded. "Please, you know I can't lie to you."

My free hand shot out and caught her by the jaw. Through my gloved hand, I felt fear. Concentrating, I drew Agatha's memories. As her emotions poured into my head, I became her, feeling the things that she had felt. I felt pure horror as I watched Kathryn attacked by a man with a skull for a head. I felt disgust as Tammy Angel forced drugs on a little girl. I felt heartache when I shot Mummy's Magic Mix into Peroxide's mouth.

I pulled away from the Scan and became me again. It

was totally weird to see myself in somebody else's memories. Agatha liked me. That was unexpected. I tweaked a nerve on her neck, and lowered her to the floor beside the others. She was innocent. Spineless, but innocent. She didn't like Angel, and hated when she forced her to hurt people. Agatha was having second thoughts about being on the Red Team.

I scanned Rubric and saw horrors…drug deals, violent bullying…all useless. He knew nothing about Susie.

Then I scanned Tammy Angel, allowing myself to go deep.

I did what you asked, Mr. Scallion. I made one of the boys plant the 10 in Blys's locker like you told me.

Good girl, the skull replied. *He'll back off now. And thank you for arranging little Christie's appointment with me. I trust you are enjoying your work.*

I am. Business has been good. We have plenty of fresh recruits.

The skull nodded. And you've been well rewarded.

I pulled out in shock. Angel was the brawn behind the drug ring. She had made a small fortune getting people hooked. But she had no Mental Arts skills whatsoever. She set up Christie Jasmine, but didn't kidnap her. She set Bobby up, too, but it wasn't her idea. She wasn't Scallion. She was simply Scallion's pawn. He was still out there.

I quickly unmasked and left the boiler room. Running around the corridor, I found Bobby waiting on the other side.

"Get out of here, Bobby."

Bobby disappeared down the hall, and the boiler room door screeched open. Rubric stumbled out rubbing his head, followed by Angel and Chew.

"Mr. Rubric!" Mrs. Bagley's voice echoed down the hall. "The boiler room is off limits to students. Would you like me to extend your detention?"

Mrs. Bagley smiled grimly at me as she strode past, heading straight for Rubric and the Red Team, wielding her yardstick like a broadsword.

I caught up with Bobby near the library. "I have to leave school," I told him. "I need you to cover for me."

"How am I supposed to do that?"

"I don't know. Improvise."

Bobby threw his hands in the air, then looked around like he would find the answer somewhere in the hall. "Oh," he said slowly. "Okay, go. You're covered." He was staring intently at the fire alarm on the wall.

I shook my head. "No, Bobby, that's a bad idea."

"I'm not that stupid," Bobby said. "Now go."

I turned and sprinted down the hall, my feet never making a sound. Short of having my uniform with its Shimmer Mode, I would have to rely on pure stealth. I slipped around corners, watching and listening, making certain no one was near before speeding ahead. I slowed to a dead stop and slipped into an empty classroom next to the school's back exit. Voices. I should have known better than to try that way out.

I quickly left the classroom and headed for my next option, the girls' locker room. It had a back door to the track field. If I could get there in time, it would be empty and nobody would notice me leaving. The shortest route to the locker room was through the gym, so I cut through the open doors and walked quickly across the floor toward the locker room entrance.

Suddenly, the fire alarm blared. Seriously? I could have sworn Bobby said he wasn't that stupid. His definition was obviously different from mine.

Since the gym's side doors opened into the school parking

lot, it was also a fire exit escape route. The gym quickly filled with students and teachers, and I found myself in a crowd. Plenty of people to hide me, but the locker room exit wasn't good any more. Then another exit came to mind, one that I should have thought of in the first place. All I had to do was find it.

As I made my way through the crowd, I saw Egon pushing toward me, panic in his eyes.

"Rinnie, Bobby told me what happened." Egon opened his arms, and I threw myself into them, resting my head on his chest. Hope washed through my anxiety-ridden body as he squeezed me tight.

"I knew you were involved in something dangerous," he said, caressing my hair. "We'll get through this. Together."

That sounded so good. I desperately needed help. But reality smacked me hard between the eyes. Egon couldn't help me against a Knight. It was too dangerous. I might have to become masked. As much as I wanted my lovable, understanding bodyguard, this was way out of his league.

My heart broke as I pushed gently away. "I have to go."

He took my hand. "I'm coming with you."

I needed an excuse to keep him from coming, but excuses required thinking. I didn't have time for thinking. "No, Egon, you can't. I'm sorry. I have to call the police."

I kissed his cheek and walked away into the crowd of students. Egon stood dumbfounded for an instant, then tried to follow me. I was almost ashamed of how easily I lost him using my art-of-stealth training. From behind the bleachers, I watched him pass by, searching the gym. A frustrated sigh escaped my lips.

I would allow myself to feel bad later. I needed to move,

quickly and alone. When he exited the far door, I took off, and worked my way back to the boiler room. I had to find that secret entrance Andy had told me about. It was the quickest way to the Academy, and I needed speed. The hall was luckily empty when I got to the boiler room.

I opened the door and entered into total darkness, hit the light switch, and made my way to the electrical panel. Somewhere on that wall, there was a hidden electrode plate that activated the secret entrance, but I couldn't see it. I searched all around the panel, but turned up empty.

The plates in every other entrance Andy built were brass or silver. There was nothing that remotely resembled an electrode plate around that panel. Nothing but a stupid warning sign—which, I suddenly realized, was classic Andy.

Danger! Shock Hazard! Do Not Touch!

I reached for the hazard sign. Instantly, mental sparks jumped from my fingertips. I pressed my hand lightly against the sign, concentrated, and released a light stream of mental energy. The electrical panel collapsed into the wall, a section moved sideways, and a toilet slid into view. I made a mental note to buy Andy some chocolate, then eat it right in front of him.

I made it to the Academy in what seemed like minutes. The boiler room toilet didn't plummet straight down like the one at the library. Andy must have been in a roller coaster mood, because this ride whipped over steep underground hills, down sheer drops, and around sharp bends. Thankfully, Andy had included a seatbelt. If you've never worn a seatbelt while on the toilet, I can't even begin to explain how weird it feels.

The Academy training room was empty. I searched the halls, hoping Andy would be there, even though I knew it was early and class wouldn't start for hours. I sprinted to his technology lab, but it was sealed. Andy was nowhere to be found. He never taught me how to use his scanning equipment, but I was determined to fire it up anyway. How hard could it be? I placed my hand against the metallic plate, and released a powerful stream of mental energy. Something clicked, and a light came on above the K-Mart sign.

Andy's voice boomed from a speaker hidden somewhere in the ceiling. "Please accept my humble apologies. My security is far too powerful for your feeble mind to break through. Besides, I'm not home right now. Actually, I am home right now, which is why I'm not here to open the door for you. This is a recording…this is a recording…please leave a message at the sound of the insult. That outfit *does* make you look fat."

Batting down a new anxiety attack, I pulled the ransom note from my pocket. It was written in blue ink. I didn't recognize the handwriting. It could have been anybody's. Then I noticed a scribble at the bottom. A little doodle. I couldn't be sure, but it seemed to be heavier, different from the handwriting. Like someone else had scratched it on the paper as an afterthought. And it was in pencil.

When I'd tried to scan the letter from Munificent, I'd been too exhausted to get anything. Hopefully, this time would be different. I concentrated and placed my palm against the letters.

Nothing.

Then I remembered how Andy had rubbed his fingers across the writing. I stared hard at the letters, and touched them. The ink smeared.

Still nothing. Then I rubbed the scribble.

I know where Susie is echoed in my mind. Mason! I felt

fright, I felt nervousness, but strangely, I felt no menace in his thoughts. Then a skull grinned at me and said *Deliver this*. Mason was still involved with Scallion. So much about Mason confused me, but I was very clear on one thing. He was going to tell me where Susie was if it was the last thing he ever did. And if she was hurt, it almost certainly would be.

It was 11:45. I had fifteen minutes to make it to the alley.

Chapter Thirty

Dead End Alley

I burst from the secret entrance of the Academy and sprinted straight for Dead End Alley, angry with myself for letting the Knights lead me down so many wrong trails. But that *was* their specialty.

Mason's change of heart may or may not have been a ruse. He seemed so sincere before I overheard him calling Old Torrents, but the ransom note left no doubt that he was still doing the bidding of the Nicolaitan's apprentice. Same M.O. as ten years ago—kidnapping and drugs.

One thing didn't make sense, though. Scallion didn't take Susie for LaReau. LaReau was dead. So why?

Then it hit me.

It was me he wanted. He knew I was the Morgan girl. Scallion would be waiting in Dead End Alley with Mason. The Knights were trying to lure us out. They wanted to finish what they had started ten years ago, and I was their key. Again.

Yeah, right. Not on my watch. Scallion was going down. I knew I was walking into a trap, and I pitied the poor boy once he caught me.

I rushed through the back streets of Greensburg, planning to enter Dead End Alley from behind the Shadow Passage instead of from the rooftops. The main streets were empty, but soon would be filled with the lunch crowd. If anyone saw me, they'd mistake me for one of the hundreds of lunchtime joggers.

I had decided against wearing my mask and armor. Scallion was expecting me. If a Psi Fighter showed up, my identity would be needlessly revealed. He may have guessed who I was, but I wasn't about to prove it to him.

When I was half a block away, I slowed to a prowl, moving without sound, careful to be unseen. I checked my belt for my Amplifier. Mental sparks jumped to my fingertips when I touched it. Last resort.

I sunk low to the brick street. My heart pounded as I peered cautiously into the alley behind the Shadow Passage. There was no movement, no sign of life. A pile of old crates and rubbish sat like twisted artwork against the wall at the dead end. The stench made me hold my nose.

I decided to take a chance, and walked slowly toward the mass of filth and waste. Then a tiny, pathetic voice froze me.

"Nothing, nothing, nothing…"

Mason Draudimon moved quietly through the piles of garbage, talking to himself, gently picking up crates and stacking them. Scallion was nowhere to be seen. Mason seemed to be searching for something.

Then suddenly, he shouted, "Here we go!" He picked up a

long crowbar and started prying at one of the crates.

I saw the crowbar and lost it. A picture of the note taped to my broken locker flipped through my mind. "Where is my sister?" I screamed, running at Mason.

"You came," he said, smiling, ripping the crowbar from the crate.

I was on him in an instant, and grabbed the crowbar with both hands, twisting it from his grasp. With a flick of my wrist, I threw it across the alley. It clanged against the brick wall and fell ringing to the street.

"I asked you a question," I said, slamming a side kick into his gut.

Mason grunted and doubled over, holding his stomach.

"What did you do with my sister?" I dropped and swept Mason's legs out from under him. He landed hard on his back.

"Rinnie, please, don't." Mason pulled himself to his feet, gasping for breath. "She's here. I'm trying to help."

"Then help." My hands shot out like twin vipers, clamping on Mason's jaw and the back of his head. I was prepared for a struggle, but Mason never moved. Big puppy-dog eyes locked on mine, then slowly closed. As his memories entered my mind, fear took me.

"Leave me alone," Mason said. "I told you I want out."

"There is no out," Scallion said. He held up a sealed envelope. "Deliver this. No questions."

Then Scallion was gone. Mason opened the envelope and read the note. He dropped to his knees. I have to find her, he thought. I have to stop him. He studied the picture. He took a pencil and started to doodle on the note. Think, think, where would he keep her?

Then despair overcame him.

A terrible foreboding washed over me. I pulled away from the scan, beyond panic now, almost beyond any feeling at all. I was no match for the Knights. I felt so tired, so utterly defeated.

"You can't help me." I sobbed quietly, my fingers caressing Mason's cheek as I released him. "This time it really *is* my fault."

Mason took my hand. "Rinnie, it's okay, Susie is—" Then his eyes focused behind me and narrowed. His mouth twisted into a grimace. "*You!*"

I turned to see what Mason was glaring at, and hope filled my heart.

"Egon!"

I pulled away from Mason and flew into Egon's open arms.

"I'm here," Egon said, cradling my face in his hands. "You needed me, and I came."

"Get away from her!" Mason growled. He stalked toward us, his sledgehammer-sized fists balled.

Egon snarled, pushing me behind him. "Go home, Mason."

"I know who you are. I believed you. I trusted you."

"Shut up and go home."

"I don't take orders from you anymore. Did you really think I wouldn't figure it out? Get away from Rinnie, or I'll rip you apart."

Mason grabbed Egon by the arm and jerked him away from me, tearing his jacket open. Egon turned and caught Mason's wrist in a lightning-fast lock. He twisted, and it snapped loudly. Egon was good, much better than I had expected. But it was Mason who genuinely impressed me. He shoved Egon away and shivered a little. He rubbed his wrist, and pulled it straight with a sickening crunch.

I almost heaved.

"Let's see how tough you really are, Judo Boy." Mason attacked like a panther, leaping straight for Egon.

Just when Egon was about to be slammed to the ground, he simply stepped aside and used Mason's momentum to hurl him face first into the alley wall. Mason hit hard and slid to the ground, leaving a bloody splotch on the bricks.

"Tough enough," Egon said.

Mason was out cold. Panic started to set in again, and I looked quickly around the alley. No Susie. I grabbed Egon by the jacket. "Please help me."

Egon stood glaring down at Mason, hair wild like he had been in a wind tunnel. The buttons of Egon's blue denim jacket had popped off. I noticed a secret agent pocket inside.

"You shouldn't have run away," he said.

He was right, and I felt awful about it. But I had to. "I know. I'm sorry. Please, I need—"

"Please help me," Egon said mockingly, waving his hands and shaking his head. "Now that your sister's missing, you need me. And you see I came. I dropped everything for you. I make time for you, Rinnie. I *always* make time for you."

"Egon, you—"

"You're into something that got your sister kidnapped."

"I know, and I need your help."

"And I want to help. But you don't trust me enough to tell me what's going on. How can I help if I don't know what kind of trouble you're in? What will it take for you to trust me? I came. Doesn't that prove anything to you?"

"I'm sorry I didn't hang out as much as you wanted. Please, help me find my sister," I pleaded. "I trust you, Egon. I do."

"Okay, then. Listen to me." He took me by the shoulders. "I'm working with Dalrymple. I've been trailing Mason. Susie's kidnapping has something to do with your kung fu school. My information says they're holding her there. If you want to save her, I need you to take me there."

I looked up into his eyes. Egon was an informant, too? How many of these people did Dalrymple have? And how clueless could they be? If Susie was at the Academy, I'd know it.

Egon brought his face close to mine. "You want to know what really bugs me?"

"No. I don't. I want to find Susie." This was not the time for a needy boyfriend, and I felt the first twinges of becoming majorly annoyed.

"Okay, I'll tell you," Egon said as though I had never spoken. "Every time I want to be with you, you hit me with an excuse—not allowed out on a school night, not feeling up to it, being late for something—always an excuse. I know it's that school. Why is it so important to you?"

"What I am worried about," I said, growing suddenly angry, pulling out of Egon's grip, "is my sister. The Academy is a part of my life I was starting to regret. I was planning to quit. Because of you. I thought we had something special. But if that were true, you'd be more worried about where my sister is than about how neglected you are."

"You *are* special," Egon said, reaching for me. "And if we have special feelings for each other, we should trust each other."

I felt anger for only a second, until Egon took my hand in both of his. Warmth and calmness washed over me. All I could feel was his soft touch, all I could see were his beautiful green eyes. Such a nice touch. Such loving eyes. So special. We belonged together.

Just like Romeo and Juliet.

Who, it occurred to me, both woke up dead.

I pulled out of Egon's grip and my mind instantly cleared.

"How did you find me, Egon?"

Egon's eyes narrowed. "Bobby."

"I never told Bobby where I was going."

"He must have read the note."

"I never told him about any note." I stared at Egon's open jacket. A pen poked out of the secret agent pocket. I did a double take. Red and silver barrel with a white rectangle.

Suddenly, I understood. I backed away.

"That's how Mason knew," I said quietly. "Scallion hands him a ransom note, and Egon shows up. You're the Knight."

"Yeah, right from King Arthur's Court, babe," Egon said. "You're out of your mind with fantasies about shining armor, and I love it."

I stood up tall and straight. Mental energy rampaged through my body and concentrated in my palms. My hair poofed. "Tell me where my sister is."

"At your school. She's probably frightened out of her mind."

I had never faced a Knight before, but the idea didn't bother me anymore. In fact, I looked forward to it. My patience was below zero. Susie might already be dead. I needed answers and Egon had them. He had one more chance to tell me what was on his so-called mind before I surgically removed it. I took a menacing step toward Egon, and he backed against the alley wall.

"Babe, don't do something we'll both regret."

That did it. Last chance officially withdrawn. "Don't call me babe." I thrust my palm forward, straight at his chest, and discharged the Mental Blast of all Mental Blasts. Egon's hand shot out like lightning, deflecting my attack. My hand smashed into the wall, and the Blast exploded. Dust and brick shards flew everywhere.

"Is that all you got?" Egon asked, smiling at the gouge in the bricks.

I drew my Amplifier. "Not really."

Egon laughed.

Chapter Thirty-one

Scallion Unmasked

My Thought Saber burst out in a searing flash of mental energy, screaming in anger as I attacked. Egon's Amplifier was in his hand in less than a heartbeat. A Shield exploded out, stopping my Saber in mid-cut.

He grinned. "You fight like a girl."

"Practice harder, and maybe someday you can, too." I cracked a side kick through Egon's Shield, right into his pearly whites. Good form, solid hit. Definitely a ten. Egon let out a howl of agony. His knees buckled and he crumpled to the ground. He shook his head and snarled up at me.

"Impressive." Blood dripped from the corner of his mouth. He spit out a tooth. "I didn't think I'd have to kill you, but maybe I'll change my mind."

"You give yourself a lot of credit." I wasn't nearly as brave as I sounded. Egon was way tougher than I had expected. I held back on that kick and was thinking that maybe I shouldn't have.

"I deserve a lot of credit." Egon's foot shot out and hooked me by the ankle, dragging me to the ground. He leapt on top of me, pinning my wrists. I struggled, but couldn't break his grip. He was strong. Fortunately, I knew how to deal with strong.

"Now, tell me where your school is." Egon's eyes were inches from mine, his breath hot on my face. "We'll get Susie and take her there with us. I just want to see it."

"Having trouble keeping your story straight? You said she *was* there."

Egon smiled. Blood dripped from his chin and landed on my cheek. He bent closer, licked it off, and kissed me right on the lips. With his entire mouth. I felt him try to scan, so I slammed my mind shut. Egon pulled away with a jerk.

"Why does my first kiss have to come from someone who's trying to kill me?" I growled. That totally shot his chances for a second date.

"First kiss? I am honored. Maybe we should rethink this relationship."

"Rethink this." I flicked the Amplifier in my pinned hand. A shadow shot around Egon's arm like an eel.

I tugged, and he screamed. Suddenly, I was on my feet, his ghastly memories flickering through my mind like a strobe. I became Scallion.

My reflection glared back at me from the window of the dark room. I looked good. Awesomely good. The mask was a nice touch. White cranial cap, sharp mandibles, deep black eye sockets. You have done well, the master said. Now find the girl. The master wore a mask similar to mine. But I looked better. Thank you, master, I replied. You know I will. He liked it when I called him my master. He actually believed he was.

My mind flickered, and Mason stood staring at me, a mixture of terror and fury on his face. You're not the man who murdered my mother, he said. Of course not, I told him. But I know where he is. All you have to do is whatever I tell you, and I'll take you to him.

Then I was at the elementary school. The little girl looked at me and screamed. She was so small. I wondered why LaReau wanted her. The man had issues. But he also had money. The master didn't know about my side job. He wouldn't have approved. Like I cared.

Don't touch me, the little girl yelled. Right. I struck a pressure point on her neck, and oh, it felt good! I wished I could have hit her harder. She collapsed. I covered her head with a black hood, carried her through an alley and handed her to Norman. Not now, LaReau whispered. I think I'm being followed. The coward. Maybe one day I'd take him out. I pulled off the girl's hood and Christie Jasmine stared wide-eyed at me. That's okay, I said. I have a place to keep her.

The image changed. I was in the back room of the Shadow Passage. Mason came through the door, concern on his face. Captious took her, he said. I tried to stop him. Not your concern, I told him, wondering whether he was going soft on me. Let's talk about the Class Project. Have you made the changes I asked for?

Then Tammy Angel's face was in my mind. She wanted me. If only she knew how close she had been to me. So easy to control. I touched her hair. Tell Rubric to make Mason kill Blys. He'll never listen, she said. When Mason asks you for 10, give it to him. Then he will do whatever Rubric tells him.

Suddenly I was in the girl's bathroom at school, moving

soundlessly toward Kathryn from behind. I held a syringe of 10 in my hand. The new 10, guaranteed to satisfy. The babes who called themselves the Red Team watched me in terrified silence. They knew to be quiet. I hated Kathryn's goodie-two-shoes life. And her hair. I grabbed it and jerked hard. She squealed and her head snapped back. I wrapped her in a choke hold and jammed the needle into the crook of her elbow. I thought about snapping her neck, but pressed the plunger instead. Kathryn grew limp and her eyes rolled back. I shoved her hard into the stall. She hit her head on the toilet with a wonderful, bone-wrenching crunch. I pulled the stall door shut and locked it with my mind, laughing. That felt great.

The memory flickered, and Rinnie's little sister got off the bus. She waved and smiled, and my heart raced in anticipation. Hurry, Susie, Rinnie was in an accident, I told her. Come with me, I'll take you to the hospital. I giggled a little as her eyes filled with tears. I could smell fear on her, and worry, and a dozen other delicious emotions. Then I pulled a cloth sack over her head.

I was me again, suddenly aware that Egon was screaming in anger to take the nasty bag off his head and fight like a man. I released him from the Lash, breathing hard, soaked in sweat. An image of Susie's angry face burned in my mind. She fought back, just like I had.

"Why?" I sputtered, shaking my head. "Egon, why?"

Egon pulled himself to his knees and stared up at me. He began to giggle under his breath, then completely lost control of himself laughing. "A Memory Lash? I can't believe you actually thought that pathetic thing would work on me."

He leapt to his feet and looked straight into my eyes, that expressionless expression filling his face. "I am Walpurgi.

Penitence has no place in my life."

Before I saw him move, his fist struck me across the cheek. Bright lights pulsed in my head, and I found myself looking up from the street at Egon. He was good. I shook my head to clear the cobwebs. Not even Andy had ever hit me so hard. I had to give that one a ten plus.

Egon turned toward Mason's unmoving body and shook his head. "He was a real disappointment. I think remorse may have gotten the best of him. I assumed he was stronger than that."

"Is this where you reveal all your evil plans to me? That's what bad guys do, right? You have some code or something that says you have to." Spots floated in front of my eyes.

Egon's gaze softened, and he shrugged. "You'll be giving me some very important details before long, so it's the least I can do. Where do I start? Mason was a lost soul looking for someone from his past. I needed a flunky. It was a beautiful arrangement. Christie was business, a little extra cash. Kathryn...well, Miss Popularity was taking too much of your attention. When she went down, there I was to console you, good old Egon. You could have avoided that if you'd made me a little bit more of a priority. No matter. You're mine now."

"But why Susie?" I asked, buying time for my vision to clear. "She never did anything."

"Bait. I needed to catch a gift for my boss. Somebody wrecked a project I was responsible for. When I find out who, he's going down. A lot of work went into it for nothing, and my boss wasn't happy. He's not very forgiving, you know."

"Nicolaitan?"

"You know more than is healthy for you, Rinnie Noelle. Or should I say Lynn Morgan?"

My breath caught, but Egon didn't seem to notice.

"He wanted retribution," Egon continued. "I thought I could make him happy, be a hero, you know, all that good stuff. You were kind enough at the dance to let me know that you're a Psi Fighter. When I opened your purse to take back my Amplifier, imagine my surprise when I found two! Did you really think that hidden pocket would conceal it from me? Then I learned from Bobby that you were adopted, put two and two together, and voilà! The ever-elusive Morgan girl. I was going to give you to Nicolaitan as a surprise gift."

"Me, the legendary Morgan girl?" I was suddenly terrified for my family, but couldn't let him know. "Wouldn't that be something? Imagine Nicolaitan's disappointment when you show up with the wrong person. Will he kill you?"

"I haven't told him yet. That would ruin the surprise. Don't worry, I'll scan you first to make sure."

Relief. My secret was still safe. If I could believe a Knight.

"But you know…" Egon smiled. "After that kiss, I might keep you for myself. I can give old Nico an even better surprise."

"Let me guess. My school."

"Your school. I don't need the Morgan girl now that I have you. I don't suppose you'll make it easy and just tell me, will you? Of course, you could always join me. We'd make a great team."

"I used to think so," I said. "But even then, I wouldn't have told you anything about my school."

"Thought not. Guess I'll have to loosen you up a bit. Psi Fighters are supposed to be tough to scan, but I think I can work around that."

I struggled to sit up, but my body wasn't cooperating.

Egon laughed. "Takes a while to recover from that, doesn't it? I hit you with my special one-two combo. A sucker punch and a Mental Blast all in one. Don't bother trying to get up. It'll be a while."

That explained why I couldn't control my limbs. I felt as though the connection between my body and mind had been scrambled. I could feel everything, and my muscles worked, they just refused to do what I told them.

Egon held up his Amplifier. A whip with nine tails hissed from the end, each tail tipped with a smoky barb. "This works just like a real cat-o'-nine-tails. It won't cut your body, but when I'm done, your mind will be so shredded you won't be able to think. You'll tell me everything just to make me stop."

A wild scream rent the air, and Mason yelled, "Don't touch her!"

Egon grunted as Mason crashed into him like a linebacker. They sailed through the air. Egon twisted, turning himself and Mason in a slow spiral. Before Mason could slam him to the street, Egon was on top, and Mason landed with a sickening crunch. Egon leapt to his feet, and began flailing Mason with the psionic cat-o'-nine-tails. The misty whip slashed across his body again and again, hissing and yowling like a cat with distemper.

Mason just sat there with a strange look on his face. Then he jumped to his feet and belted Egon right in the jaw, knocking him against the alley wall.

Definitely an eleven.

"I don't know what you're trying to prove with that stupid thing," Mason said, his broken wrist pressed against his chest. "You better try something else unless you want your butt kicked. Dude, don't you have a real weapon?"

"So it's true." Egon tucked the Amplifier into his secret agent pocket. "The Memory Lash changed you. You're protected by remorse. Otherwise my Psi Cat would have ripped out your soul. Back off, Mason. This is between Rinnie and me."

"Wrong, Egon," Mason said. "*I'm* between Rinnie and you."

Mason dove at Egon with catlike speed, hitting him waist high. They both went airborne, but with a sudden twist, Egon was out of Mason's grip, and back on his feet. He folded his arms and stood motionless. "I was really hoping for a bit more competition, Mason. I realize your wrist hurts, but maybe you want to put on your big girl panties and try again?"

Mason pulled himself up from the ground, got in Egon's face like he was going to start yelling, then head-butted him with the force of a battering ram. "Maybe you should put *your* panties on."

The head-butt drove Egon to his knees. He got to his feet, rubbing his forehead, smiling sadistically. "Want to play dirty? Let me show you what I'm really capable of."

Egon threw a lightning-fast kick at Mason's head, but pulled it short, stopping an inch from his face. "Oh, that would have been painful. Maybe you should try to hit me instead."

"You got it." Mason tucked his broken wrist against his waist. I watched in horror as he lashed out with a series of powerful punches, driving Egon backwards. Mason was fast and extremely strong, but Egon moved like a spider. Mason couldn't touch him. Egon was playing with him, like a fly in his web.

I concentrated, ignoring the pain in my cheek caused by the punch, and focused on clearing my mind of the effects of the Mental Blast. My limbs began to feel less out of control as the connection strengthened.

Mason struck again and again, but Egon dodged with ease, taunting him with each missed blow. Suddenly, he hooked Mason's fist and tossed him to the ground. Mason regained his feet quickly, but Egon blasted a knee into his ribs, doubling him over, then lashed out with a powerful uppercut that left Mason lying motionless on his back.

"Now," Egon said, drawing his Amplifier, "I want to try something. This is really gonna be cool."

A weapon slowly formed from the tip of the Amplifier, solidifying into a long-handled medieval War Hammer, the head flat on one side, spiked on the other.

Egon swung the Hammer at the wall with both hands, and chunks of brick and mortar exploded from it, landing on Mason's face. I saw no fear in Mason's eyes as he sat up, leaning on his elbows, glaring at Egon.

"Sorry, Bucko," Egon said, raising the Hammer above his head. "Now that you know my secret, I'm afraid I'm going to have to kill you. You'll have to be patient with me, though. I've never killed anyone before, so it'll probably be very sloppy. And extremely painful."

"No!" I screamed, forcing myself to my feet. My Thought Saber hissed through the air, searing a vicious arc toward Egon's arm.

Egon took the Hammer in both hands and blocked my blow with the shaft. Then he thrust the smoky weapon forward at my head. I ducked and slashed at Egon's legs. He blocked and resumed his attack.

We battled, each parrying with skill and riposting viciously. Egon attacked nonstop, wielding his War Hammer like a baton, spinning and slamming, but I easily kept him at bay with my Thought Saber.

"You're pretty good with that scrawny blade." Egon pounded his Hammer at me with an overhead two-handed blow. "You'd make a great Knight."

"Sorry, I have a job," I said, stopping the Hammer dead with a ferocious upward block. The Hammer screamed in anger, and my Saber laughed. "Getting frustrated, are we?"

"Maybe. Sure you won't change your mind? Think of the things we could do together. We'd be unstoppable." Egon swung the Hammer at my leg.

"Unstoppable? Really. You need to work on your battle rhetoric. That was so movie villain cliché." I slammed his Hammer with a fierce downward slash, nearly knocking it from his hands.

"Rinnie, no!" a muffled voice said.

I felt the color drain from my face.

"Susie? Susie! Where are you?"

Chapter Thirty-two

Susie's Fury

The second my attention was pulled from Egon, his Hammer's flat head crashed through my shoulder. Sharp coldness like slivers of frozen glass shot down to my fingertips. My sword arm went numb, my Thought Saber fizzled out. The Amplifier fell from my hand and bounced in the street.

"Easily distracted, I see," Egon said, extinguishing the Hammer. "I thought Psi Fighters were challenging. Guess not. Now, let me tell you my plan. The War Hammer is such a cool weapon. It can crush brick, smash steel, bust up just about anything I like. But, as you know, Psi Weapons don't have the same effect on flesh. I would have crushed Mason's mind if you hadn't interrupted. I'm pretty sure his heart or lungs or something important would have stopped once I destroyed his mental connections. But I have a better plan for you. Okay, I realize you're slowly becoming paralyzed, and to tell you the truth, I could have a lot of fun with that. But what I'd really like is for you to bleed. And for that, I need a good, old-fashioned hunk of iron."

Egon motioned toward Mason's crowbar lying against the brick wall. It jumped through the air and into his hand like he was holding a giant magnet.

"What are you, a Jedi now?" I said.

"Surely, those useless Psi Fighters taught you telekinesis."

"I'm in the slow group."

"Well, enough babbling." Egon stared admiringly at the crowbar in his hand. "Do you know how many nerve endings you have in your toes?"

My legs gave out and I fell. "Enough to feel it when I kick 'em up your butt." The numbing effects of the Hammer were spreading, and soon, I wouldn't be able to move at all. I had only seconds to do something. I just wasn't sure what.

"Leave her alone, coward," Mason hissed weakly. "Come fight me. Let's finish what we started."

"Mason, buddy, you're no challenge. I'll get to you in a minute."

Mason's eye was rapidly swelling shut, his head bleeding badly. He struggled to pull himself to his feet, but collapsed. I was on my own.

My Amplifier lay just out of reach. I tried to crawl, but my paralyzed body parts wouldn't cooperate. My sword arm flopped like a gummy worm, my legs were like anchors. This was so much worse than the Mental Blast. I still had some feeling in my left hand, so I stretched it toward my Amplifier. I concentrated, imagining the Amplifier flying into my hand like Luke Skywalker's light saber. I pulled hard with my mind, reaching out with everything I had.

The stupid Amplifier refused to move. It had apparently never seen the movie.

I looked up helplessly.

Egon's face had become a canvas of insanity. Grinning like his skull mask, he held the crowbar in both hands and spread his feet. "Interlocking grip, nice wide stance. Head down, eye on the ball, and *fore!*"

Egon whipped the crowbar back above his head, then sliced it down toward my shoe. I closed my eyes. Suddenly, a high-pitched scream reverberated through the alley. Egon stopped in mid-stroke.

I felt a maelstrom of mental force gushing from the garbage pile. Tattered paper and plastic bags swirled as though they were in a cyclone. Garbage hurtled through the air and splattered against the bricks. Suddenly, a crate exploded with an ear-shattering crack, scattering wooden fragments and filling the alley with dust.

When the dust cleared, a tiny figure levitated a foot off the ground, centered in a ten foot circle emptied of all debris, her hair suspended as though she were floating underwater.

"Susie," I whispered.

"You didn't tell me your sister is a Psi Fighter, too." Egon twirled the crowbar. "Bonus!"

Susie sat in midair, cross-legged, hands dangling at her sides, appearing perfectly relaxed—except for her face. Her eyes burned with a terrible hatred that frightened me, and her mouth was twisted with rage. Susie was silent, but her mental attack screamed like a small child in agony. It struck Egon and shattered his crowbar like cheap glass. Steel shards embedded themselves in the brick walls of Dead End Alley.

Egon's scream was real. He covered his ears and sank to

his knees. His whole body shook as Susie's attack strengthened.

Susie stepped out of midair and stomped toward Egon, her fists clenched, her hair floating on a mental tsunami.

"Don't you ever hurt my sister!" she screeched. Her eyes became narrow slits as her anger took physical form. Her shoulders twitched. Her fists jerked and lurched forward like twin cannons. Egon wailed again, grabbing his leg.

"*Ever!*" Susie thrust both palms into the air and a loud crack like a lightning strike echoed down the alley. Egon was thrown backward as though he had been struck by a battering ram. He slammed off the brick wall and landed facedown on the pavement, unconscious…or worse. I had never felt such power from a Mental Blast.

Dead End Alley became silent.

I sat up and shook the numbness from my aching limbs. "Hi, Susie. I found you."

Susie ran toward me and flung her arms around my neck, sobbing.

"I knew you'd come. Did he hurt you?"

"He tried," I said, hugging my little sister with what little strength I had in my left arm. "But you protected me. Hey, where'd you learn to levitate?"

"That was awesome," a weak voice said. Mason limped toward Susie and me.

"Mason, I—" The words caught in my throat. Mason's wrist was twisted at an awful angle, his eye was swollen shut, and his face was bleeding badly.

"Hey," he said, touching my cheek. "Do you know if the Dweeb League is accepting applications? I need a new job."

Chapter Thirty-three

Another Day in the Life

The school library was deserted, and we huddled in our little study room. Bobby gently caressed Kathryn's forearm. Wouldn't you know it? Even after nearly dying from a horrible overdose of the deadliest, most addictive drug on the street, Kathryn was beautiful.

"I have the best friends in the universe," Kathryn said. "I mean, I was totally out of it, but you washed my hair *and* did my nails. If I had died, I'd have looked good."

"You almost did die," I said.

"Now, Rin, you know that would never happen. Who would look after you? Hey, did you know that whispering lady stopped to see me?"

"Mrs. Simmons?"

"Yeah, she came after visiting hours one day. At least I think she did. I wasn't too coherent. Maybe it was a dream, but I don't think so. She just sort of appeared, like that day in the library. She talked weird, real formal. Like Mrs. Bagley. She told me that the Whisperers are the protectors of the protectors. They guard the Psi Fighters' secret identities, but whisper of their existence to give hope to victims in times of trouble. She said I might be a Whisperer one day. Rinnie, I think she made me a job offer. Do you think I'm Whisperer material?"

"At one time, I might have thought so. But I know now you can't keep a secret." I nodded toward Bobby.

"Oh, hush, Bobby doesn't count." Kathryn waved me off. "Besides, you're the one who has trouble keeping secrets. You go rushing off into the park, attacking with no mask, and we have to play cleanup. My Bobby could have taken care of himself. I think you just like the attention."

"No, your Bobby needed help that day," Bobby said.

"Well, maybe. But Rin should still be more careful. Batman never made it so easy for the Joker to figure out who he was."

"Batman is a comic book character," I said. "Sometimes being real stinks."

"Speaking of things that stink," Kathryn huffed. "What a jerk Egon turned out to be. I think he was in love with you, though, in his own deranged, psychopathic, controlling way. But the B-movie ninja outfit? Really? Rinnie, please tell me that you don't wear that corny skull hood and leotard when you're out doing your Psi Fighter thing."

I laughed. "When it comes to fashion, the Psi Fighters have it all over the bad guys."

"Thank goodness." Kathryn patted my hand. "Are all Knights such nutjobs?"

"Maybe." I sighed. "At least my secret is safe."

"So he doesn't remember anything?" Bobby asked.

"Susie went a little overboard with her Mental Blast. She hit him hard. Not much physical damage—except for slamming him off the wall, which he totally deserved—but she wiped his mind clean. His memories were totally blasted. Gone. Kaput."

Kathryn did a double thumbs up. "So, technically, he's been destroyed, and he'll be put away for a long time for his evil ways. A jail will hold him now."

"But I can't use him to find Nicolaitan. Susie's attack obliterated Egon's Amplifier. The Psi Fighters and all of Greensburg are still in danger until we find him."

"You can't avenge your birth parents' murder," Bobby said quietly.

"Yeah." I shook my head slowly.

Kathryn sighed. "It's nice to know Mason has lost his wombat status. He had a conscience after all. Did you know he came to the hospital every day?"

"As much as I hate the Memory Lash, I guess it has its moments."

"What did you see when you Lashed him?"

The image of a young Mason bound to a tree with a dog leash flicked through my head. "Mason didn't have a nice childhood."

Bobby nodded. "So what was really going on between him and Scallion? I mean Egon?"

"It's confusing," I said. "During the assembly when Munificent told us that a student had been in contact with the man in the skull mask, I was certain he meant Mason, but Mason knew he meant Tammy Angel. Mason believed that Nicolaitan had returned. He asked Tammy to arrange a meeting. He wanted revenge. But when Scallion showed up, Mason knew he wasn't his mother's killer. Scallion convinced Mason that he could lead him to the man he was looking for. He said he would take Mason to him if Mason would modify the Class Project and bring samples to him. Scallion tricked Mason into turning the Class Project into Psychedone 10. Mason didn't realize what he was doing until Kathryn overdosed."

"Even though I kept telling him," Bobby said. "I can't believe he actually tested that crap on himself just to prove I was wrong. How stupid can a guy be?"

"You know," I said, "I was wondering the same thing. I thought you told me you weren't stupid enough to set off the fire alarm."

A huge grin crossed Bobby's face. "Wasn't me. I dared Rubric to do it. Bet him that he was too chicken."

I laid my head on the table with a clunk. "We really have to talk."

Out in the hall, the bell rang.

"Oh, what a world, what a world," Kathryn said in her best Wicked Witch of the West voice, waving her arms and swaying. "Who would have thought that a good little girl like you could destroy all their beautiful wickedness? Oh, look out! Look out! I'm going. I'm going. Ooooh. See you after class, Rin."

"See ya, Witchie Poo." Kathryn was absolutely back. Life was good again.

The hall was packed, and I headed toward the locker rooms to find Mason. He had stuck a note on my locker asking me to meet him. I really wanted to see him. He wasn't who I had thought he was. Or maybe it was more accurate to say that he *was* who I thought he was. Beneath that big, pantherish exterior was a genuine sweetheart who I wanted to get to know better.

I rounded the hall to the gym when, without warning, something slammed into me from behind. My forehead bounced off the locker, and I saw stars. I caught my balance and spun. A huge fist flew at my face, and I slapped it into the locker. A loud clang echoed through the hall. I turned to see Rubric's face grinning sadistically. Boot Milner and Agatha Chew grabbed my arms and pinned them behind my back. Agatha looked at me, then turned her gaze away.

Tammy Angel strutted up beside Rubric. "Social Graces 101. Let the training begin."

"Just when I think you four can't get dumber without a lobotomy, you prove me wrong." I pulled lightly against the Red Team's grip. Their balance shifted just enough for me to toss them at my convenience. "Let go of me, or I'll flatten you."

Rubric laughed. "I doubt it. Egon isn't around to protect you anymore."

"But I am," a small voice said.

A ninth grader I didn't recognize stood with his hands on his hips, staring up at Rubric. "Touch her and you touch all of us."

"How about if I touch you first?" Rubric shoved the boy on the floor. "Now you owe me five dollars!"

"I was really looking forward to a peaceful day." I flipped my hands around and jerked. The Red Team yelped in pain as I wrenched them both into wrist locks. I released Agatha, then gave Boot a little extra twist, tossing her into Tammy. They both landed on the floor with a thud.

I bent down to help the boy up, glaring at Rubric.

"What are you looking at?" he barked.

"Trying to decide which of your appendages I should rip off and shove up your butt."

"Tough guy, aren't you?"

"Don't know your males from your females. That's sad, Art."

"I told you it isn't over," Rubric said. "There's still the matter of that five dollars you owe me from last time. Now it's up to ten. Plus five for the dweeb. Pay up, or get messed up."

"Arturo!" a voice called. "Mi amiga!"

Mason came strolling around the corner, his arm in a cast, the left side of his face bandaged. He walked with a slight limp.

Rubric's face puckered. "Dude. What happened to you?"

"Cut myself shaving. What are you doing?"

"Hall monitor. It's collection day."

Mason eyes met mine, and he fought back a smile. Then he noticed my forehead, and his mouth tightened. He turned to Rubric with fire in his eyes. "Nice. How's that working for you?"

Rubric stared arrogantly at me, then looked at the ninth grader. "I got fifteen coming from Peroxide. That's just for today. Not bad, huh?"

"Nice bump on her head. You do that?"

"Yep." Rubric looked at me and sneered. "Had to loosen her up."

Mason got in Art's face. "I'll take my cut now. Thirty ought to do it."

"Your cut?" Rubric squeaked in a suddenly girlish voice, taking a step back. "When did you start taking a cut?"

"Just now. Fork it over." Mason held out his uninjured hand.

"Dude, that wasn't the deal."

Mason balled his hand into a fist. "New deal." He drew his arm back and Art's eyes nearly popped out of his head.

I reached out and gently put my hand on Mason's fist. "That's not fair. You wouldn't let me hit him in the gym."

Mason smiled slyly and dropped his arm. "True. Okay, Art, give me my money. Peroxide's all yours."

"Well, I didn't collect yet," Rubric said. He seemed suddenly nervous.

"Hop to it, then," Mason said, folding his arms.

Rubric slowly turned to me. "Fork it ov—"

"Did you know she's a black belt?" Mason interrupted.

"Huh?" Rubric stared down at Boot and Angel, then drew back a step from me.

"Yeah. Kung fu. Moves like lightning. Knocked Chuckie out. You were there, don't you remember?"

"I was—"

"Oh, I guess you were trippin' a little, huh? Yeah, knocked him cold. Hit him three times—*bam bam bam*! He never saw her move. He was so sore the next day he could hardly walk. I don't mess with her anymore. Glad you're collecting for me. I don't want to get hit like that again. Not by a girl."

"Chuckie…three times?" Rubric gaped at me.

"I only hit him twice," I said.

"Only twice!" Mason shouted. " And you did *that* much damage? Impressive! Okay, Artsy, give me my money, I gotta get to class."

Rubric looked at Mason's cast, then his bandaged face. "Did she do that to you?"

"Cough up, dude, I'm a busy man."

"I'll, uh…" The color drained from Rubric's face, and he began backing away. "I'll leave it at the Shadow Passage tonight."

"I don't go there anymore," Mason said. "The place is a hole."

Still backing away, Rubric rounded the corner and disappeared. "I'll get back to ya." The sound of running feet echoed down the hall.

Mason smiled down at Angel, then turned to me. "Hi."

"Is that all you have to say to Peroxide after she almost broke my butt?" Tammy snapped, still sitting on the floor, clenching her sore behind.

"How stupid can you be, Angel? The Cool no longer Rule."

"This isn't over, Mason. My daddy will have something to say about it."

"There'll be no one to listen this time, Tammy. It's over."

"Mason—"

"Finis."

"What about Peroxide?"

"I don't have anything to say to Peroxide." Mason turned toward me.

Tammy got up. "This stinks, Mason. Let's go. Boot! Chew!"

"You go. I gotta get to class." Agatha glanced quickly at me, smiled shyly, then left.

"All right," Angel yelled. "The Red Team doesn't need you!" Then she walked away, dragging Boot with her.

"I have a *lot* to say to Rinnie, though." Mason touched my arm.

"I have a lot to say to you, too. You saved my sister and me in the alley. You risked—"

Mason put his hand over my mouth. "Me first."

"Don't make me break that other arm." The little ninth grader pushed between Mason and me, crossing his arms.

"It's okay," I said. "He's one of the good guys."

The ninth grader surveyed Mason with his head tilted, lips pursed. Then he looked up at me and nodded as if he approved. Turning to walk away, he said, "We aren't afraid anymore. Call if you need me."

"I will. Thanks."

Without warning, Mason picked me up in his arms like I was a toothpick, and hugged me. His cast dug into my ribs, but it was okay. He felt warm, and suddenly a memory flashed unasked into my mind. Mason was hugging his dad, and they were both crying. But it was happy crying.

"I helped my dad and Dalrymple round up the drug ring," Mason said. His blue eyes glistened. "Some pretty important people went down. That's the phone call you heard me take in the hall."

"Mason, I'm so—"

He held up his hand and smiled. "It's okay. You didn't know. And I never really gave you any reason to trust me, did I? So let me set the record straight. I don't make drugs. I don't push drugs. I never did drugs."

"Psychedone 10. In the park."

"Never knowingly did drugs. And once I figured out what Scallion was up to, I went straight to my dad."

"How's your dad taking it?"

"It's weird, you know, I thought he'd be pretty mad. But he told me he's proud of me. Says Mom would be, too. I don't know why. I probably ruined his political career."

"Maybe he thinks there are more important things."

"Yeah. Maybe."

"Thanks for saving my sister and me in the alley."

"Any time." Mason gazed at me thoughtfully. "Thanks for whatever it is you did to me that day in the park."

"You're welcome."

Mason smiled, and turned to leave. Then he stopped. "Hey,

I'm on the Dweeb League now, so if you have an opening for a body guard, I'd like to apply. I have good references."

"So I hear. As a matter of fact, I have the first interview question. Why did you always act like you were so afraid of Egon?"

Mason did the cutest eyebrow raise at me. "Because...he could kick my butt. That was no act."

"And you still protected me against him in the alley?"

"Thought it would look good on my résumé."

"Okay. Good enough." I suddenly felt an overwhelming urge to throw my arms around him.

He turned to leave again, but stopped one more time.

"Rinnie?"

"Yeah?"

"The hole I told you about? I think it's getting better."

That made me smile.

Chapter Thirty-four

The Looking Glass

The Four rarely show up in class at the same time. When they do, we never know what to expect, but one of them always has a surprise—sometimes bad news, sometimes good.

It's very difficult to tell them apart. Their masks aren't identical, but the differences are subtle. Andy explained to me once that they are each named according to kung fu tradition by *dan*, which is like level of expertise. Kilodan, Teradan, Gigadan, and Megadan, the highest levels in the Mental Arts. Traditional kung fu skill is mostly physical, but the Psi Fighter's power comes from her feelings. A master of the Mental Arts has reached the highest levels of compassion, kindness, and love. These are the most powerful of all emotions. And, I have to admit, the hardest for a teen to deal with. I tend to get wrapped up in bitterness, jealousy, and fear of spiders. Maybe it gets easier when you get older. Although I can't imagine ever liking spiders.

Susie stood in the center of the training floor surrounded by The Four. She looked so tiny, but stood confidently in the midst of the Psi Fighters' most powerful members. The Kilodan hovered beside her like a mother hen. A thick oak board dangled in front of her, suspended by a string. I tensed in my seat as my sister slowly extended her hand. Susie's fingers shot out like tendrils and rested delicately on the board.

"Concentrate," I said under my breath.

After what seemed an eternity, Susie's hair poofed, her shoulders twitched, and the board exploded with an ear-shattering crack. Shards flew everywhere, and one landed in my lap. I squeezed it in my hand, overwhelmed with joy. The room was silent.

Suddenly the Kilodan stopped hovering and did the Curly Shuffle as his emotionless electronic voice hummed, "We have a winner." Apparently this whole ordeal had loosened him up a bit.

"I did it!" Susie shouted, and joined the Kilodan in his dance.

Beethoven's Fifth came blaring across the sound system, and Andy waltzed across the room to the beat. He stopped in front of me, held out his hand and bowed. "May I have this dance?"

"You can't dance to this."

"I," Andy said, placing his hand over his heart, "can dance to *anything*. But, if you insist…" He pressed a button on his armor and "Save You Tonight" blasted.

"You've upgraded your iTunes library?"

"Expanding my horizons," Andy said. "The sacrifices I make for you."

The whole school jumped to its feet and began dancing.

Andy leapt to the sparring floor and performed an extraordinary One Direction.

A gong rang, signifying the end of our little break. The Four bowed, and we returned the salute. The Four were usually very somber, but tonight they seemed as cheerful as emotionless people could be. Their masks were angelic like the rest of ours, but whereas mine and Andy's had beautiful smiles and happy eyes, theirs were wide-eyed and completely unexpressive, like angels in deep thought. They all seemed tall, but I knew that was an illusion they somehow created when they were together. Their Mental Arts skills were so powerful they didn't need Amplifiers.

The Kilodan stepped back, and the Megadan held up his hand. We all became quiet.

"It is no longer news to us," he started, his voice completely without inflection, "that Nicolaitan has resurfaced after ten years. Some of you will recall the devastation he caused, and how Andor Manchild defeated him in single combat after he murdered the Morgan family. He escaped before we were able to end him."

I touched Andy's shoulder. He turned to me and smiled, but pain filled his eyes. He leaned close and put his arm around me.

"He, like we, does not show himself," our masked leader continued. "Rather, Nicolaitan makes his presence known by his actions. Lynn and Susan have defeated his Knight, but you can be certain that he will continue to pursue his heinous mission to destroy us. He will terrorize innocents to draw us into the open. The drug ring has been rounded up, but we do not know the location of their production facilities. The police searched Old Torrents Labs but found nothing. The danger is not yet over.

We are on full alert. Assignments will be made. Patrols must be established. If there are no questions, class dismissed."

Wow. Short and to the point. That's how The Four did things. The students filed out. I started for my changing closet when I felt a hand on my shoulder.

"You did well," the Kilodan said.

I'm pretty sure it was the Kilodan. They all look alike, and they all stood right behind me. "Thank you. I can't believe Susie levitated. I always thought that was a myth."

The Megadan stepped forward, hands behind his back. "It is a poor myth that doesn't have some basis in truth." He leaned toward me. "*We* are a myth, aren't we?"

"More like a fairy tale. Does Psychedone 10 really enhance mental abilities, or is that just a myth, too?"

The Megadan's mask let out a flatulent sound. "The Knights have always looked for an easy way. Always without success."

"What do you mean?"

"Mental Arts mastery can only be achieved by faith, practice and dedication. Nicolaitan created Psychedone 10 to give the illusion of mastering the Arts. He is all about illusion. In the end, drugs kill. But you, young lady, are much more than illusion, aren't you?"

"Well, sometimes in school I give the illusion that I'm paying attention."

"I know. And I may have to give you detention if you don't stay out of that boiler room." A psionic yardstick burst from the Megadan's hand.

My heart stopped. I looked at the Kilodan, then back to the Megadan. "Mrs. Ba—"

"In time, my dear, you will learn all our identities, as we feel the need to reveal ourselves. You and I have much to do.

Our school is not yet safe."

"I—"

"Naturally, I need not remind you that, while Kathryn is approved by the Whisperers…"

I shook my head, still in shock. "No, this is something even Kathryn can't know. I'm not sure it's such a good idea that I know."

"Of course it is," the Kilodan said. "Enough talk. It's time for you to practice."

I got the distinct impression that the Kilodan was laughing his butt off. "Umm, okay. I'll get Andy."

"No need." The Kilodan bowed. "Today, you train with The Four."

I blushed. Me, training with The Four. Everything had turned out so much better than I could have imagined. Life was good. Sometimes I just forgot.

My reflection stared at me from the mirror on the classroom wall. Tall and thin, I stood up straight. My feet were sort of big, and my knees were maybe a little knobby. My blond hair wasn't luxurious like Kathryn's, but it was kind of pretty. I still wasn't allowed to wear jeans with holes in them, but holes just let cold air in, so who needed them? I pictured my house and my family. Then I thought of Mason, and I felt warm.

I searched the mirror, and saw an ordinary girl smiling back at me. She was a Psi Fighter, and ordinary was a requirement for hiding in the open. She wasn't glamorous like a movie star. She looked as ordinary as any person walking down the street. Just ordinary…in a real butt-kicking sort of way.

I giggled a little, then laughed out loud.

Ordinary, I decided, was really pretty great. I dropped into my fighting stance, ready to take on The Four.

Chapter Thirty-five

Here We Go Again

A softly flickering light and a voice I could barely hear woke me from a beautiful dreamless slumber. Ugh. I rolled over toward the glow. There on my nightstand stood a tiny Andy, bent over an R2D2-shaped garbage can. He wore a Princess Leia wig.

"Help me, Rinnie-wan, you're my only hope."

Andy's hologram floated irritatingly over an MP3 player that he had given to me earlier that day. He told me to keep it beside my bed at night, because he was testing out some new technology he had just invented. I should have known it wasn't a normal MP3 player. Nothing Andy did was normal.

"What!" I snapped, irked to be ripped from my much-needed beauty sleep.

The little Andy stepped away from the garbage can and looked up at me. "Somebody's cranky." He adjusted his wig.

"Does this make me look fat?"

"No. It makes you look annoying. Like that stupid alarm clock you're standing on."

"Alarm clock? Do you think I would waste precious moments creating something that does nothing more than wake you up at inconvenient hours?"

"You've wasted precious moments on other useless things."

"True, but I have redefined uselessness with this baby. HD video, play and record, oodles of music in any format you like, and holographic communication, anytime, anywhere. The Psi Fighter's dream. Comes in blue, red, and metallic purple."

"So this irritating little device is your version of the Bat Signal?"

"Close. I call it—are you ready for this?—the psiPhone."

I pulled my pillow over my head and moaned. "I need sleep."

"See, this is the downside to successfully completing a big mission. You get more missions."

"I don't want another mission," I mumbled into the mattress. "I want another twelve hours of sleep." Then I popped up. "What kind of mission?"

"Dalrymple called. Apparently, there's about to be a murder."

"Apparently? He's not sure?"

"Well, there's no body. Just an ominous note hinting that there will be one soon."

"How ominous?"

"It's a badly written limerick."

"That's ominous." I lay back down under my pillow. "Does this thing have a snooze button?"

"Forgot to add that feature. Okay, let's make a deal. I'll

show you the note. You tell me what it means, then if you think it's not important, you can go back to sleepy time. Deal?"

"Deal."

"Take a gander at this." Little Andy pulled a tiny piece of paper from his pocket and held it up.

"And how exactly am I supposed to read that itty bitty thing?"

"Hit zoom. Duh."

"Oh. Right." I double-tapped the screen and the note grew in Andy's hand. Soon it was the size of a suitcase, and covered Andy completely. Smooth cursive writing jumped out at me. I pushed myself up on my elbows to read.

> There once was an old high school robber,
> Who over a young lass did slobber,
> But the Passage was home,
> And it caused him to roam,
> Which led to one fine Danse Macabre.

"Whoever the bad guy is, he can't spell. Dance has a C, not an S. He murdered the poem, but that's the only crime I see."

"Do you know what the Danse Macabre is?"

"Yeah, it's like macramé, right? You knit little quilts and scarves and things when you're old and senile."

"Remind me never to interrupt your sleep again."

"Didn't I already make that clear?"

"Let's make something else clear. Think back to the events of the past few weeks. Somehow, Nicolaitan got into Munificent's head and saw the Morgan girl that he had kidnapped ten years ago. That would be you. He rightly assumed that the girl had been placed in the Academy's version of a witness protection program with a new identity. There's no way he could make the connection to you and your new family, but he deduced that the girl was a student at the Greensburg High School. So he planted Scallion, disguised as Egon, to learn her identity. He told Scallion to cause pain and suffering to innocent victims, because that would draw any Psi Fighter into the open. Hence the Psychedone 10."

"And what does this have to do with dunce macabre?"

"*Danse* Macabre is a play where Death summons people to follow him to the grave. Nicolaitan has a twisted sense of humor, and loves theatrics and poetry. The heat is officially on. He's taunting us and making no bones about it. His little scheme at your school failed. His plan was to find out if the little girl he kidnapped ten years ago is indeed back and enrolled in Greensburg High School. Thanks to Egon's massive ego, he didn't learn anything useful. So now, he plans to murder people and leave us clues to the identity of his next victim. He wants to find us. He wants to find you. Now, who in your school fits this description?"

"Description? How can you get a description out of such a lousy limerick?"

"Let me ask this, O Sleepy One. Who in your school could be described as a robber?"

"Oh, that's easy. The Red Team, every one of Mason's former cronies, and three or four hundred others."

"Now we're getting somewhere. And who, out of that group of Greensburg's finest, hangs out at the Shadow Passage?"

"All of them, Andy."

Andy's hologram banged its head off the garbage can. "You're not trying."

"Andy, it's three a.m. in the morning."

"Three a.m. is always in the morning."

"Ugh!" I pulled the pillow back over my head and mumbled, "Good night, Andy."

"Let me ask you this. Which of them had a crush on a young girl?"

"Well, Chuckie Cuff liked Tish, but Tish was with Whatsisface, so that went nowhere. Rubric's main squeeze was Psychedone 10, so there were no girls that I know of, thank goodness. Mason had a crush on me, which I wanted nothing to do with."

"I noticed you used past tense, darling."

"Did I?" I got warm at the thought, but a disturbing idea popped into my head. "Andy, the Shadow Passage was Mason's home away from home before he turned into a good guy."

"I know. And he tried to steal Christie Jasmine from Scallion."

"He thought he was saving her from Captious. Oh, Andy, no…" I sat up in bed.

"Afraid so. I believe Mr. Draudimon is the target, and unless you want to attend his funeral, you'd better get your butt out of bed and down to the Academy."

"I'm on my way," I said, and I leapt from beneath the covers.

Acknowledgments

I want to thank all the wonderful people who helped produce this book.

To my Agent Extraordinaire, SuperNic Resciniti, for taking a chance on me simply because of the "birds have smooth brains" line.

To The Publisher Who Will Change the World, Liz Pelletier, for her visionary mind.

To my Amazing Editors, Stacy Abrams, Guillian Helm, and Nancy Cantor, whose brilliant ideas and very hard questions really whipped the story into shape.

To my Incredible Publicity Team, Morgan Maulden, Katie Clapsadl, Debbie Suzuki, and Heather Riccio, whose awesomeness will make the Psi Fighters a household name.

To Every Author's Go To Girl, Sarah Weiss, who can answer questions we haven't even thought of.

To my family, for putting up with me.

And most importantly, to God. He made me, and I'm happy about that.

Take a sneak peek at **Leah Rae Miller's**

THE SUMMER I BECAME A NERD

and embrace your inner nerd!

On the outside, seventeen-year-old Madelyne Summers looks like your typical blond cheerleader—perky, popular, and dating the star quarterback. But inside, Maddie spends more time agonizing over what will happen in the next issue of her favorite comic book than planning pep rallies with her squad. That she's a nerd hiding in a popular girl's body isn't just unknown, it's anti-known. And she needs to keep it that way.

Summer is the only time Maddie lets her real self out to play, but when she slips up and the adorable guy behind the local comic shop's counter uncovers her secret, she's busted. Before she can shake a pom-pom, Maddie's whisked into Logan's world of comic conventions, live-action role-playing, and first-person-shooter video games. And she loves it. But the more she denies who she really is, the deeper her lies become…and the more she risks losing Logan forever.

Only one copy left.

I have to take the chance.

I take a fortifying breath and square my shoulders before I stroll up to the glass door of The Phoenix.

I can't believe it. The Phoenix. I'm about to go into The Phoenix!

I pull the door open, and the twinkly bell I heard from the alley sounds above me. The store is set up like a book itself. I'm standing at the end of a long empty walkway. On both sides of me, metal, A-frame racks are lined up like pages waiting to reveal their awesomeness. Spinning racks are scattered throughout the store. Collectable action figures mint-in-the-box and key chains featuring superhero logos dangle from the racks' hooks. One spinning rack is covered top to bottom with slim foil packages containing *Magic: The Gathering* playing cards. If I wasn't trying to be sneaky about this whole thing, I'd give that rack of commons, uncommons, and rares a big ole whirl just to see the shimmery packets reflect the summer sunlight filtering through the windows.

"Welcome to The Phoenix, can I help you find anything?" a guy's voice asks from the end of the walkway.

Keeping my head down, I dart down one of the aisles on my left. "Just looking," I say and then snort at my own silly attempt to sound like a man.

"Let me know if you need any help."

There's a hint of suspicion is in his voice, but I stay hidden. Superspeed would be handy right now. I could find my book and leave the money on the counter without being seen. "Okay."

Then, I get lost. Lost in the bright colors of the covers,

lost in the stacks and stacks of lovely, numerically organized issues. The comics are grouped by publisher and alphabetically by series. There's Marvel's Ant-Man next to The Avengers. Booster Gold and Blue Beetle from DC. By the time I come across Fables, my number three favorite Vertigo title, I've run out of shelves on this side. I zip across the empty aisle and try to focus on the task at hand. The Super Ones must be somewhere in the middle of these shelves. There's Sandman, Superman, ah ha, The Super Ones.

I slide out the last comic in the stack.

#399?

I search the surrounding stacks, thinking maybe that money-exploiting jerk hid it from me, but I can't find it.

Here's the part where any normal person trying not to be recognized would give up and leave. Actually, a normal person wouldn't have disguised themselves in the first place, but that's a whole other matter. I, being a very nonnormal person, am going to have to ask the cashier and hope he's some college kid that won't give me a second look.

I take another fortifying breath and walk up to the counter. The guy is bent so far over a comic I can only see the top of his head, which is covered with brown, messy hair. I make an "ahem" noise to get his attention, but he doesn't look up. I raise my sunglasses up a little to glance at the book he's reading. I see a full splash page of Marcus. His whole body is contorted in agony as he screams—and I know he's screaming because the speech bubble next to his head is all pointy— "NOOOOOO!!!!" I squeeze my eyes shut, not wanting the book to be spoiled for me, but the damage is already done. I'm at the end of my rope.

"Do you have a copy of *The Super Ones* #400?" I say,

abandoning my faux-guy voice.

He finally looks up, and I recognize him. Not only do I recognize him, I *know* him. I could probably tell you what shoes he's wearing (black and white chucks with frayed laces) even though his lower half is hidden behind the counter. I know this because he's kind of been my geek idol for a while now and I've…paid attention.

Last year, he got in trouble at school because he was wearing pornography. At least, that's what the students were told, when in reality, he was just wearing a T-shirt sporting an Adam Hughes drawing of Power Girl. Ridiculous, I know. I mean, Adam Hughes is one of the best purveyors of the female form in comics today, even if he has a tendency to overexaggerate certain body parts.

Ever since then, I've had a thing for Logan Scott. Not an actual *thing* since I have a boyfriend and that would be bad, but he's got these cute freckles on his nose and cheeks, probably from playing soccer—he's the Natchitoches Central High School's goalie—and he's always reading, comics mostly, but every once in a while, I'll catch him with a high fantasy book with dragons or elves on the cover. Not that I'm stalking him or anything.

He has really nice eyes, though.

His brow furrows when he looks at me. "Sorry, we're all out."

"Really? What's that?" I point at the book he's currently stuffing under the counter.

"It's…" He trails off as he takes in the way I'm dressed. He tilts his head to the side like he's trying to see behind me. I whip around, thinking someone else is there, but the store is still empty. When I turn back, a knowing smile plays at the edges of his mouth. Sighing right now would be bad, but he has perfect boy-lips—not too full, not too thin.

He props his chin on his fist. "Do I know you?"

"Uh, no, I mean, I don't think so. I'm just passing through town. I mean, I don't live here or anything so how could you know me?" I say in a rush.

"Okay." He squints like he can pull a confession out of me with his eyes alone. "That's too bad, because this is the last copy."

He pulls #400 out and waves it around, which sends electricity shooting through me because: (1) it's right in front of my face, and I can see the amazing cover, and (2) the way he's flopping it around is breaking the spine, which breaks my heart. You'd think a guy who works at a comic shop would be a little more careful.

Instinct kicks in, and I throw out my hands like he has a gun pointed at a puppy. He stops and lays the book on the counter between us.

"Why is it too bad?" I ask. "I'm a paying customer. I give you money, you give me #400. That's how these things work." I tentatively reach for #400, but he slaps his hand down flat on top of it.

"It's too bad you're just passing through, don't live here, and don't know me, because this is my copy, and if you *weren't* just passing through, lived here, and knew me, I might let you borrow it."

He smiles that knowing smile, and more of that electricity shoots through my body, but for completely different reasons: (1) that smile is the irresistible kind I can't help but return, and (2) his voice has a soft, smooth quality that makes my brain turn to jelly.

I shake these thoughts from my mind when a voice in the back of my head shouts, "Quarterback boyfriend!"

"Well, by passing through, I meant visiting. I'll probably be around for the next couple of days so I could have it back to you pretty quick."

He scratches the back of his neck. "Hmm."

"I promise," I blurt out, my hands clasped together. I can't believe I've been reduced to begging. "I'll have it back to you in a couple of hours even."

There's that smile again. He might be adorable, but he's not being very nice, teasing me like this.

"We'll be closed in a couple of hours, so I'll give you my number, and you can call me when you're done."

"Perfect. No problem at all." I nod again and again until I think I've given myself whiplash.

He presses a button on the cash register, and blank receipt paper rolls out of the slot on the top. He hands me #400. I devour the cover with my eyes as he rips the receipt paper off and jots down his number. When he reaches for the book again, I jerk it away, thinking *Mine!*

"I just want to put this in there so you don't lose it," he says slowly, like he's trying to calm a hostile beast.

"Oh." I hand him the book. He slides the piece of paper behind the last page. "Can I get a bag? I don't want it to get any sun damage."

The bag might be another piece of evidence I'll have to find a hiding place for, but I might never have the guts to come back to The Phoenix. I want a memento, darn it.